Was this foreplay or warfare?

And, at this moment, did Dylan really care? As he pulled Sadie's bottom lip into his mouth, he knew their differences didn't matter. She moaned low in her throat and dug her fingernails into the muscles of his back. He swept a path across her cheek to the sensitive skin beneath her ear, leaving her neck, then biting her. Her hips bucked against his and she slid a hand down his back to grab his butt and drag him even more tightly against her.

He needed more. He needed skin, had to taste her, know her, have her. He stared down into her glittering eyes, taking in the rapid rise and fall of her breasts as she gasped for breath, the flush on her cheekbones, the tumbled, sexy mess of her hair.

She was everything he hated in a woman. But he was going to have her or die trying.

Blaze™

Dear Reader,

It was inevitable that I'd wind up writing a series of books set behind the scenes of a soap opera—I've spent more than three years working in-house for various TV dramas in New Zealand and Australia. It's a crazy, pressured and often hilarious way to earn a living, and I figured it would be the perfect place for people to fall in lust—and love—with one another.

Coming up with the heroines for my three stories was equally easy—Sadie, Grace and Claudia just seemed to jump right out of my keyboard, along with their heroic counterparts.

I hope you enjoy getting a behind-the-scenes glimpse into the way serial drama is produced via Sadie and Dylan's story. These two stubborn people have some serious ground to cover before they can let go of past misconceptions—but I hope you'll agree it's worth the risk.

I love to hear from readers. You can contact me via my Web site, www.sarahmayberryauthor.com, or c/o Harlequin Books, 225 Duncan Mill Road, Don Mills, ON M3B 3K9, Canada. And, of course, keep an eye out for the next installment of the SECRET LIVES OF DAYTIME DIVAS miniseries, *All Over You*, due out in April 2007.

Until then, happy reading!

Sarah Mayberry

TAKE ON ME
Sarah Mayberry

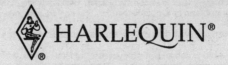

TORONTO • NEW YORK • LONDON
AMSTERDAM • PARIS • SYDNEY • HAMBURG
STOCKHOLM • ATHENS • TOKYO • MILAN • MADRID
PRAGUE • WARSAW • BUDAPEST • AUCKLAND

ISBN-13: 978-0-373-79318-1
ISBN-10:   0-373-79318-9

TAKE ON ME

Copyright © 2007 by Small Cow Productions PTY Ltd.

This edition published by arrangement with Harlequin Books S.A.

® and TM are trademarks of the publisher. Trademarks indicated with ® are registered in the United States Patent and Trademark Office, the Canadian Trade Marks Office and in other countries.

www.eHarlequin.com

Printed in U.S.A.

ABOUT THE AUTHOR

Sarah Mayberry lives in Melbourne, Australia, with her partner, Chris. As well as penning romance novels, she also writes scripts for television. She has plotted TV births, deaths, betrayals, marriages, first kisses, divorces and innumerable cliff-hangers in both Australia and New Zealand, but for now is content to stick with true love. May it ever run smooth...

Books by Sarah Mayberry

HARLEQUIN BLAZE
211—CAN'T GET ENOUGH
251—CRUISE CONTROL*
278—ANYTHING FOR YOU*

*It's All About Attitude

Thanks to all the *Shortland Street* and *Neighbours* people who have inspired this book—
bits of all of you are in there somewhere.
As always, thanks to my faithful readers—
La-La, the fabulous Miss Moneypenny and
Hanky Panky—and to Wanda, the maple syrup queen, who always knows best.

Prologue

Grovedale Senior High Prom, 1994, Los Angeles, California

SADIE POST STARED at her reflection in the girls' bathroom mirror. More specifically, she stared at her chest. Her flat, featureless, pancake of a chest. Her mother kept telling her she was a late developer, but Sadie had given up on hoping for late development two years ago. At seventeen, with a chest like an ironing board, she was officially a freak of nature. One day soon, a documentary crew would turn up on her doorstep and she'd be starring as *The Girl Who Skipped Puberty.* They'd have a doctor and diagrams, and they'd explain how all the stuff that was supposed to go toward breasts and hips in her body had instead been used by Mother Nature to stretch her out to a skinny six feet tall, with no extra to spare for luxury items like curves.

No wonder Dylan Anderson didn't know she existed. She'd sat next to him in American Literature for a whole year, and he'd barely glanced her way. The one time he had, she'd been doodling his name all over a page in her notebook, and she'd barely managed to slam it shut before he saw it.

She bit her lip, thinking about what had happened in class today. He probably knew she was alive now. And not in a good way.

Why had she suddenly decided it would be good to stand up for herself?

She knew why. She might not have breasts, but she had

desire to spare. In the privacy of her bedroom, she'd mapped the silky smoothness of her own body, discovering what felt good, what felt great, and what made her lose control when she did enough of it. And it was always Dylan's name she whispered into her pillow when she climaxed.

The door suddenly swung open and music filtered through into the bathroom as two girls entered, their high heels click-clacking on the tiled floor. They were giggling, their blond heads leaning toward one another as they whispered conspiratorially.

Sadie stepped back from the mirror, allowing them to take her place. She knew where she fitted into the school food chain. Cindi Young and Carol Martin were cheerleaders—she was an amoeba compared to them. Less, probably.

She kept her eyes averted as they smoothed on lip gloss and fluffed their hair, finally teetering back to the gym to gyrate some more and send the boys wild with their sexy, curvy bodies and gravity-defying breasts.

Cindi and Carol and girls like them were why Sadie had done what she'd done today. She knew she didn't have what it took to get Dylan's attention the old-fashioned way. And she'd wanted him to notice her so badly. When the opportunity had seemingly fallen into her lap…she'd jumped in, feet first.

Which was probably why it had all gone so horribly wrong. She hadn't thought through her strategy enough. Usually, she liked to script important events in her mind first before she tackled them in real life. Of course, in real life, people often diverged wildly from her mental script—but for some reason it helped her feel braver if she'd already imagined a version of the scene in her head.

She took a deep breath and tried to fluff her blond hair into a semblance of Cindi or Carol's provocative hairstyles. It resolutely refused to do anything but hang limply by her face, and she finally dropped her hands to her sides. She was stalling. She had to go out there and face him.

She tried her best smile in the mirror. She had good teeth, small and straight and white. And she liked her lips—they were full and pouty, even more so with some of her mom's lipstick on. The smile looked okay. She tried a greeting.

"Hi, Dylan."

She grimaced. She sounded *way* too familiar. It wasn't as if they were friends or anything. Especially after today. But what were her options? She could hardly call him Mr. Anderson. He'd die laughing.

"Hey, do you have a moment?" she said instead, trying to sound sure of herself, a woman of the world. Her voice came out all weird and croaky, like Miss Piggy.

Her eyes dropped to the bodice of her satin gown once more. Who was she kidding? She looked like a kid playing dress-up—a really tall, skinny kid. Why would Dylan glance twice at her when she didn't even look like a real woman?

On impulse, she spun on her heel and stepped into the first cubicle. Working feverishly, she plucked again and again at the single-sheet toilet paper dispenser, her hands a blur of motion as she harvested a mountain of paper.

One nervous eye on the door, she stuffed the tissue down her bodice. It prickled against her skin as she adjusted it again and again until two respectable-looking mounds tented the front of her spaghetti-strapped, knee-length, black satin dress. She turned sideways to the mirror, then spun around the other way. A small smile curved her lips. She looked good. She had breasts! Surfing a wave of confidence, she pushed her way out into the corridor.

Music throbbed loudly as she made her way toward the gym. Madonna's "Vogue" was playing, and as she entered the cavernous gym she saw Cindi and Carol and their clique striking a series of sexy poses on the dance floor.

Immediately she began to scan for Dylan. Her eyes ran over the Jocks, lounging on the bleachers and eyeing the dancing cheerleaders with lascivious intent. Next were the gaggle of Art Geeks, their dramatic black hair and smudged kohl eyeliner making them look like extras in a Michael Jackson video in the gym's nightclub lighting. The Burn-outs and Freaks were next, then the Math Nerds. A frown pleated her forehead as she turned slowly, trying to find Dylan's tall, rangy frame in the crowd. He wouldn't be dancing—he was too cool to dance. And he wouldn't necessarily be hanging out with any of the established groups. He was a lone wolf, operating outside the cliques that made up the school's social hierarchy. Luckily for him, he was good-looking enough and funny enough and cool enough to get away with it. James Dean for a new generation, except his hair was raven-black instead of dirty-blond and his eyes a dark, disturbing gray.

The crowd parted briefly as the tide shifted on the dance floor between songs. Sheryl Crow's "All I Wanna Do" came on, and suddenly she saw him standing on the other side of the gym. As usual, her heart skipped a beat. He was so dark and dangerous and beautiful.

She moved toward him, edging past dancing teens, dodging uncoordinated elbows and knees until finally he was within reach, his back to her as he talked to another guy from their year.

Nerves tap-danced in her belly now that she was near him. She almost turned away, but instead she forced herself to reach out and touch his arm, rationalizing that he probably wouldn't hear her over the music if she tried to attract his attention verbally. Plus she got to touch him, even if it was only through his clothing.

He swung around to face her and she swallowed a lump of pure adoration as she looked into his face. His unusual dark gray eyes, fringed with sooty, wasted-on-a-boy lashes, his straight, strong nose, the carved perfection of his lips and chin—she could practically sculpt him from stone she knew his features so well.

His expression was unreadable as he stared at her, but there was no missing the way his eyes dropped down below her face for a brief moment. She felt a zing of triumph rocket along her veins. He'd noticed her cleavage! It *had* made a difference!

"I just wanted to say I'm really sorry about today. And to let you know I can help you with American Lit, if you like," she yelled over the music.

His face screwed up impatiently and he shook his head to indicate he couldn't hear what she was saying.

Greatly daring, Sadie stood on her toes to make up for the few inches of difference in their heights and leaned toward him. She was so close, she could feel the heat coming off his body.

"American Lit. If you need any help…?" she yelled.

He definitely heard her that time, but his expression was unreadable. Crucially, though, he didn't say no outright. She congratulated herself on at last getting through to him. He simply hadn't understood her earlier offer, the one she'd made in class, before she'd… Well, obviously she could make up for all that now.

He leaned close.

"Sure, Sadie," he said in her ear. "You can help me out with American Lit—but first you have to tell me something."

She was awash with relief and excitement. She could feel his breath on her ear. And he was going to forgive her. She had a second chance to prove herself.

"Sure. What?"

He pointed to her chest.

"What the hell is that?"

Sadie glanced down—and froze. A glowing nimbus of white light was radiating out of the neckline of her dress. For a moment her mind went blank with horror, unable to comprehend what she was seeing. Then she realized that the bleached tissue she'd stuffed down her dress was responding to the black-light disco lighting. Not just responding—she had a supernova in her bodice, enough light to rival the neon glow of Vegas. Astronauts were probably pointing and staring from the moon, her chest was glowing so brightly.

She gasped, clapping her hands to her breasts to try to cover the incriminating radiance. Stricken, she glanced up and saw that Dylan was grinning, a hard glint in his eye now. He hadn't forgiven her for today. Not by a mile.

"You got a cold or something?" he asked. Then he reached forward and pulled her clutching hands effortlessly from her chest. Crooking a finger into her bodice, he tugged it out so he could look down her top more clearly. "Man, you've got a whole rainforest down there, haven't you?"

She was numb with shock as he reached into the neckline of her dress, unable to comprehend what was happening. She'd imagined his hands against her skin a million times, but as she felt the warm brush of his fingers against her body there was no desire, only a rising tide of nausea and shame. Slowly, casually, he plucked the scrunched-up tissue from her dress, handing each piece to her so that soon she was holding a small pile of glowing white balls. A crowd gathered to witness the spectacle. Out of the corner of her eye, she could see the Jocks doubled over with laughter as they saw what was happening, while Cindi and her pack giggled behind their hands. Others murmured sympathetically, shaking their heads as they witnessed her humiliation.

At last she was holding all the tissue, and Dylan reached forward and covered her clutching hands with his own. Leaning in close, he squeezed her hands meaningfully with his own and looked her in the eye.

"I think we're about done, Sadie Post," he said. For the first time she smelled the alcohol on his breath and registered the glassy cast to his eyes.

He turned his back on her. She stood frozen for a few more pathetic seconds as he walked away, then she turned tail and ran, glowing balls of tissue scattering in her wake.

She wanted to die. She could never come to school again.

She could never do anything again. Within minutes, the whole school would know what had happened, and she would be the absolute laughingstock, a figure of pity and fun for everyone to take a shot at.

Tears streaked her face as she bolted down the corridor, her sobs echoing off the brick walls. She hated Dylan Anderson. She hated him as much as she used to love him. More, even.

And she was never, ever, going to forget this.

1

"SADIE, STOP FIDGETING. You're a bride. You're supposed to be serene and dignified," Claudia said.

Sadie grimaced apologetically. "Sorry. I just wanted to see," she said hopefully.

"Well, you can't. Not until I've finished," Claudia Dostis said firmly, returning to the task of lacing the corsetlike back of Sadie's ivory-silk wedding gown.

Sadie sighed and nodded, and her other bridesmaid, Grace Wellington, smacked her lightly on the shoulder.

"That includes your head, too," she said. Grace was trying to anchor a frothy veil into the upswept mass of Sadie's honey-blond hair.

"Does this mean I have to go back to bride-training school?" Sadie asked meekly.

"If you're very still for the next twenty seconds, we'll put in a good word for you," Claudia said.

They were her closest friends, as well as her work colleagues and she trusted them implicitly, so she made a big effort to calm her nerves and stand docilely for the next few minutes as they continued to fuss. Finally, she felt a last tug around her middle, then Claudia let out a sigh.

"Done!"

"Me, too," Grace said.

They both stepped back and surveyed her with satisfaction.

"Nice work with the veil," Claudia said to Grace.

"Not so shabby on the dress work, either," Grace said, returning the compliment.

Sadie raised an amused eyebrow. "Does this mean I finally get to look?"

Grace and Claudia grabbed a shoulder each and gently turned her around to face the freestanding mirror in the middle of her bedroom.

The woman facing her was a stranger, an elegant fairy princess in floating ivory silk, her blond hair swept into a sleek, sophisticated updo, her neck long and slender, her pale skin flawless, her large brown eyes dramatic and sexy.

"Wow. Is that really me?" Sadie squeaked.

"Yep. Gorgeous, as always," Claudia confirmed.

Sadie blushed at her friend's compliment, but a frown creased her forehead as her gaze inevitably drifted to her chest. It was pathetic, but she would probably never be one-hundred-percent happy with the size of her breasts, she admitted to herself. Too much baggage. Too long waiting around for the damned things to arrive in the first place. Who didn't develop breasts until they were nineteen, for Pete's sake? It was a form of cruelty, as far as Sadie was concerned.

"What's wrong? You hate the way I did the veil, don't you?" Grace asked, her clear green eyes clouded with concern.

Sadie pushed the old, old worry way. She was a B cup. Perfectly respectable. It was because she was nervous—that was why such an old, dusty preoccupation had reared its ugly head.

"It's perfect, thank you. I was just wondering if I should have gone with a white dress instead of ivory," she fibbed.

Claudia made a rude noise. "Even ivory is pushing it, lady," she said knowingly.

"Hey!" Sadie said, pretending to be offended. "Are you implying I'm not a virgin?"

"I hope you're not," Grace said. "I'll have to take down all that stuff I wrote about you on the toilet wall."

They all giggled like idiots, then Sadie caught sight of the time and a jolt of adrenaline rocketed through her. The car would be here in twenty minutes.

"You guys had better get dressed," she advised.

"Remind me again how you talked me into this dress," Grace muttered as she unzipped the long, figure-hugging, strapless red sheath that had been tailor-made for her bombshell figure.

"Let me see… Because I am Bridezilla, and I must have my way?" Sadie suggested lightly.

"And because you were outvoted two to one," Claudia said as she slid into her pint-size version of the same dress. Although she was petite, Claudia's figure was still feminine, and the red fabric clung to her curves. With her olive skin and almost-black Greek eyes, she looked stunning.

"Oh, God."

Sadie turned from contemplating Claudia's dark beauty to see that Grace had pulled on her dress and stepped into her stiletto heels. Red silk outlined her classic hourglass figure, zooming in dramatically at her tiny waist, and then out again for her fantastic, sexy hips. She looked like Veronica Lake and Betty Grable and Marilyn Monroe, all rolled into one sexy, hot mama.

"Hubba, hubba." Sadie hooted approvingly.

Grace blushed a fiery red to match the dress. "I look like an overcooked hot dog," she said gruffly. "If one of these seams gives, duck for cover."

Sadie laughed and shook her head. They looked beautiful. Red had been the ideal choice for both of them, and the classy dress set off their different figures to perfection.

"I think we need more champagne," she said, moving across to where the last bottle rested on ice. She and Grace had already guzzled a whole bottle while their hair and makeup was being done—Claudia being a staunch teetotaler—but Sadie figured the alcohol would help settle her growing nerves.

She was getting married! Her mind turned briefly to Greg

Sinclair, the handsome blond man she would soon call husband. She wondered what he was doing, how he was feeling. Was he as nervous-excited as she was? Would it be cheating to call him before the wedding?

Resisting the temptation to jinx things by making a quick phone call, Sadie concentrated on working the cork loose from the champagne bottle as Claudia and Grace put the finishing touches on their hair and makeup.

She had to stifle a smile as she heard Claudia bossily telling Grace to not even think about putting on the heavy black-framed retro glasses she habitually wore.

"Banned from the wedding," Claudia announced firmly.

She was going to make a great producer on *Ocean Boulevard,* Sadie knew. She sighed happily to herself as she poured out the champagne. Her life was so good right now. It had been cool enough working with Grace for the past two years as script producer to her script editor on *Ocean Boulevard,* the daytime soap that currently consumed her working hours, but now Claudia would be joining them as producer of the show. It didn't get much better—doing something she loved for a living with her two closest friends by her side. And, in under an hour's time, she would be married to an amazing, funny, clever, gorgeous man.

"Pinch me, quick," she said to Grace as her friend came over to collect a glass of champagne.

"Sure," Grace said, obliging with a gentle nip on Sadie's arm. "Better?"

Sadie grinned and slid an arm around her friend's waist. "Where would I be without you guys?"

Claudia joined them, and she slid an arm around her waist, too. Across the room, the mirror reflected their images back at them and Sadie couldn't help smiling. What a mismatched set—Claudia the pocket-rocket, string-bean old her and Grace the va-voom vamp.

"I love you guys. Thanks so much for doing this with me," she said.

Claudia and Grace squeezed their arms tighter around her waist, and she had to stare at the ceiling for a few seconds and blink like crazy to avoid crying.

"Suck 'em back in, Sadie—no brides with panda eyes on our shift," Claudia said encouragingly.

Sadie laughed, the humor helping to restore her equilibrium. Bang on time, the doorbell rang.

"God, the car's here already," she said, her nerves ratcheting up a notch.

The next five minutes were spent in a bustle of activity as they gathered all the items Grace and Claudia considered necessary to maintaining her appearance through the ceremony and reception—including the rest of the bottle of champagne. Her bridesmaids spent another five minutes out in the street discussing the best way for Sadie to sit on her skirt, until finally Sadie stepped past them and squished herself into the seat.

"Easy," she said when they stared at her, scandalized.

The church was a ten-minute drive away, and she sat back and tried to let the sunny blue sky soothe her. It was useless, however—her brain was like a hamster on a wheel. What if she forgot her vows? She'd always been hopeless at remembering lines. And what if she tripped when she walked up the aisle and her skirt flipped up and—God! Had she even remembered to put underwear on? She clapped a hand to her hip, but was unable to feel anything through all the layers of fabric.

She turned to Claudia on her right. "Did I put underwear on? Can you remember?" she asked urgently.

Claudia patted her arm reassuringly. "You need to stop thinking, sweetie," she said firmly.

Sadie opened her mouth to protest, then her sense of humor caught up with her and she collapsed into laughter.

Which was why she almost missed seeing her uncle Gus

standing out front of the church, frantically waving the driver on as they approached. At the last minute, however, as the car swept past the church, she registered the formally dressed man gyrating like a maniac on the sidewalk.

Swiveling in her seat, she craned her neck to look out the rear window and confirm it really was Gus, and that they really had driven straight past the church.

"Um…hello?" she said, leaning forward to tap on the glass dividing the back of the limo from the driver. "Wasn't that the church back there?"

"Yeah, but we got waved on. I'm going to do a lap," the driver explained.

Sadie sat back with a thump and stared first at Claudia and then Grace.

"What the hell?" she finally asked.

Both her friends were looking equally confused.

"Maybe they're waiting on something," Grace suggested.

Sadie bit her lip. A horrible, dark thought slithered into her mind and she tried not to look in its direction. It was useless, however—she worked on a daytime soap. She'd written or helped plot this scene too many times over the years. Happy bride, perfect day, laughter—then disaster. Dead groom. Groom gravely ill due to car accident. Revolt in groom's far-off European principality—she'd done them all over the years.

"Can we go back, please?" she asked the driver anxiously. "I don't want to do a lap of the church."

"But—" the driver objected.

"You heard the bride. Turn the car around," Claudia ordered, her producer's voice firmly in place.

Sighing audibly, the driver spun the wheel and the car turned back toward the church.

As they approached from the opposite direction, Sadie could see her uncle had been joined by her pale-faced aunt, Martha.

His shoulders were slumped and he shook his head as they discussed something intently.

"Oh *shit*," she whispered under her breath. Another series of worst-case scenarios flitted across her mind: groom runs off with best friend. Bomb threat on church. Groom turns out to be bride's secret brother.

"I know what you're thinking, and I know it's hard to rein in that imagination of yours because of what we do for a living, but this is not *Ocean Boulevard*," Grace said firmly. "It's probably something lame like the priest has had too much altar wine, or Greg's allergic to his boutonniere."

Sadie took a deep breath and forced herself to let go of the awful, over-the-top scenarios racing across her mind. Grace was right. She was overreacting. She wouldn't go borrowing trouble—she'd simply face whatever was wrong and deal with it.

Her uncle must have heard the car, because he turned and frowned as the limo came to a halt.

Despite her vow to herself, Sadie leaned across Claudia to push the door open, unable to wait for the chauffeur to do it. Claudia slid out instantly, turning to help Sadie drag herself and her silk train from the car. The click of heels on the pavement told her that Grace was circling the car from the other side, but all Sadie's attention was on Gus.

"What's going on?" she asked. She was clutching her bouquet in a death grip, her knuckles white.

"I'm sorry, sweetheart," Gus said, and Sadie knew then, without a doubt, that she was about to have a Soap Wedding.

Behind her, she heard Grace's swift, shocked intake of breath, and Claudia muttered a four-letter word.

"He's not here?" Sadie guessed, taking a stab at which soap cliché she was about to get sucked into. Of course, she could rule out a few right from the start. To her knowledge, Greg was not the prince of some far-flung European country. And she was pretty sure he wasn't her brother, given that he was the spitting image of his father. Also, her two best friends in all the world were standing behind her, so neither of them had run off with him.

"He had a note delivered," Martha said, handing over a plain letter-size envelope.

Sadie stared down at it for a long moment before passing her bouquet to Grace. Her hands were trembling as she slid a finger beneath the seal and tore the envelope open. There was a single piece of paper inside. Greg had gone to the trouble of printing it, she saw, rather than writing it by hand. She had a flash of him mulling over the composition of the letter on his notebook computer, adding and deleting words as he pondered how best to break it to her. He obviously hadn't mulled for too long, however. The note was devastatingly short.

Dear Sadie,
I know I'm the one who wanted to hurry, but you were right. It's too soon to get married. Don't worry, I'll pay for everything. I just need some time to get my head together. Forward the bills as they come.
Yours, Greg

Her hand dropped to her side and she blinked back the storm of tears that was pressing against the backs of her eyes. That was it? He was dumping her at the altar, and she only got a handful of words?

"What did he say?" Claudia asked.

Sadie held out the letter. There was a short silence as Claudia and Grace read the note then passed it to her aunt and uncle.

"He never said anything, hinted at anything…?" Martha asked, bewildered.

Out of the corner of her eye, she could see Claudia's head come up.

"You mean like, 'Sadie, I don't think I'm going to turn up

tomorrow'? That kind of thing?" Claudia asked in a dangerously calm voice.

Sadie laid a hand on her arm. "Claud," she said. This was
not her aunt's fault. She was a good woman who'd done her
best to fill in the gaps in Sadie's life when her parents were
killed in a car accident seven years ago. Martha was blown
away—as they all were.

"I can't believe this," Grace said, her eyes scanning over and
over the few words on the note. "This is…unbelievable."

Sadie lifted her eyes to contemplate the stately church in
front of her.

Inside, more than two hundred of her and Greg's friends and
relatives were waiting to celebrate their wedding. The men
would be in suits, the women in gorgeous-but-deadly designer
high heels that they knew they'd regret by the time the reception was over. In their cars, presents would be sitting, wrapped
and ready to put on the gift table once they arrived at the reception. Toasters, kettles, towels, glassware. The wherewithal
to set up a new home. Her and Greg's new home.

She hoped they'd all kept their receipts.

She clenched her hands together as a wave of humiliation
and hurt threatened to descend. She wanted nothing more than
to turn on her heel and get the hell out of here. To pretend that
she had never been so foolish as to believe the words of
handsome Greg Sinclair when he'd looked into her eyes and
told her he adored her. That he wanted to marry her, as soon as
possible. That he'd never felt more sure of anything in his life.

"Let's go," Claudia said decisively. She gestured toward the
waiting car where the chauffeur was doing his best not to look
too interested in what was going on. This would be a bit of a
treat for him, Sadie reflected distractedly. A twist on the usual.

"Yes, your friend is right, sweetheart," Gus said. "You go,
and we'll let everyone know that there's been an incident, and
the wedding's been postponed."

Sadie winced at her uncle's choice of words. She knew he thought they'd save her face, but everyone in the church would know the truth. It was pretty damned obvious what had happened—the groom hadn't shown up.

She could imagine them all whispering behind their order-of-service booklets while she stood outside trying to work out what to do. *Why is it all taking so long? Where's the groom? Shouldn't he be waiting at the altar?*

Suddenly it all felt suffocatingly familiar. The refrain from Sheryl Crow's "All I Wanna Do" tinkled its way through her mind, and for a horrible moment she was standing in the middle of the gym again as her classmates mocked and pitied her.

"No!" she said suddenly, determined to shake the past off.

Everyone stared at her.

"No, what?" Grace asked.

"No, I'm not going," Sadie said. She turned toward the church and started walking before her courage failed her.

The others scrambled to keep up.

"You don't have to do this, Sadie," Claudia said, trying to hustle in her ankle-length sheath and high heels.

"Yeah, I do. They're my friends and family. I invited them all here," Sadie said with determination.

"We can do it," Grace said, dodging in front of her. "Let us do it. Please."

"I want to do it," Sadie said through gritted teeth. "I *need* to do it."

It was true. She knew they'd all feel sorry for her, and she didn't want or need their pity. Would do anything to avoid it, in fact.

Grace slowly stepped aside, and Sadie continued her headlong march toward the church door. The coolness of the vestibule enveloped her as she pushed open the ornate double doors. She almost tripped on her voluminous skirts, and she looked down to see her train had gotten caught in the door. She felt tears looming again as she tugged her dress loose, as though the act of pausing had allowed the shame and hurt to catch up with her.

God, she couldn't do this. But she had to. For herself. She took a step forward.

"Wait," Grace said.

Sadie steeled herself to be firm again, but Grace pointed at her mouth.

"You've got lipstick on your teeth," she said quietly.

Sadie rubbed her thumb across her incisors and smiled for her friends.

"How's that?"

"Good," Grace said tightly.

Nodding her thanks, Sadie grabbed a big fistful of silk and lifted it to her waist so she could walk more freely. Claudia and Grace stepped ahead of her, their expressions tortured as they shoved the inner doors open for her.

An abrupt silence fell as two hundred and twelve people swiveled in their seats to stare at her as she stood at the top of the aisle. At the front of the church, the organist gasped with surprise and automatically dropped her hands down onto the keyboard. The first few notes of "Here Comes The Bride" sounded before the woman snatched her hands away, blushing furiously.

Humiliated heat rushed to Sadie's cheeks as the echoes died. Eyes straight ahead, she strode briskly up the aisle toward the altar where the priest, Father Baker, was eyeing her sympathetically.

Claudia and Grace flanked her, their faces set. Sadie had no idea what her own face was doing. She was just concentrating on not crying, not throwing up and walking. That was about all she could handle at the moment.

The priest came down off his three-step elevation to meet her.

"Sadie, my dear," he said, reaching out a hand.

"I'm sorry for wasting your time, Father," she said stiffly. "If you'll give me a moment, we'll get out of your hair."

He looked surprised when she swept past him and stepped up to the microphone on the pulpit. Flicking the switch on the microphone's side, she took a deep breath and lifted her gaze at last to confront her waiting audience.

Every last person was holding their breath. Some of them were even leaning forward in anticipation. It was almost funny. Almost.

"Sorry to keep you all waiting," she said. Her voice broke on the last word, and she cleared her throat and blinked back the tears that had rushed to her eyes. She was *not* going to cry. Not yet.

She felt Grace's hand on her back as her friend moved behind her. The warm knowledge that Grace and Claudia were here helped her focus.

"As you might have noticed, we seem to be short a groom. Don't you hate that?" she said wryly.

Her audience stirred, and a few people tittered. They hadn't expected wise-cracking, but it was all she had to offer at the moment.

"I don't suppose anyone wants to volunteer on short notice?" she asked, raising an eyebrow and looking around, pretending she was waiting for someone to step up to the plate. More embarrassed laughter and uncertainty from her audience. "Can't be tempted? Bummer. I guess it's party time, then. And I expect to see each and every one of you at the reception—Greg has assured me he's paying, so let's make sure we blow out the bar tab."

Pinning a bright, confident smile on her face, Sadie stepped back from the mike.

Claudia's face was pale as she helped gather up Sadie's skirts so she could march back up the aisle.

"Are you sure…?" Claudia asked in an undertone. "I mean, the reception…?"

"Yes. No. I don't know."

Sadie had no idea how she was going to get through finger food plus three courses, but somehow she had to.

There was a muted murmur as she strode up the aisle, head high.

Then she was outside, heading toward the limo. The chauffeur hastily butted out his cigarette and leaped to open the door for her. She practically dove into the rear of the car, one hand reaching for the half-full champagne bottle before her dress train had even made it through the door. All pretense at grace or composure gone, she lifted the bottle to her mouth and guzzled greedily. A small rivulet of golden champagne trickled over her chin and down between her breasts. She didn't give a hoot.

Claudia and Grace wedged themselves in beside her, and Claudia reached over to secure the seat belt over the scrunched-up folds of Sadie's dress.

Sadie took another hearty slug of champagne before speaking.

"I hope you've broken those shoes in, ladies, because tonight we are *dancing*," she announced bravely.

DYLAN ANDERSON SMILED to himself as he pulled down the last photo from the corkboard in his office. It had been taken using a Polaroid camera during a long, crazy afternoon in the story room when everyone had been banging their heads against the wall, trying to come up with something to fill sixty minutes of commercial television for Box-Office Cable's hit drama, *The Boardroom*. The smile turned into a grin as he studied the shot—six grown, adult people crowded together, their features hopelessly distorted by the adhesive tape they'd used to fix their faces into weird, strange configurations. It was puerile, adolescent—and that was being generous. Particularly given the net total of their salaries. But sometimes the pressure cooker of the writers' room had to blow. And, in his experience, something strange, funny and wonderful always came out of it.

Okay, maybe the day of the taped faces wasn't the best example of the phenomena—but it was a great memory, which was why he was taking all his Polaroid shots with him. Each one represented a moment he wanted to remember. *The Boardroom* had been his best TV writing experience to date, a rare convergence of inspired creator, simpatico writing team and talented directors, cast and crew. An absolute gift, from beginning to end. But Dylan had still opted not to renew his contract with the show for another year.

He'd been tempted. It was always tempting to stay where you knew you were appreciated, and your work was consistently affirmed by the television industry in the form of award nominations, stellar reviews and high ratings. But Dylan had never been the kind of guy to rest on his laurels. Despite what certain people in his past might think. He had goals, and nothing short of the extinction of the entire human race was going to stop him from achieving them.

His hand dropped to the thick envelope sitting on his desk, already addressed and ready for the courier to pick up. His feature screenplay, finished at last. The first of many, he hoped. Ready to send off to his agent so she could begin shopping it around. He patted the envelope, thinking of all the long hours he'd spent plotting the damned thing, writing, rewriting, then rewriting again to get it where he wanted it.

He allowed himself to feel a small moment of pride as he contemplated the achievement on the very simplest of scales—he, personally, had written over ninety pages of screenplay. Spelled the words correctly. Even got the grammar and punctuation right, give or take a few colloquial exceptions. The man—boy, really—he'd been fourteen years ago would have been astonished. But that boy hadn't known that he had dyslexia. That boy had whipped himself daily for being an ignorant half-wit who couldn't understand even the basics of stuff that other kids seemed to take in as easily as air. He'd been on a road to self-destruction, spiraling out of control, furious at himself for being kicked out of school, looking for some way to ease the pain…

Realizing that he was standing in his almost-empty office dwelling on his misspent youth, Dylan gave his head a brief, impatient shake. All that stuff was history, water under the bridge. Long gone, done and dusted. Unimportant in the world of here and now.

Stacking the screenplay on top of the carton of personal effects to take out to his car, Dylan spent the next few minutes checking his desk drawers for anything he'd forgotten. Apart from stray paper clips and Post-it notes, he was home free.

His heart felt lighter as he grabbed the box. *The Boardroom* team were holding a goodbye dinner for him tonight at his favorite Mexican restaurant in Hollywood, and he'd say his final goodbyes then. For now, he was content—happy, even— to be moving on from this stage in his life.

He'd made it to the office door and was balancing the carton on his knee to flick the light off when his phone rang. Frowning, he contemplated not answering it, but his conscience wouldn't let him walk away without picking up. Sighing, he dumped the box on his visitor's chair and scooped up the phone.

"Anderson, here," he said.

"Dylan, it's Ruby. You got a sec?" his agent asked rhetorically. Rhetorically because, no matter what his response, she always kept talking. She could talk under wet cement, his agent. One of the reasons he paid her a small fortune every year.

"I know you're keen to put your feet up for a while and give that enormous brain of yours a break, but I've just had a very interesting call," Ruby said. Dylan smiled to himself, recognizing the *enormous brain* reference as Ruby's way of softening him up.

"Forget it," he said firmly. "No. Negative. Non. Not interested. I officially do not exist for the next two months. Then you can start fielding job offers for me again."

"Dylan, baby, you haven't even heard what the offer is!" Ruby wailed.

Dylan rested his hip against his desk. Ruby was only getting warmed up, he could tell.

"You're going to have the screenplay on your desk tomorrow morning. That should keep you busy enough."

"So you don't even want to know who's desperate for a story editor on short notice? Not even a tiny inkling of curiosity?" Ruby asked.

"Nope. Not interested," Dylan said smugly. He had the next two months of his life planned down to the second—three concepts to develop further for network pitches, and several more screenplays in various stages of plotting. Only when he'd laid the groundwork for the next step in his career would he start looking at in-house jobs again.

"Fine. I'll ask around the traps, see if anyone else good is available."

Off the hook, Dylan felt free to be helpful. "Try Olly Jones. I know he was keen to stop freelancing and go back in-house."

"Yeah, I know. They signed him to *Crime Scene* last week."

"Hey, that's great," Dylan said, pleased for his friend and making a mental note to give Olly a call. He couldn't remember the last time he'd had a full weekend to himself or caught up with his friends.

"You got your big goodbye bash tonight?" Ruby asked.

"Yep. Gotta go home and stock up on the tissue," Dylan said.

"Yeah, right, because you're so sentimental," Ruby scoffed.

"I'm an emotional guy," Dylan defended.

Ruby made a rude noise. "Anyway, I'll call you once I've read the script," she said.

"Sure. See you."

Before he could put the phone down, Ruby spoke up again, her tone exasperated. "You're really going to let me hang up without even asking which show it was? You could really do that?"

"Yep."

"And you call yourself a writer! Where's your natural-born curiosity and nosiness?"

"It's not going to work, Ruby," he said good-naturedly. "I've got too much to work on to even consider it."

"Fine. It's just I know you like the show, I thought you'd be tickled to work on it," Ruby said. He could almost see her shrugging her big shoulder pads.

"Ruby…"

"Fine. Don't work on America's number-one daytime soap. See if I care."

He was about to end the call, but he hesitated for a beat, his interest well and truly caught.

"You mean, *Ocean Boulevard?*"

"The one and same," Ruby said smugly. "Apparently, their story ed's written himself off for six months or so in a car accident."

"Yeah?" Dylan said, his mind ticking over at about a million miles a minute. Sadie Post worked on *Ocean Boulevard,* had done for the past four years. He'd have to be deaf, dumb and blind not to know that in the small industry they worked in.

He couldn't even think her name without feeling a burning resentment. A series of images flashed across his mind's eye—Sadie staring at him with burning intensity as she humiliated him in class by peppering him with questions she knew he couldn't answer; the impatient disgust on his guidance counselor's face as he kicked him out of school; his father's contemptuous acceptance that flipping burgers was all his ignorant son was good for.

"Dylan. You still there? Hello?" Ruby said.

"Keep talking," he said after a long moment.

Maybe he wasn't as busy as he'd thought.

TEN DAYS LATER Sadie drove into her assigned parking spot at the *Ocean Boulevard* production offices in Santa Monica and pressed the button to bring the roof down on her Audi TT convertible. She checked her appearance. Her hair looked windblown, but it matched the tan she'd gained on her honeymoon-for-one in the Caribbean and she figured it was the least of her problems. It was amazing how things like convertible-hair suddenly gained perspective when you had a real crisis to deal with. Nothing like being stood up at the altar to give a girl a reality check.

Grabbing her satchel, she swung her legs out of her low-slung car and pushed herself to her feet. She couldn't wait to get into work. She imagined her desk, overloaded with scripts and story lines for her to read, and felt pathetically grateful. *Ocean Boulevard* was her sanctuary, her solace. She knew it would take all her energy and focus, and then some. Its comforting embrace would get her through the next few months. She was banking on it.

Not that she was a basket case. Far from it. She was good, solid.

Okay, she wasn't about to kick up her heels and dance a jig, but she wasn't a sniveling wreck, either. After ten days of self-pity in the Caribbean, she'd picked herself up and dusted herself off. Life went on, and so would she. It was that simple.

Recovering was a little easier given that she still hadn't heard from Greg. She told herself she liked it that way. If she never spoke to him again, she could pretend the whole six months she'd thought she was in love with him had been a hallucination.

Striding toward the building, she switched her focus firmly to work. She hadn't had a chance to download any of the story lines that had been written while she was away, but she could spend the day catching up before the team pitched her their ideas for the week's episodes on Tuesday morning.

She mentally reviewed the show's story strands from a week and a half ago as she breezed past the receptionist and into the open-plan office. Set in Santa Monica, *Ocean Boulevard* centered around a group of people living in a Spanish mission-style apartment block on the street of the same name. The show ran an hour a day, five days a week, so there was always plenty of work to keep her busy.

A couple of heads came up as they spotted her, but she waved and flashed a bright, confident smile. *Nothing to see here,* her expression said. *No tragedy to pick over. Please, move on.*

Her office looked exactly the same as when she'd left it, except for a vase full of fresh tiger lilies on her desk return. Claudia being thoughtful, she guessed.

Slinging her satchel on top of her filing cabinet, she hit the power button on her computer and waited for it to boot up. She was typing in her password when Claudia appeared in her office doorway.

"I knew you'd be in early, you workaholic," Claudia said. Her tiny frame was encased from head to toe in black, her signature color.

"Holiday's over," Sadie said, clicking through to her e-mail program.

"Hmm. I don't suppose the gutless wonder has made contact yet?" Claudia asked, referring to Greg.

"Nope, thank God," Sadie said. "I have nothing to say to him."

Claudia raised a disbelieving eyebrow, but let the subject go.

"We need to have a quick work powwow," she said, switching to producer mode. Propping a hip against Sadie's bookcase, she tucked her hands into her trouser pockets. "Don't freak, but Joss had a car accident while you were away. Broke his pelvis in three places."

Sadie gasped. "Oh, my God. Is he okay? Was anyone else hurt?"

"No. The idiot was test driving a Porsche on Toyopa Drive in the Palisades. A dog ran across the road and he smacked into a tree." Claudia shook her head as though she still couldn't quite believe it. Joss was notoriously accident prone. He could find a way to hurt himself in a rubber room.

"Wow. But he's going to be okay?" Sadie asked.

"Six months before he'll be out of rehab, but he's fully covered by insurance, so apart from the joys of physiotherapy et cetera, all is good. Except, of course, we kind of need him."

Sadie's eyes widened. For a moment she'd been so worried about Joss's health that she'd forgotten about the show.

"God, yes. We have to find a new story editor," she said, her brain hitting a brick wall at the very thought. Story editors—good ones—were like hen's teeth, difficult to find. Usually it took months to woo someone away from another show, or to headhunt a promising up-and-comer. The story editor was the focal point of the story team, the person who said yes or no to plot lines and drove a show forward. As script producer, the story editor and his or her team were Sadie's direct reports. It would be her responsibility to find someone to stoke *Ocean Boulevard*'s furnace with new and innovative ideas now that Joss had taken himself out of the game. Automatically, she reached for her address book, but Claudia waved a hand.

"Relax. I sorted it out while you were gone. We got lucky," she said.

"Yeah?" Sadie asked doubtfully.

"You're going to love him. Five years experience in London working on various shows, including their top-rated police procedural, and he's coming off three years with Box-Office Cable on *The Boardroom*. I still can't believe we got him, but he was between contracts and he loves the show."

Sadie frowned. European experience, credits on *The Boardroom*—BOC's gritty depiction of high-stakes corporate life. It was all starting to ring a bell in the back of her mind. A very large, very noisy, alarm bell.

"I'm not sure if…" she said, but Claudia spoke over her.

"Look, here he is now. You guys can chat a little before everyone gets here."

Sadie felt the blood drain from her face and her stomach drop to the floor as she saw the tall, dark-haired man approaching over Claudia's shoulder.

He still had to-die-for good looks. His eyelashes were still too long and dark. And his gray eyes were still cocky and overly confident.

She stared at him, all her nightmares rolled into six-foot-two-inches of strong, supple male.

Dylan Anderson. Her teen nemesis. And her new direct report.

2
―――――――

As soon as Dylan saw Sadie Post, all his expectations about working on *Ocean Boulevard* went out the window.

After initial talks with Claudia, he'd been genuinely intrigued about the idea of working on a soap. The demands of the show—five one-hour episodes per week—meant that an enormous amount of material had to be produced by the writing team. It would be a challenge, and an opportunity to push the envelope. Just talking to Claudia had given him ideas. But he'd be fooling himself if he pretended that was why he'd walked away from his own plans so easily—learning from Claudia that Sadie would not be a part of the hiring process had been the clincher. The thought of her returning from vacation in the Caribbean to find him ensconced as her new story editor had been irresistible.

Despite all his achievements and how far he'd come, the memory of his humiliation in American Lit at her hands remained a sore spot in his psyche. It wasn't the most mature or rational or noble motivation for taking a contract with *Ocean Boulevard,* but he figured a guy was allowed a moment of weakness every now and then.

Then he walked in her office door and all his expectations hit an unexpected slippery patch and went skidding out of control.

When he'd pictured this moment in his mind, Sadie had been as forgettable as she'd been throughout their school years—same blah blond hair pulled back into a tidy ponytail, same raillike body in baggy clothes.

But the woman rising from her office chair to face him was an Amazonian goddess. Nearly six foot—had she always been so tall?—with long, flowing Pamela-Anderson-just-rolled-out-of-bed-hair. And her body was no longer skinny. In fact, it looked as though the curve fairy had paid her a very substantial visit since he'd last seen her. Perky breasts thrust up from a slim torso, their curves outlined by a tight black T-shirt. Dark denim jeans clung to legs that were long and lean and seemed to go on forever. Just the way he liked them.

For a second he was so thrown he could only stare and blink. Then he got his game face back on. So, she'd turned into an okay-looking adult. Big deal. It didn't change anything.

He'd already decided how to play this—supercool, not a single allusion to school beyond the mandatory acknowledgment, nothing that would give her the satisfaction of knowing that he attached any significance or power to her memory whatsoever. This was about burying the past, not resurrecting it. Just because she looked like a bikini model from *Swimsuit Illustrated* didn't call for a change of plans.

"Sadie. Great to see you again," he lied through his teeth.

He even managed a smile—nothing too effusive or sucky, just bright enough to be professional. Extending his hand, he waited for her to shake it.

There was a long, long pause before she extended her own hand. Her skin felt cool and silky as her palm slid against his, and his gaze was caught by her velvety-brown eyes. Warm chocolate spiced with caramel, he decided before he registered what he was thinking and gave himself a mental slap.

Where the hell had that come from? She could have shriveled currants for eyes, or big Bambi numbers—it didn't matter one iota to him.

"You guys have met before?" Claudia asked, her gaze alert as she glanced back and forth between them, probably wondering why he hadn't mentioned it in their interview.

"Sadie and I went to school together," he supplied innocuously.

He was holding Sadie's eyes as he said it and was thrown when something soft and vulnerable flashed behind them. Another expectation blown away. He'd imagined defensiveness when she saw him. Even indifference—after all, she probably had dozens of scalps on her belt from all the people she'd stomped on over the years. No doubt it was a real bitch for her to remember what she'd done to whom.

But the hurt, tortured look that had raced briefly across her face threw him. Again.

"That's right. Dylan and I went to the same senior high," Sadie clarified.

"Really. Dylan didn't mention it when we talked," Claudia said, her near-black eyes fixed on him questioningly.

Dylan shrugged self-deprecatingly. "Didn't see the point. It was a long time ago," he said. "To be honest, I wasn't sure Sadie would even remember me."

A muscle tensed in Sadie's jaw, the first and only sign that she felt any discomfort at all. Dylan noted the moment with satisfaction.

"Just goes to show, it's a small world," Claudia said, obviously accepting his explanation. "Kind of takes the wind out of my sails, though. I was pretty proud of finding you all on my own."

Sadie's face was once again under control as she eyed him.

"I thought you were contracted to *The Boardroom*," she said.

Betraying color instantly stole into her cheeks. She'd been keeping an eye on his career. Probably waiting for him to be run out of town or told to sit in the corner with a pointy dunce cap on his head.

"I was packing up my office when Claudia's offer came through," he said. Settling his shoulder against the wall, he turned the conversational spotlight on her.

"I hear you were on holiday in the Caribbean. Where'd you go?"

"Um, St. Barts," she said. Her eyes darted to Claudia, and he got the sense that a secret communication was passing between them. Out of the corner of his eye, he saw Claudia shake her head minutely.

What was going on?

"I was there a few years back. Did you try the scuba?" he asked, probing a little more. What was the big secret about St. Barts?

"No. I mainly hung out on the beach and read and caught up on sleep. You know," she said dismissively.

He narrowed his eyes assessingly. He'd assumed she'd gone on holidays with a friend or boyfriend, but it sounded as though she'd gone alone. Was that what the look between her and Claudia was about? He couldn't quite believe that a woman as attractive as Sadie had to go on holiday alone. Even with his built-in prejudice against her, he could see that many men—okay, most men—would find her attractive.

Of course, there was that personality of hers to consider, he reminded himself. There was only so much bitchiness a man could tolerate for the sake of a sexy body.

"Sounds great," he said.

"Yeah, it was," she replied. She shifted her head a little, her hair rippling over her shoulder as she tilted her chin at him. As though she was daring him to challenge her on her answer.

Definitely something going on there, but he was in no rush to find out. Television production offices were always rife with gossip. All he had to do was tee up the right conversation with the right gossip-monger, and he'd know everything from her shoe size to the last time she flossed.

"Why don't I leave you guys to it, then? Sadie probably needs to be brought up-to-date with what's happened while she's been away," Claudia said, moving toward the door.

Dylan decided to take her departure as the cue to crank things up a little. Time to let Ms. Post know that she wouldn't have things all her way this time around. Without asking permission, he sank into the chair opposite her desk and propped the ankle of one leg confidently on the knee of the other.

He'd been thrown off guard for a couple of moments there by the discovery that Sadie the Stick Post had turned into a whole handful of woman. But he was over that now.

Time to start setting the record straight.

SADIE FELT A STRESS twitch break out under her eye as Dylan Anderson leaned back in her visitor's chair and locked his hands behind his head. As though he owned the place, king of all he surveyed.

She felt as though she was in a human-size snowglobe, and someone had just shaken the crap out of it. In fact, if all her furniture started floating around her, she wouldn't be a bit surprised—she felt utterly, completely at sea. Flummoxed. Thrown. Terrified. Furious. In fact, there was a whole mental ward of violent emotions wrestling for supremacy in her brain. For the moment, she was a helpless bystander, waiting to see which emotion would be the final victor.

Dylan Anderson. *The* Dylan Anderson. Star of her nightmares for at least five years after that horrible, crushing senior prom. The man voted Most Likely to Be Hit by a Car in a Dark Alleyway in her own private, personal yearbook.

And now he was here. Sitting opposite her—slouching, really, already supremely at ease.

She wanted to scream. She wasn't up to this. She was already on her knees after Greg's betrayal. This was too much.

Over the years, she'd imagined running into Dylan again. For a while, it had been her favorite indulgent daydream. In her version, she was wearing a designer gown, looking blindingly beautiful as she sauntered up the aisle after accepting her Best Original Screenplay Oscar. He'd fallen on hard times and was working as a seat warmer, filling in for celebrities when they needed to go to the bathroom. Their eyes met briefly—and she sailed right by, cutting him dead, ignoring him completely. Or, in her alternate fantasy, she stopped and took pity on him, insisting he give her a call—she was sure they could find something for him to do around the production office. Emptying bins, cleaning toilets, licking her shoes. That kind of thing.

Instead she got this—him sitting cockily across from her, making the room feel smaller and putting her whole body on red alert.

Whenever she'd cast him in one of her revenge fantasies, he'd always been balding and paunchy, with a pronounced stoop. Sometimes she even gave him missing teeth. Why the hell not, after all? It was her fantasy, and she was in charge of hair, wardrobe and makeup.

But, unfortunately for her, the years had been kind to Dylan. Not just kind, generous. Really, really generous. Although he'd retained his lean, rangy physique, his shoulders had broadened with age, his chest deepened. His thighs were stronger, his biceps more pronounced. She could even see the smooth curve of pecs beneath his dark green T-shirt. He'd moved on from the rebellious long hair of his youth and wore it cropped short and tousled now, one lock flopping over his forehead. Even the lines around his eyes and mouth only made him more attractive, if that were possible. The bastard.

God, she despised him. For a moment, reconstituted hate threatened to overwhelm her as she stared at him. The things she could say to him. Had wanted to say to him, all those years ago once she'd moved beyond mortification and into rage. In the very early days, she'd written him letters. Long, scathing, insulting letters that told him exactly what she thought of him. She may have even been tempted to deliver one of them to him if he hadn't disappeared after prom. She'd never seen him again after that night.

She'd thought him blessedly gone forever from her world

until she'd had the horrible shock of seeing his name on the end credits of *The Boardroom* three years ago. It couldn't be the same man, she'd told herself. But a subtle check through industry sources had quickly proved it was. It had been the career equivalent of finishing her breakfast cereal to find a cockroach in the bottom of her bowl. No, worse—half a cockroach.

Since then, she'd checked up on him every now and then, so she knew where he was, what he was doing. Like keeping an eye on a spider that had found its way into her home.

And now he was here, sitting opposite her, oozing masculine confidence like a miasma, waiting for her to say something.

Thank God Claudia hadn't told him about her disastrous wedding. She'd almost sobbed with relief when Claudia had given a tiny shake of her head to indicate he didn't know anything beyond the fact that she'd gone to the Caribbean. If there was any justice in the world, he'd stay in the dark, too. Just the thought of him knowing about her humiliating private life was enough to make her feel nauseous.

The silence stretched a long, long time as she tried to shuffle her disordered, chaotic thoughts into some kind of shape. He waited her out, his eyes steady, his expression unreadable. The bastard.

What got her the most was the benign, butter-wouldn't-melt way he'd mentioned that they'd gone to school together, and that he didn't know if Sadie would remember him or not. As though his cruelty hadn't been one of the pivotal moments of her life.

The thought that his treatment of her had barely registered a blip on his personal radar was the jolt she needed to find her backbone.

Last time she'd seen this asshole, he'd bested and humiliated her in grand style.

He wouldn't be getting a second shot.

Squaring her shoulders, she cleared her throat.

"I gather that you came on board last week, is that right?" she asked.

To encourage the illusion of professionalism, she grabbed a notepad and pen, and hoped like hell that her hands weren't shaking with reaction.

"Yep. Pretty much just picked up where Joss had left things. The team was great, really on top of it all," he said.

She bristled at the proprietorial way he handed out the compliment—as if he'd handpicked the team and trained them up personally, not her. As though he was telling her something she didn't know.

"Yeah, they're a great team. Very experienced. I'm surprised Claudia didn't consider getting one of them to step up, actually."

The moment the words were out of her mouth, she knew she'd made a tactical error. For starters, none of the team was really at the stage where they could step up and take over the show at the drop of a hat. And he'd know that after a week with them. The bastard.

Second—and more importantly—she'd tipped her hand. He knew she didn't want him here. She could see it in his eyes— along with the fact that he didn't give a damn how she felt.

"Guess you'd have to talk to Claudia about that." He shrugged, supremely cool.

She swallowed the swearword that sprang instinctively to her lips.

"Since you seem to have landed on your feet so well, we'd best get straight down to business," she said tightly, determined not to give him another inch.

"Sure. You want me to recap last week's episodes, or did you get a chance to read them before you came in?" he asked.

She resisted the urge to respond defensively by blaming her late flight for her lack of preparation. She was *his* boss, not the other way around.

"Just walk me through the salient points," she said calmly.
"Sure."

Tilting her chair back a little, Sadie steepled her fingers and tried to look confident and in control.

Anything to survive this first encounter with some dignity intact.

DYLAN TOOK A MOMENT to gather his thoughts before launching into a summary of last week's stories. Not easy when his eyes kept drifting to the neckline of Sadie's tight T-shirt.

"Basically, we picked up on the six strands you guys had going—Gabe and Hannah's romance, Kirk and Loni's divorce, Garth's malpractice suit, Honey's pregnancy, Luther's machinations regarding the family business and Angel's high-school dramas. Going over the previous few weeks' worth of story lines, I thought we'd pretty much milked the divorce scenario as much as we could. So last week we got Kirk to the point of agreeing in principal to a settlement, and signing the papers," Dylan said.

Sadie's eyes narrowed as she processed what he'd said. Dylan waited and watched, his eyes drifting of their own accord over her face. She had great skin—sun-kissed, clear. *Glowing* was probably the way the cosmetic companies would describe it. Except it didn't look as though she was wearing a lot of makeup to him.

"Future planning for Kirk and Loni is that they reconcile. We don't want them getting a divorce," she said.

"I saw your forward-planning stuff," he said. "I thought we could get a few more twists and turns in there before we got them back together. So, Kirk's signed the papers—but he hasn't sent them anywhere yet."

She stared at him, that muscle flexing in her jaw again. Good skin, and great eyes. Why hadn't he remembered her eyes? She must have had those back in high school, even if the breasts that thrust up beneath her T-shirt had been conspicuously absent back then.

"And what's going to stop him from handing the papers over to his lawyer?" she asked.

"This week, I figure Loni's going to have a visit from an old flame. Someone to turn the heat up," he said. He grinned cockily, daring her not to like it.

"And next week Kirk learns his brother has died?" Sadie asked, carefully not passing comment yet.

"Maybe. If we can't find any more twists and turns before we get there," Dylan said noncommittally.

Her eyes flashed once, briefly, then the calm, unreadable mask was back in place.

"That all sounds very interesting," she said. "Rather than you going through it all verbally, though, I think I'd prefer to read the episodes, so I can really absorb the nuance."

Her lips thinned for a moment, but nothing could disguise their plump poutiness for long. She had a very sexy mouth, he judged. Belatedly, he became aware of what he was doing: checking Sadie Post out.

Wrenching his brain back on track, he focused on the main event.

"Sure. You're the boss, after all," he said.

She'd been making a note on her pad, but her head shot up at that. They stared at one other for a long moment, then her gaze shifted to something over his shoulder.

"The rest of the team is here," she said. "I don't want to hold you up."

He could have sworn she sounded relieved. The suspicion was reinforced when she stood, signaling the meeting was over. She was rattled. He relished the realization, even as he made himself a promise—he planned on shaking her cage a lot more than this over the next few months.

Instead of responding to her cues, he remained seated,

wanting to see how far he could push her. Slowly, deliberately provocative, he slid his eyes over her body.

What was supposed to be a goad quickly turned into a pleasure tour. It wasn't exactly a hardship looking at her, he admitted to himself as his gaze lingered on the firm, uptilted mounds of her breasts. She had the sort of lithe, elegant body that would look amazing naked. His eyes dropped to her hips. He hadn't seen her butt yet, but he bet it was peachy. He wondered what kind of underwear she wore, whether she was a believer in the thong.

"You know, I would have walked past you in the street," he said once he'd lifted his eyes back to her face. He was satisfied to see that she was blushing, her eyes sparkling with anger. "You sure have changed a lot."

"Yes. You're still pretty much the same, though," she said. She didn't mean it as a compliment, he knew.

He stood, taking pleasure from looking down on her, even if he only had the advantage of an inch or two.

"You'd be surprised."

He drilled her with his eyes before he delivered his parting words.

"I'm really looking forward to the next few months, Sadie."

SADIE CLUTCHED at her desk as he exited her office, allowing herself to at last register how weak her knees were, and that her entire body was trembling with reaction.

Automatically her eyes followed his rangy body as he walked away, dropping to catalog his strong back and lean, trim hips. Well-worn denim sculpted the perfect male ass she remembered from all those years ago. It was still extremely grabbable, she decided dispassionately, the kind of perky male butt that made most women drool.

Every woman except her, of course. She was forever immune to any so-called charm Dylan Anderson had to offer.

She sank into her chair and stared at the notes she'd taken. Jumbled words and a messy, violent doodle filled the page. A pretty accurate depiction of her mindscape at present.

She felt blindsided, overwhelmed. He was the enemy. She didn't want him at *Ocean Boulevard.* How could Claudia have done this to her?

As soon as the thought crossed her mind, she wiped it out. This was not Claudia's fault. If Dylan Anderson wasn't who he was, he'd be the find of the year. A huge feather in their caps, in fact. He'd been nominated for a number of awards for his work on *The Boardroom.* As much as it galled her, she knew he was well respected. Admired, even.

"Gag me with a cheese grater," she said out loud, reverting to one of her favorite high-school phrases. For some reason, it felt appropriate.

"Talking to yourself. Second sign of madness."

It was Grace, already sliding into her visitor's chair. Sadie felt pathetically pleased to see her, and had to bite back the overwhelming urge to blurt the whole sad saga out on the spot.

"I'm not even going to ask what the first sign is," she said, hiding the revealing doodle in a desk drawer.

"You know, I can never remember. Is it hairy palms? Or is that masturbation?"

As always, Grace managed to tease a smile out of Sadie, despite her preoccupation. "Sorry, I didn't have a Catholic education." Sadie shrugged.

"More pity you. If only you knew the guilt you could be enduring on a daily basis," Grace said as she crossed her legs. Sadie's eyes were drawn to the dark purple stilettos on her feet.

"Hey. They're new," she said, desperate for distraction.

"Yep. Found them in a little flea pit off Sunset Strip," Grace said smugly.

The fact that Grace wore a lime-green vintage fifties dress

with white piping and belt should have made the shoes a big mistake, but, as usual, her friend managed to pull the look off. With her dark burgundy hair worn long with very short, straight bangs, Sadie reflected that Grace had been born about half a century too late.

"So, what do you think of Mr. Studly?" Grace asked, twirling a strand of hair around her finger.

"I hate him," Sadie said, then immediately clapped a hand over her mouth. She honestly hadn't meant to say anything. She'd planned to hold it all in and try to work out some strategy. But the words had leaped out of her mouth as though they had a life of their own.

Grace blinked.

"Really? God, what did he say? He was only in here for half an hour."

"We went to school with each other."

"No way." Grace's eyes narrowed. "Why am I sensing pent-up teen angst here?"

Ridiculous tears suddenly welled in Sadie's eyes and she blinked furiously.

"Hey, are you okay?" Grace asked, really concerned now. She stood and started to move around the desk to comfort Sadie.

Sadie held up a hand to forestall her. "Don't! Please! I don't want him to know I'm upset," she said, shooting a wary look out her doorway to where she could see Dylan talking casually to two of his team members.

"Okay."

Grace sank back into her chair, her face creased with worry. "This guy really did a number on you, didn't he?"

Sadie took a deep breath and sighed heavily.

"It's ancient history. It shouldn't have this much power over me," she said ruefully.

"Yeah, right. In my opinion, the years between thirteen and

nineteen keep therapists all over the world in ski holidays and suntans. Kids can be cruel, man," Grace said.

"It's stupid to even think about it. I mean, I'm an adult now. None of that stuff counts anymore," Sadie said. She didn't sound even remotely convincing.

Grace wasn't buying, either.

"I think you should tell Claudia," Grace said firmly.

"No."

"Why not? There's no way you would have hired this creep on your own. Claudia will understand."

Sadie loved that her friend had already consigned Dylan to the creep category without even hearing her story. She was a true friend.

"I can't. What am I going to say? 'He was mean to me in school, make him go away'? There's no way I can put Claudia in that position."

"What's the point of being friends with the boss if you can't exploit it a little?" Grace joked.

Sadie managed a halfhearted smile.

"What are you going to do, then?" Grace prompted, green eyes worried.

"I don't know. Suck it up, I guess. It's only a six-month contract, right?"

From where Sadie was sitting, it seemed like a life sentence, but she knew she wasn't entirely rational right now. She'd been taken off guard, and all the old memories had rushed up to swamp her. Once she'd had some time to reflect and strategize, she'd be fine.

"Tell Claudia," Grace repeated firmly.

"The show needs a story editor, Grace. I won't put her in the position of doing me a favor at the expense of the show. She's only been producer five weeks. It's not fair."

She felt tired all of a sudden. She *was* tired—she'd been fighting with her back to the wall for too long. Ever since the wedding-that-never-was. All she wanted right now was to close her office door and hibernate for a while. Sensing this, Grace stood.

"You know where I am. And that there's an obscene chocolate stash in my bottom drawer."

"Thanks," Sadie said, smiling for her friend's benefit.

Once she was alone, the smile faded from her face. Could her life suck any harder right now? She didn't think so.

She was still in emergency-response zombie mode by the time she got home that evening. She'd managed to avoid anything but the most brief and superficial of contacts with Dylan all day. But she knew that wasn't going to last.

A hot shower and her floppy pj's went a long way to restoring a sense of normalcy. An indulgent dinner of Chunky Monkey ice cream and Oreo cookies papered over any remaining cracks in her equilibrium. By the time she'd immersed herself in a couple of chapters from her favorite romance author and was ready to switch the light off, the world had resumed its rightful perspective.

Dylan Anderson being at *Ocean Boulevard* was a pain, sure it was. But she could handle it. The past was the past, after all. She was a grown, mature woman. She'd learned to drive, voted, had sex and become a homeowner since she and Dylan had last seen one another. None of that old stuff mattered. At the end of the day, he was the same as any of her other direct reports.

She curled into her pillow, anticipating the release of sleep. A few hours of blessed nothing, and she'd be ready to face the world again.

Then she had The Dream.

As soon as she realized she was standing in the school gym, she tried to wrangle her subconscious under control, but it was too late—she was being sucked into the old, old memory.

It was after school, and all the other kids had gone home. She was about to enter the girls' change room when she heard someone singing, the sound echoing out from the boys' change room next door. It only took a moment for her to recognize the voice. Immediately her heart kicked into overdrive.

She hesitated at the junction of the two change rooms. Then her feet drifted toward the boys' entrance. She could hardly believe she was doing what she was doing, but her fingers were already trailing along the cold tile wall as she eased her way toward the door.

Heat rushed into her face as she heard the sound of running water beneath the sound of Dylan Anderson's singing.

He was in the shower. Heat rushed to an entirely different part of her body as she imagined him naked and wet beneath the rushing water.

Her feet moved forward again, and she was powerless to stop them. Her breath was coming in little soundless gasps as she slid along the final row of lockers separating her from the showers. The splash of water and Dylan's voice seemed preternaturally loud to her sensitized ears. A part of her was astounded at what she was doing. She never did anything daring or wrong. She was a straight-A student, punctilious, safe. She'd never been in trouble for anything at school, but here she was, in the boys' change room, about to sneak a peek at Dylan Anderson under the shower. Was she insane? Had some vital part of her intellect flipped out all of a sudden?

But despite the clamor of alarm bouncing around her brain, she slid forward. One step. Two. Three. She held her breath as she ducked her head around the corner.

And stared. His back was to her as he stood in the middle of the shower bay, the water pummeling him as he took his time washing. His body was tall and firm, his shoulders broad, and his back tapered down to a rounded backside that made Sadie's mouth water for something she didn't even have a name for.

His overlong dark hair was wet, trailing over his down-turned face, and his back muscles flexed as he washed his belly. She forgot to breathe entirely as he lifted his head and turned in profile to her. Her rounded eyes took in the smooth, sculpted planes of his pectoral muscles, quickly dipping below to trail greedily down his rippled abs to the area she was most curious about. Between his thighs she saw her first real live penis, and the sight of him, long and substantial, made her press her knees together. Oh boy. Oh boy, oh boy, oh boy.

He turned fully toward her then, arching his neck back so that the flow of water washed his hair away from his handsome brow. She ate up every inch of the body on display. His thighs were long and lean, his calves curved and in perfect proportion to the rest of him. One hand washed idly at his belly as he closed his eyes and swept his other hand up across his forehead and into his hair.

He was magnificent. So much better than all her fantasies. The thought of him touching her, of being held against his hard chest, of touching the strength between his legs… She was dizzy with desire.

She was so mesmerized, she didn't register that he was nearing the end of his shower. Suddenly, however, he flicked the taps off and reached for his towel. Her heart nearly exploded in her chest—she would die if he caught her. Just die. She managed to get her frozen limbs together enough to slide behind the shelter of the first locker aisle. Looking around desperately, she saw too late that she was standing right in front of his open locker, and that his clothes were thrown haphazardly on the bench that ran between the rows. She heard the slap of bare feet on wet tile. He was coming her way. Desperate, she fled to the end of the aisle, diving behind a bin full of dirty towels.

Hunched on the ground, arms wrapped around her knees, eyes squeezed tightly shut, she waited to be discovered. Surely he'd seen or heard her? Surely she was about to be punished for her moment of daring audacity?

After a few seconds, she slowly opened her eyes again. The pounding of her heart subsided enough so that she could make out the sound of Dylan dressing. He hadn't seen her. Chin resting on her drawn-up knees, she tried to interpret the sounds she could hear, willing him to get dressed and leave.

The hiss of an aerosol can: Dylan putting on deodorant. God, she loved the way he smelled. The thump of something heavy hitting the ground: Dylan dropping his shoes, ready to put them on. The clink of metal on metal: Dylan doing up his belt.

She waited for the telltale clang of his locker closing, but it didn't come. Time stretched, and still it didn't come. She frowned. Had he gone or not? He'd sounded fully dressed to her. Why would he hang around?

The cold from the tile floor was seeping through her thin gym shorts, and she cursed herself for her impulsiveness. Now that the excitement of seeing Dylan naked was wearing off, she could see how stupid she'd been. How reckless. If he'd seen her, her life would, quite simply, not be worth living.

Finally, after a long, long time, she dared a peek over the top of the bin.

She immediately ducked down again. Dylan was still there—sitting slumped on the bench between the lockers. Curious, she dared another peek. He had something in his hand—a piece of paper. But it was the look on his face that transfixed her. He was upset about something—very upset, if she had her guess. His handsome face was twisted into a sort of desolate resignation. Suddenly, he swore and balled the paper up, then shot it toward the nearest trash can. Slamming his locker shut, he grabbed his beat-up leather jacket and strode toward the exit.

Sadie waited until his footsteps had well and truly faded before pulling the paper from the can and racing to the safety of the girls' change room. Locked in a toilet cubicle for extra safety, she smoothed the crinkled page flat on her knees. It was the pop quiz they'd just had handed back in American Lit. Dylan had scored an F.

It was no newsflash to her that Dylan wasn't exactly acing the class. She sat next to him—she knew how often he got reprimanded for not doing homework, or for having the wrong answers when called upon by the teacher. She'd tried to shield him as many times as she could—jumping in to answer for him, distracting Mr. McMasters with questions—but she'd always suspected that she worried about Dylan being embarrassed far more than he did. He was so cool—she'd figured he didn't give a hoot about anything to do with American Lit. He never so much as twitched when Mr McMasters took a shot at him, and most of the time he had a smart-ass response ready to throw back.

But now she realized he did care. He cared a lot.

And for the first time in over a year of loving Dylan Anderson, hope flared in her heart. Because she knew she could help him. She had something to offer him now. She'd never had a chance of attracting him the traditional way, not with her concave chest and gangly legs. But she could help him pass Lit. It was one of her best subjects. He'd have to look at her then, wouldn't he? He might even be grateful. They might even become friends.

And then, maybe, he might—

Sadie sat bolt upright in bed, the sheets twisted around her legs. She kicked at them until they loosened, then rolled to her feet. Her skin felt clammy, overheated. Flicking her bedside lamp on, she paced.

At least she'd managed to wake before the rest of the dream unfolded. She pushed her damp hair off her forehead, wishing she could push the old memories away as easily.

If she could take back one moment in her life, she'd erase those few, fateful seconds when she'd heard Dylan Anderson singing in the boys' locker room. If she hadn't snuck into spy on him. If she hadn't seen the look on his face. If she hadn't been so determined to help him...

Sadie wrapped her arms around her chest, then frowned as she felt the insistent press of her erect nipples against the soft skin of her inner arm. That was the most pathetic, infuriating part, she decided—not that this ancient dream she'd thought she'd banished had returned to haunt her, but the fact that the memory of Dylan Anderson naked in the shower still had the power to turn her on.

She hated him. At the very least, she had nothing but contempt for him. Unfortunately, her body still remembered how much it had yearned for him, how many times she'd cried his name into her pillow when she touched herself all those years ago.

Pathetic. For one thing, she was damned sure Dylan wasn't pacing the floor somewhere in L.A., thinking about her naked body right now.

It was the wake-up call she needed. Her spine stiffened and the tingling feeling in her limbs subsided as her adrenaline levels dropped.

After a day of reeling in reaction, she suddenly had clarity. The past didn't matter. What she used to feel didn't mean squat. This was her turf. She was the boss. This time, things would be different.

She'd show Dylan Anderson that Sadie Post wasn't a pushover anymore.

If it killed her.

Jaw set, she climbed back into bed. She couldn't wait till the morning, she told herself. She was actually looking forward to it. He wasn't going to know what hit him.

3

THE SUN WAS WARMING the edge of the world when Dylan steered his motorcycle into his parking space at *Ocean Boulevard* a week later. He told himself he was starting early because he liked to be prepared. It was true, to a certain extent—his dyslexia had made him a stickler for research and preparation; it was one of the ways he harnessed his unique way of thinking.

If he hadn't spent half the night staring at the ceiling, he'd have been willing to buy his own excuse, too. The truth was, he hadn't been able to stop thinking about *her.* Every time he'd closed his eyes, a dozen different images of Sadie flashed across the movie screen in his mind. Those legs. Those velvet eyes. That bedroom hair. The tight black jeans she'd worn last Thursday. The flash of cleavage he'd caught at yesterday's lunch break. The long, sensuous curve of her neck…

It had taken a whole week for him to admit it to himself, but he finally had—Sadie Post, poster child for snarky academic bullies, was a bona fide hottie.

He'd never been the kind of man to have too many illusions about sex and his own desires. He was scrupulously honest with the women he dated, and had never told any of them that he loved them, despite knowing that was what some of them wanted to hear. He wasn't even sure he believed in love— except in a fictional sense, for the characters he wrote about. And it certainly wasn't something he was looking for in his own life, not for a long time yet, anyway. But he'd also never found himself in a situation where he was attracted to someone he didn't even *like*.

And he definitely didn't like Sadie. The past week had been one long extended wrestling match with his new boss. He said black, she said white. Simple decisions became drawn-out discussions, meetings went overtime—work was a war zone, pure and simple.

Despite all that, the image of Sadie's long, lithe body refused to leave his mind. He hadn't had a good night's sleep since that first day when he'd walked into her office and she'd stood from behind her desk. He told himself that it was irrelevant that parts of his anatomy found Sadie Post appealing. The last thing he was going to do was to lay a finger on her. He might have had sex with women for a lot of reasons over the years but he wasn't about to stick it to a grade-A bitch like her just because she had great legs and breasts he itched to get his hands on.

Being so certain on that one point didn't make sleep come any easier, however, and early this morning he'd finally given up on staring at the ceiling and saddled up his Ducati motorbike for the commute into work. Now he pulled his helmet off and ran a hand through his hair. His eyes naturally gravitated to the lone car in the parking lot, a silver Audi TT convertible. It was a great little car, and he'd toyed with the idea of buying one for a while, but he hated traffic, and the Ducati made short work of L.A.'s world-famous congestion.

Since TV writers weren't exactly known for being early risers, he guessed the car had been left overnight. Probably someone had tied one on after work and caught a cab home. Grabbing his satchel, he headed into the building, looking forward to several hours of quiet before the rest of the team descended.

Swiping his way through security, he moved toward his office. And froze in midstride as he registered that he wasn't alone. She was standing in the kitchen area, arms crossed in front of her face as she pulled her sweater over her head. It was an innocuous act—except for the fact that the shirt she was wearing underneath clung stubbornly to the sweater fabric. As she lifted her arms, the shirt rode up her body, revealing an expanse of trim, tanned torso and a flash of lacy white bra.

He couldn't help himself—he took a step forward, toward her. Then the sweater was over her head, and Sadie was tugging her shirt down and shaking her long blond hair back into place.

As quickly as that, he was hard for her, his erection straining against the fly of his jeans. He grunted his self-disgust. Clearly, his penis was under the illusion that hell had frozen over, that being the only time he'd consider having sex with his new boss and old enemy.

She must have heard him, because her head swung up and her eyes widened as she registered his presence. A hand strayed to the hem of her stretchy white shirt, and Dylan guessed exactly what she was thinking. *How long had he been standing there?*

His self-disgust at his own lack of control morphed into satisfaction as he saw her uncertainty. He liked her uncertain, wanted to see more of it. Wanted to rock her boat as much as he could, give her a little taste of what she'd no doubt been dishing out to others her whole life. A slow smile curled his lips as he sauntered toward her.

"Morning, Sadie," he said.

Her eyes narrowed, then her shoulders straightened as she squared up to him.

"Good morning, Dylan. You're here bright and early," she said primly.

"Yep," he said. Then he let his eyes dip below her face, sliding over those high breasts of hers, discovering the denim miniskirt hugging her hips, lingering on the length of tanned leg on display in between the hem of her skirt and the black cowboy boots she wore.

His intention was to keep her off balance, encourage her to

worry a little more about whether he'd seen her impromptu striptease or not. He hadn't considered what effect his leisurely inspection might have on his nether regions—desire simply wasn't on the agenda between him and Sadie Post. His body was going to have to suck it up.

Unfortunately, his body had other ideas. Without any permission from him, his erection grew harder still, throbbing with the need to get closer to the tall goddess standing in front of him.

Feeling like a hormonal teenager, Dylan moved his satchel ever so casually in front of his groin. The last thing he needed was for Sadie to realize he wanted her. Not that he actually did, of course—but she might get other ideas if she caught sight of the giant boner in his jeans right now.

His momentary preoccupation had given her time to regroup, and there was no doubt or embarrassment in her eyes now.

"I've got notes for you on last week's block," she said, crossing to the coffee machine to collect a mug. "Nothing major, just a few continuity issues we need to clear up."

Dylan waited for her to say anything more, like maybe comment on the high tension in the stories they'd crafted last week, or the powerful emotion of Friday's cliff-hanger moment—a tear-jerker if ever he'd plotted one. But she didn't. In fact, she appeared to have said all she was going to as she poured milk into her coffee, apparently supremely unaware of him standing there staring at her, willing her to say more.

"No problems with the Friday cliff-hanger moment?" he asked, immediately kicking himself for fishing. He didn't need her approval.

She eyed him blandly, not giving him an inch. "It was fine. I expect you'll be picking it up for Monday's episode?" she asked.

Fine? His cliff-hanger was going to have fans screaming at the TV set, and she thought it was *fine?* Dylan clenched his hand on his satchel but deliberately matched her innocuous tone.

"We can discuss it in the pitch meeting at ten," he said.

She obviously didn't like the fact that he hadn't answered her directly. He saw anger flash behind her velvet eyes, but she quickly put her mask back in place.

"It will certainly be interesting to see what you've come up with," she said.

He didn't miss the challenge in her words. *Interesting,* his ass. She planned to make this as hard for him as possible. Last week's pitch meeting had been a polite standoff, but they'd only been warming up. Now, with a full week of push-and-shove behind them, he knew the gloves would be off. He found himself grinning. There was nothing he liked more than rising to a challenge.

"I'm all for interesting," he said.

She narrowed her eyes at him again, then picked her coffee up decisively.

"I don't want to keep you from your work," she said, moving off.

His eyes instinctively dropped to her butt as she walked away, mapping her sweet curves and the lean muscles of her thighs. The surge of renewed desire in his groin annoyed him so much that he called out after her. She was not going to get the better of him, even if her miniskirt was doing most of her dirty work at present.

"Actually, I wanted to have a word," he said.

She hesitated for a second, then turned back to him.

"Sure. In my office," she said smoothly.

He followed her with his eyes for a moment more before starting after her. Grudgingly he admitted to himself that she had one of the sexiest damn walks he'd ever seen.

She was sliding into her seat behind her desk when he

entered. It was obvious she expected him to take the subordinate's chair opposite. Instead, he tossed his satchel onto it and took up a position leaning on her filing cabinet, more than aware that she was at a disadvantage with him looming over her.

He could see the exact moment she understood her little ploy to undermine him with office geography had failed. He didn't even try to repress the cocky grin that curved his lips. As long as he could keep his unruly gonads under control, he was going to enjoy poking a stick at Sadie as often as possible over the next six months.

"How can I help you?" she asked, tilting her head back to look up at him.

His grin widened at her phrasing. As if he was going to let her *help* him.

"I wanted to discuss the idea of doing a feature-length episode during our peak viewing time over winter to capitalize on the audience. It's a concept a few of the European and Australian soaps have had a lot of success with," he said.

She frowned. "You've been doing your homework."

He shrugged. "*Ocean Boulevard* has a reputation for taking risks. I'm surprised you haven't gone down this route already."

She opened her mouth to say something, then shut it with a click. Clearly frustrated, she swiveled her chair to face him more squarely and crossed her legs.

"The idea has been floated a number of times, but the previous producer wasn't keen. Claudia is more openminded, however."

He could see it was killing her to give him even that much information. If he wasn't mistaken, the only thing she wanted to tell him was how far to shove his head up his own butt.

"Great. Let's pitch the idea to her," he said.

"Not yet. This is only your third week, Dylan."

"So?"

"You'll have enough on your plate just getting up to speed. Taking on a feature-length episode on top of that would be fool-hardy."

He straightened with annoyance.

"I'll cope. I think we should do this. Or don't you want the ratings?" he challenged.

She uncrossed her legs and his eyes fell to skim their tanned length.

"Our ratings are the best they've been in ten years," she said coolly.

"So you're happy to rest on your laurels, is that it? Don't want to push to the next level?" He made it sound like an idle question, but they both knew he was goading her.

"We start plotting the winter blocks in five weeks' time. That's not long enough for you to get a grip on the show, the characters and the team, let alone be ready to tackle a feature-length episode on top of the normal workload. You've never had to produce this volume of story week-in, week-out in your career before. I think you should be careful not to bite off more than you can chew."

Dylan swallowed a four-letter word. She looked so prissy, sitting there with her back straight and her knees pressed together. Even the plumpness of her full bottom lip had disap-peared as she fed him her uptight little diatribe. This was the girl he remembered from American Lit—the girl who always had to be right and always had to have the teacher's attention.

"You sure your problem with this isn't that it's not your idea?" he asked.

"Very," she said succinctly. "I'm also sure that I don't need to justify my decisions to you, hard as that may be for your ego to comprehend."

Dylan smirked. "I don't have ego problems, sweetheart. I know exactly what I'm worth."

"Do you? I didn't know you were such a pragmatist."

His smirk turned into a grin. He was enjoying himself.

"I'm going to pitch my idea to Claudia, see what she thinks," he said.

That got her goat. She surged to her feet in one lithe move, body tense as she leaned toward him for emphasis.

"Don't even think about it. You've had my answer. Learn to live with it. Once you've found your feet, we can talk again."

"I don't need to find my feet," he said through clenched teeth.

She snatched a copy of last week's block from her desk. Dozens of Post-it flags bristled from the side of the document, a testament to how many changes she wanted made.

"Are you really so arrogant that you think you can walk onto a show that's been running for over fifteen years with multiple, complex story lines and back-stories and think you've got it whipped in a couple of weeks?"

She slapped the document down onto the desk to punctuate her challenge. He eyed the many flags assessingly.

"There were bound to be continuity issues. They'll shake out in a couple more weeks." He shrugged confidently.

"You really do have a colossal ego, don't you?" she said, one hip jutting out as she gave him a dismissive head-to-toe.

"Takes one to know one, baby," he said.

She jabbed a finger at him and her breasts jiggled in reaction. "First, don't ever call me *baby* again. I am your script producer, and you'd better not forget it. Second, I worked twenty-four hours a day, seven days a week when I did your job three years ago. I'm not ashamed to say it took a good six months before I knew what I was doing. I'm not afraid of admitting I have things to learn. How about you?"

He stared at her. Her moment of surprising humility and candor took the wind out of his sails.

"I think you're making a mistake," he said, some of the heat gone from him now.

"I can live with that," she said, her gaze steely.

She'd left him nowhere to go—bar throwing a complete hissy fit. Without a word, he swiveled on his heel.

"Thanks for the chat," he said over his shoulder as he stalked from the room.

"Any time, Dylan. My door is always open," she called after him sweetly.

He screwed up his face as he did a silent, mocking imitation of her as he crossed to his office. *My door is always open.* What a load of horse shit. She wasn't fooling anyone—she wanted to stomp on him until he was confetti.

Snapping his notebook computer open, he hit the power button. She might have won the battle, but she was going to lose the war. He wouldn't have it any other way.

SADIE SANK INTO HER CHAIR as Dylan walked out of her office. Her heart was racing so fast she was sure her chest must be visibly vibrating, and she thanked God that Dylan's office was out of her direct line of sight.

Damn him, she thought as she pressed a hand to her breast. *Damn his insolent gray eyes and his too-tall body and his too-wide shoulders. Who the hell does he think he is, crowding my office and standing over me like he's emperor of all he surveys?*

She felt a surge of satisfaction as she reminded herself that she had won their little skirmish—decisively. It was the first time she'd triumphed over him so unequivocally, too. Last week, they'd had confrontation after confrontation, but she'd always been left with the distinct feeling that they'd ended each battle in a draw. He was such a smart mouth; he always seemed to have an answer for everything.

She felt a smile tugging at the corners of her mouth as she relived the confounded look on his face. She'd whipped his ass good and proper—and it felt good.

An insidious thought slid into her mind as she pulled her notepad toward her, ready to start work. If she wanted to take advantage of it, she had an amazing opportunity in her hands. If she wanted to, she could wipe out the ignominy and humiliation of the past in one fell swoop. She could beat him, humiliate him, emasculate him. Pound him down until the memory of what he'd done to her was nothing but a faded, sepia moment that had no power over her anymore.

She was his boss. She could hurt his career, get him sacked. Destroy him.

Maybe it was the residual adrenaline from their fight, but the idea was suddenly incredibly appealing. For the next two hours before the rest of the office came to life, she even allowed herself to believe she was capable of it, too. She could lure him into some kind of disagreement, then use it as a pretext to sack him. If he kicked up a stink, she could make sure enough rumors got around to make him appear difficult, moody and intractable. The kiss of death for a TV writer. Still enamored with the notion, she dug out her address book and jotted down a few names for potential replacements for Dylan. She'd told Grace last week that she couldn't get rid of Dylan without having a suitable candidate in mind. But if she had that person waiting in the wings... There'd be no stopping her from kicking Dylan's arrogant ass out of the building the next time he tried to bully her.

Feeling as all-powerful and godlike as Donald Trump in *The Apprentice*, she put a call through to her first prospect. As she waited for the line to connect, Claudia walked past her doorway and flashed a smile her way. Sadie felt a surge of guilt as she considered what she was doing—sneaking around behind her friend's back to make her own life more comfortable. That quickly, reality rushed in and all the reasons why she could never be hard-ass enough to go through with such a cutthroat scheme tumbled into her mind. She couldn't even say no to door-to-door charity collectors, for Pete's sake, let alone be cold and calculating enough to squeeze Dylan from the building without just cause. Hell, she still had a cupboard full of peanut-butter Girl Scout cookies from last summer—and she was allergic to peanuts.

Relieved that sanity had come calling before she'd done anything stupid, she was about to put the phone down when a voice sounded in her ear.

"Olly Jones speaking."

She should have ended the call, but she was so surprised she spoke up.

"Um, Olly, it's—it's Sadie Post calling from *Ocean Boulevard.* We spoke last year at the Writer's Guild seminar," she said. *Shit.* What was she going to say to him now that she'd decided she wasn't up to being Machiavellian?

"Sure, Sadie. How're you doing?" Olly said, his Southern accent pouring as smooth as syrup down the line. "How's the show going?"

"Show's going great. Really great. Everything's good."

"Good to hear," Olly said.

She could hear the curiosity in his voice. He was wondering why she was calling. With good reason. She tried to think of a viable excuse, but her mind was a complete blank. The silence stretched awkwardly, and in desperation she fell back on her original reason for calling. It wouldn't hurt to sound the guy out, would it? Even if she never did anything with the information, it was a legitimate reason for calling out of the blue like this.

"Listen, I was wondering if you were still looking for in-house work?"

"I was, but I've just signed with *Crime Scene,*" Olly said apologetically. "It never rains but it pours, I guess. Been sitting at home waiting for the phone to ring for months."

"Well, you know the industry," Sadie said, trying not to sound too relieved. Thank God he had work, since she had nothing to offer him.

They chatted for a few more minutes about mutual friends, and Sadie put the phone down feeling as though she'd had a close call.

Who was she kidding? She wasn't the conniving Alexis Carrington type, always with a sharpened knife at the ready to stab someone in the back. If she was going to get rid of Dylan, it would be open and honest—no matter how intimidating that might seem when she remembered the dark resolve in his eyes and his ready, quick tongue.

She checked her watch. It was 10:00—time for the pitch meeting with Dylan and his team. Gathering her notes, she stood and took a deep breath. She had no illusions. It was going to be a battle of wills from beginning to end, a clash of the Titans. Last week's meeting had been bad enough, but she knew he'd come out fighting hard today after their disagreement earlier. But she'd already decided that beating him at his own game was the only way she was going to manage him, so there was nothing left for her to do but endure. Teeth gritted, she strode forth.

The moment she entered the meeting room, her stomach clenched. Because she'd dallied making her stupid call to Olly Jones, the rest of the team had filled up the available seats, and the only spot remaining was to Dylan's immediate left. She stared at it for a full ten seconds as she hovered in the doorway, hating the idea of sitting so close to him. Why hadn't she come sooner to grab a spot as far from him as possible? Last week, they'd sat at opposite ends of the table and stared icily at each other all meeting. It was an arrangement that had suited her just fine, but this week she would have to make do.

Lips thin, she slid into the seat, her body tense and stiff. They were sitting so close, she could smell his aftershave—something mellow and delicious—and out of the corner of her eye she could see the dark hairs on his tanned forearm as he tapped at the keyboard of his notebook computer. She pressed her knees together and kept her arm tightly by her side, determined to avoid even the hint of physical contact with him.

Around them, the rest of the team and Claudia chatted desultorily, chewing over last night's TV ratings, discussing the latest movie releases. Only she and Dylan were silent. Feeling ridiculously awkward, Sadie shuffled through her paperwork while Dylan continued to tap away on his keyboard. She didn't dare look at him. She didn't want to—she knew what he looked like. His image was etched indelibly on her brain.

Glancing down, she stiffened with shock as she saw that her nipples were jutting shamelessly out from her chest, fully aroused and keen for the world to know it. The realization forced her to acknowledge the illicit buzz that had stolen through her the moment she sat down—a mixture of awareness and alertness and excitement, every nerve ending on emergency standby, her blood as thick as treacle in her veins.

Angry with herself, she twitched her arms across her chest to hide her ridiculous nipples. She knew exactly what this was—a tired relic of her teen crush. It was pathetic, and shameful.

And for the life of her she couldn't make it go away. Her gaze was practically burning a hole in her notes she was staring at them so hard, but nothing could stop her from being supernaturally aware of the man sitting beside her. She could feel the heat radiating from his body and, even though she hadn't looked at him since she came in, she was painfully aware of everything about him, from the black T-shirt he wore to the way his hair curled behind his ears, to the strength of his forearms.

She shifted in her seat. She despised him. She wasn't attracted to him. He was an egotistical jerk. This physical awareness was simply a ghost from the past.

Still, her body remained on high alert. She suppressed a sigh of relief when Dylan finally pushed his chair back and moved a few feet away to the whiteboard. Perhaps now she could concentrate on the here-and-now instead of some aberrant teen urge that was about as welcome as a dose of poison ivy.

"Right. Welcome to block 735," Dylan said as he called the meeting to order. Conversation died and all eyes turned to him. All eyes except for hers. She knew better than to look at him after the way her body seemed determined to forget the humiliation she'd suffered at his hands.

"Let's start with Loni and Kirk. Last week we left Kirk feeling distinctly jealous about the way that Loni and her old flame, J.B., were getting on. He's held off on sending the divorce papers. It's time for Loni to find out about this, and for Kirk to accuse her of sleeping with J.B. In the middle of their big row, they'll get the call from the cops—Kirk's brother has died in a car accident, leaving behind an orphaned baby girl."

Sadie took notes, marking down anything she wanted Dylan and the team to flesh out in more detail for her before she signed off on it. As the minutes passed and he outlined a heart-rending, sexy story for the show's star-crossed lovers of the week, Sadie felt a grudging admiration. She wanted to hate his ideas, to find a million different ways to criticize and put him in his place. But he was good. He was very good.

By the time he'd moved on to the next major strand for the week, she'd been so lulled by his voice that she forgot to keep her eyes on her notepad. The moment her gaze slid across to his tall body she realized her mistake, but it was too late.

Standing just a few feet way, he stretched and paced and gesticulated passionately as he outlined his ideas. Strong muscles flexed in his chest, his biceps bulged, the tendons stood out in his neck. At one stage, he even lifted the edge of his T-shirt to scratch himself absently, and she was treated to a flash of firm, muscled lower back. Next her eyes dropped to his thighs, hugged so intimately by worn denim. He was bigger there than she remembered, his quad muscles fuller and firmer.

Belatedly she registered that she was staring, that her

nipples were once more erect, and that she hadn't taken a note for five minutes.

This was the last problem she'd expected to have with Dylan Anderson. She hated him. Or, at the very least, she despised the boy he'd once been. The package he came wrapped in shouldn't make an ounce of difference to her. But—apparently—it did.

It was a fairly shameful discovery to make about herself, and it made her more terse than she'd planned to be when she began her revision of Dylan's pitch.

"This situation with J.B., Loni's old school flame. How far were you planning on taking their flirtation?" she asked abruptly.

"I was thinking a kiss. A kiss that Kirk walks in on," Dylan said.

"I can see how that would be the obvious way to go," Sadie said. Dylan's eyes flickered as he registered her subtle put-down. "I think you need to be careful about making Loni look easy. He may be an old flame, but J.B.'s a new character for our audience. They want her to be with Kirk, not J.B. They're going to see her as a scarlet woman if she kisses him."

"I don't have a problem with that. We can redeem her. There are a million ways to do it, especially once the baby is in the picture," Dylan argued.

"I disagree. I think you can have your cake and eat it, too. Have a close moment between Loni and J.B., but have her back off, explaining she's too confused to get involved with anyone. Then have Kirk walk in on a later moment that looks damning, but the audience knows isn't."

Claudia shot her a searching look before speaking up. "I like both angles, to be honest. I guess the question is, which do we think is more in line with Loni's character?"

One of the team, Luke, piped up next.

"Loni loves Kirk. She always has. I don't think she'd look twice at another guy, old flame or not."

The discussion took on a life of its own and Sadie dared a

glance across at Dylan. He wasn't watching the others, however—he was studying her with a hard glint in his eye.

She looked away from the promise and the threat in his gaze. She could handle him. Of course she could.

DYLAN WAS SO RILED by lunchtime he had to do something or explode with frustration. Dragging his running kit from his bike panniers, he pulled on shorts, tank top and sneakers and took off for a long, soothing run along the Santa Monica beach.

He tried to push Sadie's triumphant face from his mind as he pounded the sand. The way she'd sat there through the pitch meeting, sniping at him, using her superior knowledge of the show to shoot him down. Not a single word had passed her lips about the level of conflict, emotion and sophistication he'd brought to the stories. He knew he was doing good work. The team was excited, Claudia was excited. But Sadie wasn't giving an inch.

It was typical of her, but he was going to force her to acknowledge him if it took the full six months to do it. And he was going to fight every battle toe-to-toe with her, no matter how small or insignificant the point. Which was why when the block was plotted this week, Loni was going to kiss her old school flame, J.B. If Sadie wanted to push the issue, they could take things up a notch. He was more than ready to go the distance.

"Hey, Dylan! You trying to outrun the devil or something, you crazy ass?" a voice called from behind him.

Dylan slowed his pace and turned to see his old writing buddy, Olly, approaching red-faced across the sand.

"I've been chasing and calling after you for five minutes, you bastard, and you didn't stop," Olly said, doubling over as he tried to catch his breath.

"Didn't hear you. Should have run faster, Olly," Dylan teased.

"Yeah, yeah. We weren't all born with stilts for legs," Olly said good-naturedly, gesturing to his own hairy, stocky limbs disparagingly.

"Don't tell me you got yourself fired already?" Dylan joked. Olly had famously been fired on the first day of a new job because he'd offended the show's temperamental lead actress by not recognizing her.

"Working from home on the plot. But thanks for the words of encouragement."

"Any time."

They fell into a slow jog as they turned toward the pier.

"How are you enjoying your break, you lucky SOB?" Olly asked.

"Says the man who's just come off two years of freelancing," Dylan reminded him.

"Yeah, freelancing—not lying around doing nothing for two months," Olly said enviously.

"Like that was what I was going to do. Anyway, save your envy gland, my time off is on hold. I took a temporary contract with *Ocean Boulevard*."

To his surprise, Olly stopped in his tracks.

"No way!" he said, looking bemused.

"Yeah, way."

"That's so weird. I had a call this morning from their script producer, Sadie Post. She wanted to know if I was available to come in-house. I assumed she was talking about story ed work, but it must have been something else, yeah?"

Dylan clenched his teeth as he processed what Olly had revealed.

Sadie had called Olly that morning to offer him Dylan's job. Nice. Really freaking nice.

An odd sort of satisfaction gripped him. This was the kind of thing he'd expected from the adult Sadie Post—the grown-up version of how she'd operated in high school. It was good to see she wasn't going to disappoint. And it might—at last— kill off his body's absurd desire to rub bits with her. At the moment, he couldn't imagine being aroused by her ever again.

"Hey. What's up?" Olly asked. "Have I put my foot in it?"

Dylan forced a smile. "Nah. Just more TV bullshit. You know how it is," he said.

But he brooded on Sadie's sneakery all the way back to the office and all through his shower. By the time he was dressed again and ready to start the afternoon's plot meeting, he'd built up a righteous head of anger.

Perhaps if Claudia and Sadie had caught him at any other time, he'd have been able to bite his tongue. But when he bumped into them on his way back to his office to dump his sweaty running clothes, he was in no mood to be fair or circumspect.

"Hey, great meeting this morning," Claudia said. "I'm really pleased with the way you guys are going."

"Thanks," Dylan said shortly. Praise was always nice, but what he really wanted right now was a fight. He eyed Sadie angrily, aching to let slip that he knew what she'd been up to.

"I'm not blowing smoke up your yoo-hoo," Claudia said, obviously sensing his distraction. "You've really hit the ground running. It's like you've been here for years."

Sadie didn't say a word, her closed-lipped silence delivering her verdict on his performance. Suddenly the perfect form of revenge popped into his mind.

"I'm glad you feel that way, Claudia," he said smoothly. "I wanted to run an idea past you."

He quirked an eyebrow at Sadie before he continued, a non-verbal *up yours* to cue her in to what he was about to do. She was quick on the uptake, and her back stiffened as she glared at him in outrage.

"How would you feel about producing a feature-length episode for the peak winter period? A stand-alone story that also feeds into our other episodes?"

Claudia's face lit up. "Hey, I like the sound of that. What do you think, Sadie?" Claudia asked, looking to her friend for her reaction.

Sadie shot daggers at him, her jaw clenched so tightly he could see the muscles working beneath the skin.

He smiled for the first time since Olly had inadvertently let it slip that Sadie had tried to shaft him.

"It was one of those things that just came to me," Dylan said brightly before Sadie could speak up. "I was out jogging with my old buddy *Olly Jones* at lunchtime, and it simply popped into my head."

The look of outrage was replaced with a guilty caught-out expression as Sadie picked up on his none-too-subtle hint. He winked at her. *Gotcha.*

"I'd have to sound out the network, but there's no reason why they wouldn't be keen." Again Claudia looked to Sadie for her reaction, and Dylan crossed his arms over his chest and waited.

"That all sounds like a really...*interesting* idea," Sadie finally said, shaking her head. She looked as though she was spitting out ground glass.

"I know it will add to the department's load, but you've got some ex-story-liners who are happy to fill in on a locum basis, haven't you?" Claudia asked, clearly taken with his idea.

"Um, yeah," Sadie said.

"Hey, that's excellent. I'm really pleased you liked the idea, Claudia," Dylan said, just to rub it in a little more.

"Definitely. We'll have to explore it further, of course, but if everything checks out I think we should go for it."

"Excellent," he said. Smiling broadly, he lifted his hand in a casual salute. "Now, if you'll excuse me, I'd better get back to my day job."

He shot Sadie one last, overly bright smile before he headed off, his eyes delivering the real message: *screw you, lady.*

Whistling quietly, he sauntered back to his team.

SADIE SEETHED for the rest of the afternoon. The sneaking, stinking, slithering snake! The way he'd stood there, cool as a cucumber, pushing her and Claudia around like pieces on a chess board. She wanted to tear him limb from limb.

Her blood had run cold when he'd mentioned Olly Jones's name. What were the odds? She was the unluckiest woman on the planet. First the wedding, then Dylan turning up on her doorstep and now this—it was almost as though she were cursed. She'd never intended to go through with her stupid plan to oust him—but he'd never believe that, even if she lowered herself enough to tell him so. Which she wouldn't. Even if it meant she looked like the worst kind of conniving TV back-stabber.

It wasn't only that he'd back-doored her. Even though she had her own personal prejudices where he was concerned, she acknowledged that he'd had a right to be pissed with her about what she'd sort of thought about doing. It was the way he'd gone about getting his own back. So smug. So clever. So in charge. It made her want to kick something—preferably his ass. Her mind kept flashing to how he'd looked as he laid his idea in front of Claudia: dark hair still wet from the shower, color in his cheeks from his run. He'd smelled fresh and powerful and vital. That was the worst of it, really—the whole time he'd been running circles around her, shafting her to her face, she'd been surreptitiously ogling him, measuring his thighs with her eyes, imagining what his chest looked like, flashing back to that time in the showers when she'd seen exactly how well equipped he was to be the school stud.

A brisk knock on her open door brought her head up. Claudia flashed a big grin.

"I'm on my way home, but I thought I'd let you know we're on for Dylan's feature idea. I've spoken to the network and cleared it with the big guys at our end. How cool is that?" she said, clearly excited at the prospect of taking on such a daring project so early in her reign.

"Fantastic," Sadie said through gritted teeth.

It was well and truly time to go home, but she stared at her desk for a good ten minutes after Claudia had gone, grinding her teeth and clenching and unclenching her fists.

She hated that he'd come into her world and turned everything upside down. She couldn't stand what he did to her equilibrium, the way her body reacted when he was close, the way he made her feel young and vulnerable and exposed again.

Abruptly she stood, her eyes narrowing. She knew exactly what she had to do. It was inevitable, probably had been since the moment he'd walked in the door.

She strode into his office unannounced. He was standing beside his desk, packing up his notebook computer for the day. His head came up as she kicked his door shut with her cowboy-booted foot. Grabbing the guest chair, she wedged it under the door handle to ensure they weren't interrupted.

"You took your time," he said coolly.

She narrowed her eyes at him.

"God, I hate you. Everything about you. The way you walk into a room and own it straightaway. The way you're never at a loss. That stupid, cocky smile—God, I really hate that," she said. All the while, her fingers were busy at her shirtfront, sliding buttons free.

Shrugging out of her shirt, she dropped it to the ground. He stood rock-still, but his eyes dropped to her breasts like heat-seeking missiles.

"You're not exactly my favorite person, either," he said, hands going to the hem of his T-shirt.

She planted herself in front of him as he peeled it over his head.

"What you did with Claudia this afternoon—sleazy is being generous," she said, reaching out to grab a handful of his hard chest.

"Right, 'cause you're pure as the driven snow," he said harshly, grabbing her and hauling her against his body. "You just can't stand it because someone is fighting back for a change."

"Arrogant pig," she snapped at him.

"Conniving bitch," he fired back.

And then his hands were in her hair and he was tilting back her head and sliding his tongue into her mouth with a take-no-prisoners urgency that took her breath away.

4

HE COULDN'T GET ENOUGH of her. The thought raced through his mind as he angled her head farther back, deepening his penetration of her mouth. Her tongue danced with his, countering each thrust with an attack of her own. Her hands curled around his biceps, pulling him closer, and her hips ground against his, the action a pale imitation of what he needed from her right now.

He pulled her full bottom lip into his mouth. She moaned low in her throat and dug her fingernails into the muscles of his back. He swept a path across her cheek to the sensitive skin beneath her ear, laving her neck then biting her. Her hips bucked against his and she slid a hand down his back to grab his butt and drag him even more tightly against her.

He needed more. He needed skin, had to taste her, know her, have her. He pulled back, and she made a small animal sound of frustration. He stared into her glittering eyes, taking in the rapid rise and fall of her breasts as she gasped for breath, the flush on her cheekbones, the tumbled, sexy mess of her hair.

She was everything he hated in a woman. But he was going to have her…or die trying.

"This has to go," he ordered, reaching for the zip on her skirt.

"You first," she said, hands homing in on his belt buckle. He was so hard, he felt as though he was going to burst right through his jeans, and within seconds she was sliding a hand inside his boxers and grasping his swollen shaft.

He groaned, his hands reaching for her breasts in retaliation. Imagining how they looked, how they felt, had been driving him wild since the moment he saw her, and he slid his hands over them with a groan of satisfaction. She closed her eyes and bit her lip as he squeezed them firmly before seeking her already-hard nipples with his thumbs.

"Yes," she whispered, the one word filled with a world of hungry intensity and demand.

Her grip tightened on his erection and her movements intensified. What was left of his self-control snapped. All he registered was need. He had to be inside her. Now. He wanted to possess her, own her, defeat her. He moved forward, pushing her back onto his desk. She went willingly, her legs spreading to accommodate him as he pressed closer. Lowering his head, he tongued her nipple through the lace of her sexy white bra. She responded by increasing her tempo as she worked his shaft and fisting her other hand into the loosened waistband of his jeans to drag him closer still.

Trembling with desire, he raced a hand up her thigh and beneath her miniskirt, spreading her legs wider as he sought the heat of her. He gave a grunt of satisfaction as he found the damp satin of her panties. She was hot and ready for him. Impatient, he slid his fingers beneath the elastic and dipped into the warm, wet velvet between her thighs.

Nothing was going to stop him from conquering her.

SADIE GASPED with satisfaction as he probed her inner lips with knowing fingers. She hated him, but she wanted him. She had to have him. She was mindless with need. She was beyond thought, beyond speech. All she knew was that he had something she had to have, and she released her grip on his stunningly hard erection to grasp the other side of his loosened waistband and drag him into place with both hands.

"Now," she demanded. *"Now."*

The gaze he shot her was fierce, devoid of anything except need, but she didn't care. She wanted only one thing from him—and at the moment that one thing was pressing against her panties, a hard, hot remedy for the desperate ache inside her.

She listened impatiently to the crinkle of a foil packet opening, then he tugged her panties roughly to one side. She felt the first nudge of his hardness against her softness. Then—

She gasped as he filled her, stretched her, almost pushed her over the edge. He was big and thick, and she greedily took him all, quickly adjusting to and then glorying in his penetration. He let out a hiss of satisfaction as he plunged to the hilt, then his free hand slicked up her torso to shove her bra out of the way so he could touch her breasts unhindered.

She wrapped her legs around his hips and crossed her ankles behind his back, ensuring he wasn't going anywhere until she took what she wanted from him.

And then he began to move. A confident, needful thrusting that exactly echoed her own wants. His head ducked and she closed her eyes and bit her lip as his mouth found her bare breast at last.

So good. It was exquisite torture: the hardness of him inside her, stroking her, the roughness of his tongue on her nipples, the urgency of his hands as they grasped her hips. She ran her own hands up and down his back, relishing the flex and release of muscle as he pumped into her. Tension ratcheted tight inside her, faster than it ever had before. She followed her instincts and closed her eyes, reveling in every sensation as she laved his strong neck with her tongue, tasting his essence. Glimpsing heaven behind the darkness of her closed eyelids, she urged him greedily on.

"Harder," she demanded, opening her eyes to lock gazes with him. "Faster."

His eyes glittered at her as he took up her challenge, hammering into her, each thrust pushing her closer to completion.

Soon it was all too much. His hardness. Her wetness. The rasp of his stubble on her tender breasts. The firm pull of his mouth on her nipples.

She raced toward the end. The tension inside her clenched… and released, and she came with a gasping sob, her fingers digging into his back, her teeth sinking into the strong muscle of his shoulder as she tried to stop herself from falling apart completely. He stiffened almost instantaneously, every muscle tense as he found his own peak, his hands clutching her hips with painful intensity as he shuddered into her.

She felt boneless. Liquid and formless. Her head lolled back, her eyes closed, her ankles unhooked themselves and her legs slid down the outside of his thighs to the carpet. One breath, two. The tingling warmth of her orgasm vibrated outward to her toes and fingertips.

Then he withdrew, and the cold rush of air where once he'd been was like a slap in the face. She jerked upright as sense and comprehension returned to her in a rush.

What the hell had she done?

Dylan turned his back on her, and after a few seconds she heard the clink of his belt buckle as he dressed himself. She stared down at herself—skirt scrunched up around her waist, bra bunched above her rosy, flushed breasts. Her nipples were still hard and glistening from their contact with his mouth, her breath still coming in pants. She felt as though she was looking at a stranger.

She jerked her bra into place with shaking hands, reaching for her shirt the second her breasts were covered. At least she didn't have to crawl around to find her underwear—they hadn't bothered with such civilized measures as actually getting properly undressed, after all. Tugging her panties into place, she buttoned her shirt and took a deep breath.

He was waiting for her to make eye contact, and she didn't want to. She didn't want to more than anything in the world.

She'd just had sex with the man who had blighted her school

years. The man who'd humiliated her and turned her into a laughingstock. She'd grabbed his erection and rubbed herself against him and demanded he give it to her. And he had. Hard and fast—exactly the way she'd wanted it.

From the moment she'd left her office she'd known what was going to happen, just as he'd known it the moment he looked up and saw her standing there. At the time, it had seemed right, the only possible outcome after all the sniping, tension and adrenaline.

Now, it felt about as reasonable and sane as taking a running jump into the mouth of a volcano.

Slowly, she raised her head. His dark gray eyes were unfathomable, but his harsh expression gave the game away. He was about as thrilled as she was that they'd had carnal knowledge of one another on his desk.

She combed a shaking hand through her hair as yet another horrible repercussion crashed in on her.

This man was her *employee.* She was his boss, for Pete's sake. And she'd impaled herself on him like some hard-up nympho.

"That," she finally said, "was a big mistake."

"No shit, Sherlock," he said.

She flinched at the absolute certainty and disgust in his tone, but was perceptive enough to understand that most of the disgust was directed at himself.

"At last, something we agree on," she said, trying to find some way through the minefield she'd created for herself.

"Don't worry, I won't be expecting champagne and roses," he said sarcastically.

Her eyes narrowed.

"Very astute of you," she said.

His eye narrowed, his hands twitching by his sides. A sudden, hot flush raced up her spine as she remembered his long, clever fingers tracing her inner lips and she swallowed an incomprehensible, unexplainable lump of lust.

How could she want him again when she was standing here wallowing in regret that she'd had him in the first place?

She fell back on the practical to get her through the impossible.

"It's well past six," she said, checking her watch. "Probably everyone else has gone, but you leave first."

He lifted a lazy eyebrow. "Any other orders, great leader?"

"Yeah—zip it," she snapped.

To her consternation, he patted his jean's fly. "Don't worry, it's staying zipped," he said with cold finality.

She had no power over the blush that stole into her cheeks. Crossing her arms defensively over her chest, she tucked her hands into her armpits and stood to one side as he packed up his computer and stuffed notes into his satchel. All the while she tried to ignore the warm throb between her legs. While every other part of her was cringing with regret over what had happened, her vagina was lying back, smoking a cigarette and vibrating with smug satisfaction.

Traitor.

After what seemed a long time, Dylan crossed to his office door. He didn't even bother to glance her way as he moved the chair, opened the door and stepped out into the open-plan area. She heard the sound of the cleaner's vacuum, and some of the tension left her shoulders. Hardly anyone stayed until the cleaners were in the building. There was a reasonable chance that no one had seen her enter Dylan's office, or heard anything they shouldn't have.

It was a tiny sop, a small crumb of comfort. After all, Dylan still knew what had happened. He'd definitely been there to see how much she craved him, how hot she'd been for him.

When she was confident he'd had plenty of time to make his escape, she took a deep breath, smoothed her hair once more, and stepped out.

Except for the cleaner working away in a distant corner, she was alone. Contrary to her irrational expectations, no alarms went off to alert the world to her gross breach of conduct, and a neon arrow didn't drop from the ceiling to mark her out as a shameless, out-of-control hussy.

Horribly self-conscious, she managed a tight-assed walk to her office where she quickly threw her things into her handbag. A Post-it note was stuck to her computer monitor. It was from Grace. "Will be late tonight. Hope 8:00 is okay?"

Sadie groaned as she remembered that Grace had arranged to return a stack of Sadie's books that evening. How was she going to look her friend in the eye and pretend she hadn't just had low-down, grubby office sex with her new story editor? Scrambling, she headed out of the building. More than anything in the world, she wanted to close her eyes, stick her fingers in her ears, sing a nursery rhyme and wish the last hour out of existence.

But, as she knew from painful experience, life didn't work that way.

She clenched her jaw as she unlocked her car. Sometime soon, she had to catch a break. She hoped she didn't spontaneously combust or get hit by satellite debris or fall victim to a superrare jungle disease before then. Because the way her luck was going, all three were more likely than her life getting out of the toilet anytime soon.

WHAT THE HELL was wrong with him?

The question echoed around Dylan's brain as he pushed the speed limit all the way home to his cliff-top house in Laurel Canyon in the Hollywood Hills. He slammed the door and threw his jacket viciously onto the couch as he strode through the living room to the deck that looked out over the panorama of tree and cliff and Hollywood that was the house's best feature. He paced up and down the full length of the deck a half dozen times before his wild, chaotic thoughts began to settle. He'd bought this house for the view—it never failed to calm him and remind him of his place in the world. Now, as the fresh-for-L.A. breeze and the swish of trees worked their magic, he forced himself to examine what he'd allowed to happen.

He'd had sex with Sadie Post. Although sex was a very gentle word for the unarmed warfare they'd waged on each other's bodies. She'd been...undeniable. The way she'd looked at him, pure hunger in her eyes. The way she'd taken what she wanted, reaching into his jeans to grab him with confident, greedy hands. And the way she'd wrapped her legs around him and demanded everything he had and more.

He swore, the wind whipping the words away. He was hard again, hot for a woman whom he genuinely disliked. Just from thinking about her.

He didn't get it. How could he want to get that close to someone he had absolutely no respect for?

Even as he pondered the point, his rational self played devil's advocate. He didn't actually *disrespect* Sadie. For starters, the team she'd assembled and trained were top-notch—all incredibly talented, clever people who were right on top of things. And they all admired Sadie a lot. A hell of a lot, given the amount of time dedicated to Sadie talk around the table. If he'd heard one wacky Sadie tale over the past week, he'd heard a dozen. Like the time Sadie made a bet that she could jam a dozen donuts into her mouth at the same time, then spent a full ten minutes looking like a surprised chipmunk as she stuffed her face. Or the time she insisted they all wear their pajamas to work because they were plotting a sleepover for the show's teen characters. And, of course, how could any of them forget the water pistol fight they'd had when the air-conditioning went down last summer? Sadie had turned into Rambo, crawling under desks and tables, leaping out from behind pillars to nail her team.

None of which corresponded to the uptight, punctilious, patronizing prig he'd sat next to in American Lit all senior year.

Then there was the show itself. He had great characters to

work with. A well-balanced cast of women and men, ranging across all age groups. Someone had spent a lot of time ensuring that the show was well structured and set up for continued rating success. And, as much as it made him grind his teeth to admit it, he suspected that person was Sadie.

He thrust the thought aside as he walked into the house, aiming for the kitchen. So, she was okay at her job. She'd have to be competent to have been promoted into her current role after only four years on the show. Even someone with her expertise in sucking up to authority couldn't get by on butt-kissing alone.

As for her coworkers, obviously she'd learned some people skills since school. That was all.

Dragging the fridge door open, he grabbed a can of soda and flipped the lid open impatiently. The burn of carbonated drink on the back of his throat didn't do much to dispel the thought growing in the back of his mind.

Sadie wasn't quite the monster he'd imagined. She might even be…human. He crushed the empty can in his hand and lobbed it into the trash can.

The memory of what she'd done to him in Lit class had been a never-ending source of fuel for the fire in his belly ever since he'd been diagnosed as a dyslexic. Once he'd understood that he wasn't stupid or lazy as so many people had told him over the years, he'd gotten angry. If his learning difficulty had been recognized by even one of his teachers, his school years would have been incredibly different. He wouldn't have wasted so much time, gotten into so much trouble. He certainly wouldn't have been flipping burgers in a greasy spoon off the 405 freeway at the age of twenty, barely making enough to pay for the roach-infested shoe box his landlord called an apartment.

But he'd turned it all around once he understood the unique way his brain worked. He'd earned his high-school equivalency diploma at night school and gone on to study at N.Y.U. School of Film.

The memory of the superior, smug look on Sadie Post's face as she systematically took him apart in front of the whole class had kept the home fires of his determination burning through every late-night study session and every setback. He'd been determined to prove her, and everyone like her, wrong. He was going to be a success.

Dylan moved through to his bedroom and started shucking his clothes. His movements were tense with self-directed anger.

Nothing was going to change the way he felt about Sadie. Not even the fact that he'd just been buried inside her, reveling in her heat and passion. It was irrelevant. Meaningless. A freak occurrence, never to be repeated.

Stepping into his ensuite bathroom, he caught sight of himself in the mirror. A half circle of pale red imprints marked his shoulder muscle, and he leaned forward to examine it. Teeth marks. A memory rushed up at him—Sadie coming apart beneath him, her body vibrating with pleasure and tension, her hands clawing at his back, her teeth sinking into his shoulder.

Jesus. He didn't need to look down to know that he was fully erect. Again. It was as though she'd made a secret pact with his penis that he didn't have any say in.

Turning, he checked his back and saw that there were two distinct sets of scratches on either side of his spine.

She was wild, that was for sure. Wild and off-limits.

Flipping the water on, he stepped into the shower cubicle. Warm water eased over his tense shoulders, and he closed his eyes and lifted his face into the spray. If only he could wash away the memory of how sinuous and alive she'd felt beneath his hands.

Between his thighs, his erection twitched as though to remind him that it was still down there, wanting another taste of Sadie. Dylan regarded his rebellious member with a curled lip.

"Never again. Get over it," he said.

Then he flipped the water to icy cold and gritted his teeth. Whatever it took. Because Sadie was the enemy, and they were never fraternizing again.

"WHAT HAPPENED to you?"

Sadie flinched and stared at Grace as her friend stood on the threshold of her condo holding a carrier bag full of paperbacks.

"What do you mean?" Sadie hedged.

Grace frowned. "Something's happened. I can tell," she said. "Lucky I bought ice cream."

Sadie shrugged her shoulders in what she hoped was an adequate simulation of someone who didn't know what her best friend was going on about. But she did. She *so* did.

She'd had a shower, trying to wash away the memory of Dylan's hands on her body. But it was as though he'd branded her. The water on her skin, the brush of the towel, the faint, silky friction of her underwear and clothes when she got dressed again—all of it was an echo of his touch. The way he'd cupped her breasts and squeezed them. The way he'd tongued her nipples, then bitten them gently. The way he'd filled her completely, the most welcome penetration of her life.

Her face was flushed with remembered desire, her eyes dark and glittery. No wonder Grace had taken one look at her and known immediately that something was up.

Because she was deeply ashamed and uncertain about what had happened, Sadie kept up a steady stream of innocuous chatter as she collected spoons for the two different types of ice cream Grace had bought—cookies and cream and triple chocolate.

Grace waited until Sadie was digging her spoon into the untouched surface of the chocolate ice cream before probing again.

"What's going on, Sade?" she asked, her wide green eyes searching.

"Nothing. All good here," Sadie lied.

Grace arched an eyebrow disbelievingly. Sadie gave in to the urge to come clean.

"Or I may have just screwed Dylan Anderson's brains out on his desk," she confessed in a rush.

She watched Grace closely, waiting—hoping, really—to see a reflection of her own self-disgust at what she'd done. But Grace only looked thoughtful.

"Well. There's a turn up for the books," Grace said, digging into the cookies and cream.

"Don't you mean 'hello, dirty slut, sleeping with the biggest asshole on the planet because he's got a hot body'?" Sadie said, not even bothering to hide how miserable and confused she was.

"No. I'd have said that if that was what I meant," Grace said mildly. "I am, however, slightly curious about how you got from 'I hate him' to 'take your clothes off, stud.' Just as a student of human nature, you understand."

Sadie swallowed a delicious, creamy lump of ice cream and wrinkled her forehead in acknowledgment of her own confusion.

"We've been fighting since he got here. Not obviously, but every decision is a struggle. And there was all this tension. Suddenly it seemed like the natural way to go, and the next thing I knew we were kissing. And stuff."

God, it sounded so...*primal* when she put it like that.

"*And stuff.* That's the good bit, right? The bit single, hard-up women like myself only get to fantasize about," Grace said.

"It wasn't good. It was...out of control," Sadie said, shaking her head as she remembered the way her instincts had taken over.

"Yeah? That good?" Grace said, eyes wide as she popped another spoonful of cookies and cream into her mouth.

"I bit him, Gracie," Sadie confessed in an embarrassed almost-whisper, pressing her hands to her hot cheeks. "And I think I may have scratched his back. I definitely ripped his fly open to get at him."

Grace made a fanning motion in the air with her hand. "Yow! You vixen! I'm impressed," she said admiringly.

Sadie glared at her friend. "This is serious, Grace. Not only do I not like the man, but he's my employee. I can't believe I let this happen."

Grace shrugged philosophically. "Something had to give, Sade, after the way you sucked it up when the wedding went wrong. All that emotion had to go someplace."

Sadie paused in the act of delving for another scoop of ice cream. She hadn't thought about the wedding, or Greg, all day. In fact, she hadn't thought about any of that stuff since the moment she'd recognized Dylan standing behind Claudia in her office doorway.

"I think you're right," she said, relief washing through her. "Of course! This was my way of freaking out over what happened with Greg. Oh, thank God."

Sadie shook her head and waved her hands in the air to indicate how relieved she felt. "Oh, I feel so much better."

Grace raised a single eyebrow. "Hmm."

"What now?" Sadie demanded.

"Well, I think it's totally understandable that you were on edge and that something had to blow. But I find it interesting that you chose Dylan to do the blowing with, so to speak."

Sadie frowned impatiently. "He was there, that's all."

"Okay," Grace said, clearly unconvinced.

"Trust me, Grace, I am not attracted to that man," Sadie said emphatically.

"Careful there, Pinocchio, you're gonna take my eye out with that nose of yours," Grace said.

"You think I'm lying?"

"To yourself more than me," Grace explained matter-of-factly. "I mean, I think you're genuinely deluded."

"Thanks," Sadie said drily. "That makes it so much better."

"There has to be something more to this than simple proximity," Grace argued. "This guy was horrible to you, yeah? Yet out of all the men you could have gone crazy with, you let him take your clothes off. That's got to mean something."

Sadie shifted uncomfortably. Most of the time, she valued her friend's sensitive perceptiveness. Tonight it was interfering with her need to stick her head in the sand.

"I had a crush on Dylan in high school," she admitted. "My body seems to still have this stupid juvenile crush on him."

"I thought he bullied you?" Grace asked, confused.

"No. He…he humiliated me in front of the whole school," Sadie said.

Slowly, with lots of ice cream to lubricate her memory, she told her friend about her senior prom. Grace was rigid with fury by the time she'd finished.

"What a bastard! My God. How can you stand being in the same room as him?"

"Better yet, how could I have had sex with him?" Sadie asked, smiling weakly. Going over the old memories had brought it all back to her. Why had she performed the most intimate of acts with the man who'd destroyed her self-esteem for more years than she cared to remember?

Grace slid the lids back onto the ice cream tubs, her eyes filled with worry.

"I don't know what to say to you," she said after a long silence.

"Yeah. I'm really messed up, aren't I?" Sadie said, managing a halfhearted laugh.

"I didn't mean that. Someone who hasn't had a social orgasm in over four years isn't really in a position to dole out relationship advice to anyone." Grace shrugged. "Unless Dylan runs on batteries, I'm all out of expertise."

Sadie laughed and slid her arm around Grace's shoulder.

"Admit it—I'm messed up. My fiancé dumped me at the

altar, I've just slept with my teen nemesis and I have a bellyache from too much ice cream. Worse, this is not the first time I've had ice cream for dinner this week. And I call myself an adult."

"I've never met an adult I liked, anyway," Grace said.

Sadie was stowing the ice cream in the freezer when Grace's cell phone chimed.

"Sorry." Grace grimaced as she took the call. The impatient expression on her face faded as she recognized her caller. "Hey, hey—slow down, Hope. I can't understand a word you're saying."

Sadie propped her hip on the kitchen counter as Grace attempted to soothe her youngest sister. Hope was the model, Sadie remembered. Superskinny, spoiled and immature, from what Sadie had seen of her over the years. Unfortunately, Grace had something of a blind spot where her sisters were concerned. Her two older sisters, Felicity and Serena, were also professional beauties—Felicity was a weather girl in the Midwest somewhere, while Serena was an actress here in L.A. For some reason, Grace seemed to think it was her duty to drop everything to tend to any of them should the need arise. Last year, she'd taken vacation time to fly out to nurse Felicity through a bad case of the flu. Felicity had repaid her by recovering early and heading off to Miami for some "much needed" sun, leaving Grace behind to house-sit her Siamese cats for a week on her own. Hope was always dropping into town unexpectedly, usually with some tale of woe that required Grace's time and attention to unravel. And Sadie didn't even want to think what Serena had done...

She frowned as she heard Grace telling Hope where the spare key to her condo was hidden and assuring her she'd be there as soon as she could.

"What's up?" Sadie asked neutrally.

Grace looked harassed and concerned as she started gathering her coat and bag.

"I'm so sorry, Sade, but I have to go. Hope's broken up with that model boyfriend of hers, the one she's been seeing for the past year. He kicked her out into the street in New York, and all her other friends are off on assignment somewhere. She jumped the first plane to L.A. so she could be with family."

"Lucky you," Sadie said. Hope was always having highly emotional breakups with her boyfriends, so it was hard for her to get too wound up with empathy.

"He hit her, Sadie. Can you believe that? He gave her a black eye when she tried to leave." Grace's voice was shaking, and tears stood out in her eyes as she considered her sister's plight.

"She's safe now, don't worry," Sadie said, wrapping her friend in a hug. Guilt pricked her as she thought of how dismissive she'd been of Hope's feelings. Was she so self-centered now that everyone else's experiences were inconsequential? Just because she'd had a run of bad luck didn't make her the center of the universe.

"I know she can be a little overdramatic at times, but I've never heard her so upset. I think getting to my condo and finding me out was the last straw," Grace said.

"You be careful driving, okay? No speeding," Sadie said as she urged Grace toward the door.

Grace hesitated in the hallway.

"I feel bad leaving you like this. After…well, you know."

"After I had sex with my new story editor?" Sadie asked wryly. "Forget it. I'm trying to. How's that for a solution?"

Grace smiled. "It's a start. I'm all for self-denial as a coping mechanism. Look where it's got me."

They hugged goodbye and Sadie shut the door on her friend. For a moment she remained leaning against the cool timber.

Forget having sex with Dylan Anderson. It was a great solution. Perfect. Except for one thing.

He was utterly unforgettable.

5

THE NEXT MORNING Dylan was writing plot points on the white-board when he saw Sadie's silver Audi flash past outside the window. He paused, marker hovering in the air, and watched as she slid her car into her assigned spot. He willed his gaze away, but it remained resolutely fixed on the scene unfolding outside the window. He lowered his arm, reluctantly admitting to himself that he wanted to watch her. They were never going to have sex again—but he needed to run his eyes over her sexy body, and was powerless to stop himself from doing so.

The seconds passed, but still she didn't exit the car. She was simply sitting there, staring straight ahead. He frowned, sliding the cap back onto the marker and moving closer to the window.

"Hey, Dylan," a voice said behind him. It was Kim, one of the story liners, ready to start the day's plot meeting.

Without turning, he raised a hand to acknowledge her greeting, his eyes—and thoughts—glued on Sadie. What was she *doing?*

As he watched, she shook her head impatiently and reached for the door. It opened a crack—then she slammed it shut again and slumped back in her seat, banging her open palm against her forehead in a classic "stupid me" gesture.

Curious. His frown deepened. Of all the scenarios he'd imagined post-desk-sex with his uptight boss, this was not one of them. He'd kicked himself sideways all evening over giving her a rod to beat him with. Women had been using sex to control men for as long as there had been sex. He'd handed Sadie the perfect tool to torture him with—his own desire for her. He'd resigned himself to six months of having what his body wanted used against him. But now… Now his conviction that Sadie was going to cold-bloodedly use what had happened between them to her advantage was undergoing a major makeover. She didn't look cold-blooded. She looked…confused. Embarrassed. Uncertain.

Outside in her car, Sadie's lips moved. She was giving herself a pep talk. Like a crazy lady. His lips curved into a smile, amused despite himself. Right now, she was about a million miles from the unapproachable, tight-lipped woman who'd been blocking him every which way all week and secretly plotting to give his job to his friend. She looked human and approachable, vulnerable. Even…appealing.

He swore under his breath as he acknowledged his own thoughts. One screw, and suddenly she was Mother Teresa. What kind of a moron was he?

Had he forgotten what she was really like? Was he really ready to brush off years of anger because she'd felt like silk beneath his hands?

His mind flashed back to that classroom and that fateful day. The memory was burned into his psyche, as vivid as the day it had happened.

It had been his turn to give a class talk on a chapter from their textbook. As usual, he'd sweated buckets trying to make sense of the squirming lines of text or to piece together the few words he could recognize on the page. He made desperate notes as another student held the floor, trying to remember exact phrases so he could regurgitate them with his own spin, an old trick he'd learned to scrape his way through class. Never Go First was his motto, and it had served him well.

But this time, his precious preparation time was interrupted by prissy Sadie Post as she leaned across from her desk next to his.

"You're looking at the wrong chapter," she said, her eyes and mouth all screwed up with tension. "We're on chapter eighteen, not thirteen."

He glanced down at the page in front of him, staring at the squiggly chapter number. He'd sworn it was an eighteen, but now that he really looked, it was more of a thirteen.

"You should talk about the way Faulkner used imagery in *The Sound and The Fury* to convey emotion," Sadie offered next. "Mr. McMasters likes that kind of thing."

Suddenly all his rage and confusion boiled up inside him and he turned to glare at her. She was always first to class and last to leave. She always had the answers, and she loved shoving her hand in the air so she could show off in front of everyone. She ate up everything Mr. McMasters threw at her, and then some, and made Dylan feel about a million times dumber than he already was just by sitting next to him. Now she was offering him charity, trying to help the stupid kid.

It was more than he could stomach.

"What makes you think I'd want help from someone like you?" he said viciously.

She went white with shock. "W-what?"

"When I want to talk to someone about Lit, I'll be doing it with Louise-Anne or Cindi Young. Someone worth wasting my time on. Understand?"

She shut her mouth with a click, and her brown eyes burned as she stared at him, her face tight.

Then Mr. McMasters called Dylan to the front of the class to begin his talk.

He stroked his way to the front of the class, doing his best to look unconcerned and confident. As usual, he started with a couple of jokes to get McMasters good and riled. In Dylan's experience, once his teachers were pissed at him, it came as a pleasant surprise if he said anything remotely sensible.

Borrowing heavily from his predecessor's comments, Dylan

bullshitted his way through a five minute dissertation on *The Sound and the Fury,* ending, as usual, with another joke. Traditionally, that was more than enough for the teacher to send him back to his chair with a C or at worst a D under his belt.

"Thank you for that, Mr. Anderson," McMasters said sarcastically. "I'm sure Mr. Faukner is rolling in his grave. Any questions from the class before we move on?"

Dylan was about to head back to his desk when a hand shot into the air. He froze, surprised. No one ever asked questions.

"Yes, Sadie? Do you have a question for Mr. Anderson?" McMasters asked.

"Yes. I wanted to know if Dylan thought Benjamin Compson was a reliable narrator?"

Her eyes bore into him as she cocked her head inquisitively to one side, challenging him to answer her. Dylan smiled casually. Miss Priss was trying to trip him up, but he'd had his ears open. He might be stupid, but he wasn't a complete moron.

"I think Benjamin's narration was pretty sentimental, so probably he fudged things a bit," he said easily. He started back to his desk again.

"What's your theory on the chronology of the novel?"

It was Sadie again, back ramrod-straight. A prickle of nervousness raced up his spine. He wiped his damp palms on the sides of his jeans.

"It…it worked okay. I thought the chronology was fine," he improvised.

He didn't even get a chance to move before she fired another question at him.

"What about Caddy's section of the book. What did you think of her narration?"

Dylan shot a frown at McMasters. "This is bull. No one else got this many questions."

But McMasters was enjoying watching him sweat.

"Answer the question, Mr. Anderson."

Dylan made a show of looking unconcerned. "I thought Caddy's section was fine. But not as good as Benjamin's," he said.

In the front row, one of the class nerds smirked behind his hand. Dylan frowned. He'd obviously got something wrong, but what?

Sadie fired again. "Would you say that her narration was lyrical?"

He shrugged. "Sure."

The kid in the front row smirked openly now, and someone at the back of the class giggled. He scanned the room, looking for clues. What was going on? What had he said wrong? His neck felt stiff with tension, and he had his knees locked so tightly they ached.

"What did you think of the section where Lenny accidentally killed the puppy?" Sadie asked next.

More sniggering. Dylan shifted his weight from his back foot to his front, and shot another look at McMasters. But the Lit teacher only nodded, indicating Dylan should answer the question.

"I thought it was sad, but Lenny had to do what he was told," Dylan guessed, taking a wild stab at what the situation might have been.

Open laughter now from his classmates. Sadie leaned forward in her chair. She hadn't taken her eyes off him once.

"And what about the time Huck and Jim were camping on the island?"

Some of the class were in stitches by now. Embarrassed heat warmed his face. She'd made a fool of him somehow, and McMasters was loving it. Dylan's hands curled into fists. He wanted to wipe the smug smile off McMaster's face and storm from the room, but pride held him in place. Pride, and Sadie Post's accusing brown eyes.

"I think you've about proved your point, Ms. Post," McMasters said. The teacher turned his attention to Dylan. "Did you even bother to read the text, Anderson?"

"Yeah, of course I did."

"Really. So you're well aware that Caddy does not narrate any section of the novel, and you were just playing along when Ms. Post threw in characters from Steinbeck's *Of Mice and Men* and Twain's *Huckleberry Finn?*"

As if McMaster's unveiling of the joke had given them permission, the class erupted into full-fledged laughter.

Dylan's chest ached with humiliation.

"I did my report," he said fiercely.

McMasters shook his head and pointed to the door. "Out. You want to be lazy, be lazy on someone else's time."

He didn't need telling twice. In two strides he was at the door.

"And I'll see you in my office after class, Mr. Anderson," McMasters said ominously.

The rustle of paper and the sound of muted chat dragged Dylan out of the old memory. Glancing over his shoulder, he saw that the whole team was gathered now, ready to start work. Out in the car park, Sadie was finally getting out of her car. He watched as she flicked a lock of hair over her shoulder and shouldered her work satchel.

Beautiful, but a bitch. She was practically a soap cliché. And he was just as garden-variety, letting his genitals dictate the running. The dumb guy sucked in by the black widow's lures.

Except it wasn't going to happen. Never again.

Jaw set, he turned to his team.

"Okay, let's get started…"

SADIE DIDN'T SEE Dylan until midafternoon. It was a point of some pride to her, in fact, that she managed to avoid him for so long, although it really hadn't been that hard. He was ensconced in an all-day plot meeting, so as long as she avoided hanging around the kitchen, all was good.

Her theory was holding up well until two o'clock when Lara popped her head into Sadie's office.

"Hey. Dylan asked me to come get you. We need your opinion on something."

Sadie stared at the other woman.

"Um… Can it wait? I'm really snowed under here." Sadie stalled, gesturing toward the paperwork strewn across her desk.

"It's a future planning question. We're starting the teen romance stuff between Angel and the geeky friend."

Sadie opened her mouth to trot out another excuse but closed it again without saying anything. She had completely forgotten about the eight-week teen romance they'd mapped out in forward planning a month ago. Of all the stories for Dylan to want help with, it had to be that one. She remembered her earlier theory that she was cursed. It was looking more and more likely every day.

There was no excuse for not responding to Dylan's request, however. She prided herself on being professional.

Forcing a smile, she stood. "Sure, not a problem."

Her legs felt shaky and insubstantial as she followed Lara back to the meeting room. Her belly did a series of flips and turns as she prepared herself for this first postsex encounter, and she could feel her heart banging against her ribs.

You're thirty years old, not seventeen, she reminded herself.

When that ploy failed, she reminded herself that even if she couldn't feel blasé, she had to act that way. Pride demanded it.

He glanced up from his notebook as she entered the room, and her breath caught in her throat as their eyes met and locked. She saw his pupils dilate, and noted the small giveaway twitch as he swallowed suddenly. Then her eyes dropped to his body and she was remembering how strong his arms had felt around her, how hard his chest had been against her breasts, the harsh sound of his breathing in her ear, the firm, muscular curve of his butt in her hands…

"Thanks for coming," Dylan said as she pulled out a chair with shaky hands.

She stiffened, her eyes narrowing. Thanks for *coming?* She couldn't believe that even Dylan Anderson would dare make a crack about what had happened between them in front of a roomful of their subordinates. Then she noted the dark blush staining his cheekbones.

So, he hadn't meant to be a smart-ass. Some of her tension eased as she slid into the chair.

"How can I help?" she asked, making a Herculean effort to sound normal and pretend she hadn't unzipped Dylan's fly less than twenty-four hours ago and helped herself to what she'd found inside.

"We're kicking off Angel's love triangle this week, and I wanted your take on the two guy characters," he said.

He leaned back in his chair as he spoke, and Sadie tried to ignore how broad his shoulders looked in the charcoal polo shirt he was wearing.

"Okay. Um, there are two main players apart from Angel, who we all know, of course, because she's a regular character on the show," Sadie babbled, trying desperately to gather her thoughts. If only he wasn't so attractive. And such a jerk. "The nerdy friend, Calvin, is Angel's constant companion, and the bad boy is in her math class. Calvin is your classic unsung, untested hero. Lacking self-esteem, but all heart. Once he gains some confidence, he's going to turn into Angel's knight in shining armor. And, of course, underneath his glasses and bad haircut he's pretty cute."

Dylan nodded as he took notes. "And the bad boy?"

Sadie swallowed nervously and reached for something to occupy her hands. As usual, the big meeting table was littered with notebooks, coffee cups, crumb-covered plates and pens and pencils. She settled on an oversize pencil that someone had brought back from Hawaii.

"The bad boy is just that—bad. Late for class. Never does his homework. Talks back to the teacher. His one redeeming feature is that he's a hunk. Angel being a teen, that's the bit she's interested in. She has a crush a mile wide," Sadie explained.

She clenched the pencil hard in her hand as she spoke. When she'd mapped out this story with the team at their forward planning weekend, she'd willingly channeled her high-school experiences with Dylan into Angel's character. It was something everyone on the story team did—steal from real life to feed the voracious story machine of the show. Not for a second did she ever think she'd be sitting opposite Dylan outlining the story inspired by her own secret crush on him. This was where the whole "being cursed" thing gained traction big-time— really, could she be any unluckier?

"So, what's the bad boy's story? Does he know she likes him? Angel's a pretty hot chick," Dylan said.

Sadie frowned. "He has no idea. And Angel's pretty, but she's not spectacular. We deliberately play her down so we can do stories like this and give the ordinary teens in our audience someone to identify with. Our bad boy's too busy trying to pick up cheerleaders to notice her," Sadie said firmly.

Dylan made another note. "So, this guy is dumb? Is that it? Nothing but a dumb hunk?"

Sadie shifted uncomfortably in her seat. Until a week ago, she'd have answered yes to that question. But clearly Dylan Anderson was not dumb.

"He hates school," she improvised. "He's too busy being the party king to care. He thinks high school is going to last forever and he's always going to be on top."

"So he *is* dumb. And shallow," Dylan said flatly.

"He's really only a distraction to stop Angel from looking too close to home for a while. But soon she's going to work out that her nerdy sidekick is her dream man," Sadie said defensively.

"Do you have any objection to us making the bad boy as three dimensional as possible?" Dylan asked.

Sadie shrugged, acutely uncomfortable. It was almost as though Dylan knew she'd based the character on him. But even in her heightened state of paranoia she knew that wasn't possible.

"Sure. Go for it. I always like shades of gray in a story," she said.

Dylan nodded and flicked over a page on the forward planning notes he was following. She saw he had underlined certain passages for ease of reference, and remembered how well prepared he'd been in every meeting they'd had so far. Whatever else she thought of him, he took his work very seriously.

"I see there's a crisis in a few weeks' time, where nerdy kid is going to leap to Angel's defense when bad boy picks on her. Did you have any ideas about how this might play out?"

Sadie slid the big pencil back and forth between her fingers nervously. She'd had lots of ideas about how those scenes might play out—but since her real-life teen costar was sitting at the other end of the table, she decided it would be better to play dumb.

"I'll leave that with you. As long as Angel gets a sharp lesson in contrasts. Just because the bad boy is beautiful doesn't mean he's worth knowing, that kind of thing," Sadie said.

"Okay, fine." Dylan's eyes dropped to her hands, and Sadie glanced down to see that she'd wrapped her hand around the fat pencil and was absent-mindedly sliding her palm up and down the lacquered wood.

Her eyes widened as she registered how suggestive the action was, and she dropped the pencil as though she'd been electrocuted. Feeling a full body blush coming on, she shot to her feet.

"If that's all, I've got a paper full of desk to get to," Sadie mumbled. She grimaced. "I mean, a desk full of paper," she said swiftly.

The blush was setting her ears on fire by the time she'd

exited the room. Prickles of sweat broke out under her arms, and she dove into her office with a sigh of relief.

Despite a few minor hiccups, she'd survived. Dylan had behaved professionally, and so had she. If she could get through another twenty-four weeks or so like that, Dylan's contract would be finished, Joss would be back and her moment of temporary insanity in Dylan's office would be dust.

Someone made a desperate squeaking noise, and Sadie realized it was her.

Things were pretty bad when a girl didn't believe her own line of bull.

BY FRIDAY, Dylan was feeling distinctly edgy, despite the fact that hostilities between him and his blond-haired opponent had been notably subdued for the past few days. He figured that was something to do with the bout of all-consuming sex they'd had in his office on Tuesday night. Nothing like mutual orgasm to bring about world peace. Unfortunately for his personal equilibrium, however, schtupping Sadie hadn't put paid to his body's obsession with her. He'd woken every night since with a raging hard-on with Sadie's name all over it. But he refused to give in to the demands of his hormones. He was old enough to want more from sex than just mindless friction. At the very least, he wanted to not actively dislike his bed partner. Sadie didn't even qualify on that most basic level.

Although she had her moments, he had to admit. Such as yesterday, when he'd arrived at work to find half a dozen big bags of candy on the story-room table. Lara and Ben had crowed with delight and dived straight in. Later he'd learned that Sadie often treated the story team, be it with bottles of wine for post-work drinks on a Friday, or with sugar to help keep them going through the long plot meetings.

And she was a lot less uptight than he'd imagined. The sound of her laughter was always echoing through the office.

Most of the time it was when she was hanging with Grace or Claudia, but she seemed to get on well with everyone. Except for him, of course. He told himself that was because he was the only one who knew what she was really like.

But he still found himself following her with his eyes when she came into his orbit. It was impossible for him not to notice her. For starters, she was so much taller than the other women in the office. And she had those amazing legs. Every time he scanned their lean length he remembered the feel of them wrapped around his hips as he thrust into her. Reason enough to look away, many men would think. Wiser men than him, unfortunately.

No wonder he was starting the day feeling cranky and tired and pushed to the limit. He made himself a double-shot espresso in the kitchen, and slid into his chair at the head of the story table with an old man's sigh. He was looking forward to the weekend. It wouldn't be a complete break, as he'd spend part of each day blocking out ideas for the following week's stories, and he had a number of his own projects on the go. The important thing was that anything he did would be a Sadie-free activity—exactly what the doctor had ordered.

"Have you got a minute?"

Dylan looked up from the draft story lines he'd been reviewing to see Sadie standing in the doorway, a sheaf of papers in hand. He was getting used to the two of them being the first people into the office in the morning. Not that they ever exchanged more than the minimum of words, but he was always aware that she was around.

"At your service," he said.

She shot him a hard look for his provocative choice of words and propped herself at the end of the table, almost as though she was afraid to come any closer. He allowed himself one quick full-body scan before putting his libido back on a tight leash. The sleeveless red cotton peasant top she was wearing was open at the throat, offering a glimpse of the shadow between her breasts. The fabric frothed out loosely over her chest and stomach, but was gathered in again around her waist. A frilly hem sat over the waistband of a pair of well-worn denims that made her legs appear to go on forever. She was wearing her black cowboy boots again, and the mere sight of them was enough to send his thoughts winging back to Tuesday night. He slammed down on the desire easing into his veins and forced his focus to work.

"What's up?" he asked neutrally.

She tapped one of the draft scene breakdowns she was holding. He'd e-mailed the drafts to her last night so he could pass her notes onto the team today.

"This story with Angel and the bad boy," she said.

"Jack," Dylan said. For some reason, the way she referred to the bad boy character so impersonally really got on his nerves.

"Fine, *Jack*. I see in Wednesday's episode you have Angel trying to get his attention and flirting with him."

"Yeah. And he ignores her, as we discussed," Dylan said.

Sadie shook her head. "She would never try to get his attention like that. It's out of character for her. She's shy, she's got low self-esteem. She's very inexperienced with boys. And she thinks this guy is a god. She would never try to get him to look at her."

Dylan snorted. "Girls are born flirting," he said.

"Not all girls," Sadie said vehemently. A little too vehemently, Dylan noted.

"So, what does she do, then? Just stare at him when he's not looking?" Dylan asked. "That's not going to make the greatest TV in the world."

"It's about small moments. She doodles his name in her book, then has to hide it when he looks across. She hangs out near his locker so she can be near him. And she tries to shield him when the teacher has it in for him. With good direction,

we can get those moments. She really loves this guy, remember.
She adores him."

Sadie's cheeks were flushed, and she didn't quite meet his
eye as she delivered her feedback.

"And this guy has no idea she likes him? Teenage boys
aren't that dumb," Dylan said disbelievingly.

She looked directly at him then, her eyes oddly fierce.

"Yeah, they are."

There was a long moment of silence, then Sadie broke their
eye lock and shuffled her papers around. Dylan studied her
closely, trying to work out what was going on.

"I wanted to talk to you about the bad boy's scenes, too,"
she said.

"Jack," Dylan corrected her again.

"Right, Jack. He's too nice," she said.

"What?" Dylan asked, a little taken aback. "He smokes, he
hassles the girls in the corridor, he gets kicked out of class.
What more do you want?"

"This scene with the teacher telling him he's dumb and that
he should just quit school now and save them the trouble of
kicking him out. I don't believe it. It's like a scene out of
Dickens or something," Sadie said.

"It happens," Dylan said flatly.

"I think it makes him too likable. He's supposed to be the
enemy," she said.

"I thought you liked shades of gray in your stories?" he
asked. "He's a person, too. He has dreams, fears, motivations.
Don't you think it makes it more interesting if we know what
makes him tick, why he behaves the way he does?"

Sadie made a disparaging noise. "It's not hard to work out.
He thinks he's God's gift to women, and he's too lazy to work
hard for anything else in his life."

"I think you're wrong. I think he's a kid who's had it tough.
I think his parents are both blue collar workers who don't give

a damn about education and don't believe in him. And I think he's had trouble with school since the moment he started because no one ever took the time to understand he learned differently from the other kids."

Too late Dylan realized that he'd just laid a whole lot of himself out on the table. But to his everlasting relief, Sadie didn't appear to pick up on the unusual level of passion in his tone.

"What do you mean, learns differently? You mean he's got a learning disorder?" she asked, a frown pleating her forehead.

Dylan shrugged, backing off now. What was he playing at, true confessions? She was the last person he wanted to trust with the knowledge of his dyslexia.

"Not necessarily. Maybe he's got eye trouble or something, or a hearing problem and he can't understand what the teacher is saying half the time," he hedged.

She cocked her head to one side, considering the idea. "That's kind of interesting," she said reluctantly. "The big bad hunk with a hidden weakness."

"It's a difference, not a weakness," Dylan heard himself say defensively.

This time she picked up on his tone, and the look she shot him was searching. She didn't say anything further, though, simply flicked through her notes some more.

"Can you get the story liners to adjust the episodes more in line with Angel's character, please?" she asked, obviously preparing to leave.

"What about the material with Jack?"

She shrugged. "Leave it in. You're right, it's more complex this way."

Dylan raised his eyebrows to signal his surprise at her ready capitulation. She read him straight-off.

"Pretty soft for a tyrant, aren't I?" she said.

She leaned forward to pass the notes over, and his eyes automatically dipped into the shadow of her cleavage. Their fingers accidentally brushed as he took the papers, and a surge of pure lust rocked him. God, he wanted her again. Too much.

His eyes lifted to her face. Her cheeks were faintly flushed, her eyelids at half-mast. As he watched, the tip of her tongue darted out to moisten her full lower lip.

"It's not going to happen again," he said suddenly.

She blinked, then took a step back.

"Of course not."

"It was a mistake. A big one," Dylan said, determined to kill whatever it was that burned between them. "We don't even like each other."

"It's not going to happen again," she confirmed.

"Just so we're agreed."

"Absolutely."

Turning on her heel, she left. For the life of him, he couldn't stop himself from following the wiggle of her butt in her faded denims.

It doesn't matter, he assured himself. *She doesn't want it, and you don't even like her. It's never going to happen again.*

SADIE WAS DETERMINED to spend the weekend doing work. She didn't have to, but she was so confused and messed up that she needed something to take her mind off its interminable circling.

An hour into her Saturday morning revision of the week's story lines, she knew she'd made a mistake. She couldn't read a scene without remembering Dylan pitching the idea. His voice kept popping up in her subconscious, and even though she kept pushing it away, it had the same effect thoughts of Dylan had had all week: it made her horny.

Which lead her straight back to being messed up. Despite their agreement that there was no chance of a rematch, she'd still woken this morning panting for breath, a handful of vivid-sense memories firmly imprinted in her mind: the feel of Dylan sliding inside her for the first time; the fierce hunger in him as he tongued her breasts; the clench of his fingers on her hips as he shuddered out his climax. If her dreams had carried on to the inevitable conclusion, she might have been almost grateful for the release. But they didn't. She always woke before her dream-self could be satisfied, and as a result she was now strung tight as a bow. A very turned-on, horny, desperate bow.

Worse, as she sat in her living room reading over the work Dylan and the team had produced for the week, she was forced to admit the realization that had been growing inside her since she'd returned from holidays—he was incredibly talented. It wasn't just that he knew how to build tension to a cliff-hanger that demanded their audience tune in the following day. It was the nuance, the feeling he captured between the characters. And, typically, it was Angel's school love triangle that show-cased his skill to perfection. It was all there—the small looks, the hesitations, the accidental touches, the unconscious snubs. He'd captured it all in painful, sensitive detail.

How could this be the same person who had treated her so cruelly all those years ago? It was a question that had reared up in her mind a number of times over the past week. She needed to hold on to the old anger so badly; his humiliation had been such a pivotal moment in her life. But the more she saw and heard of Dylan, the more trouble she was having re-conciling the smart-ass loner of her memories with the articu-late, witty, clever man of today.

He'd incorporated all her changes with no argument what-soever. He clearly wanted what was best for the show. He wanted to make good drama—as she did. And, scarily, their ideas about what made good drama were uncannily attuned. The clashes of the Tuesday morning pitch meeting aside, he'd taken on board all her suggestions and comments, bar a few exceptions. And even then, he'd made his version so undeni-able she'd been forced to concede that it was the right way to go. Such as with the whole to-kiss-or-not-to-kiss issue with

Loni's ex-boyfriend, J.B. Dylan had gone with his angle, having Loni kiss her old flame. But he'd done it so convincingly, mining all the nuances so well, that Sadie couldn't in all conscience put her foot down for the sake of it. It was good. Better than that—it was great.

After a couple of fruitless hours, she threw her pen down. She couldn't stop thinking about him. It was that simple. She might as well admit it to herself, because it wasn't going away. And while she was at it, she might as well add that she wanted his hands on her body again more than she wanted chocolate, ice cream or coffee, her three favorite food groups.

"This is crazy," she told her empty condo, bouncing up from the couch agitatedly.

What was wrong with her? How could she want someone who had been so cruel to her? Was this some twisted statement on her psyche? Was she actively seeking out a man to hurt her in some way?

Catching a glimpse of her reflection in the antique mirror above her fireplace, Sadie stopped and stared. Her hair stuck out in all directions, and her eyes were wide and confused.

"You're a mess," she told her reflection.

And she needed to get out of her own head for a while. Scooping up the phone, she hit the speed dial for Grace. Guilt and discomfort gnawed at her as she consciously acknowledged something she'd been doing all week—she was avoiding Claudia. So far, she'd ducked two lunch invites and a movie suggestion from her friend. She felt like a prize cow. But she also knew she couldn't spend time with Claudia and not give up her secrets. And it wasn't fair to dump her mess in her friend's lap. More correctly, it wasn't fair for her to dump her mess in the *producer's* lap. Which pretty much defined the problem in a nutshell. She needed her friend, but she couldn't in all conscience ask Claudia to choose between their friendship and her responsibilities. Sadie should not have slept with

Dylan. She knew it, he knew it, and Claudia would feel incredibly let down if she knew what Sadie had done. Hell, Claudia had only been in the job seven weeks, and Sadie had banged their prize new story editor in the office within days of laying eyes on him. Just the thought of Claudia's reaction to this bit of news made Sadie's stomach churn with anxiety.

The sound of Grace's voice in her ear pulled her back from her tortured thoughts.

"Hey, Gracie, it's me. You feel like shopping, or lunch or something?" Sadie asked a little desperately.

Grace made an apologetic sound. "I'm so sorry, Sadie, but I've already told Hope we'd hang out today. I've been working all week, and she's been stuck at home on her own…" Grace explained.

Sadie was confused. "I thought you said yesterday that she was going home today?"

"She was. But she's changed her mind. She's a real mess, Sade. I'm going to talk her into staying with me for a while. There's plenty of work for her out here, and I don't want her anywhere near that creep. He's called her a couple of times, but I made her block him from her cell phone, and he doesn't have my number."

"Okay. Well, maybe we could do something tomorrow?" Sadie asked.

"Sorry. Hope has booked us in for facials tomorrow." Grace sounded guilty, and Sadie rushed to assure her.

"That's great. You deserve a break. I'll see you on Monday, okay?"

"Are you all right?" Grace asked, concern lacing her voice.

"Just confused, as usual. But this, too, shall pass, right?" Sadie said brightly.

They talked for a few more minutes, then Sadie returned the phone to its cradle.

Arms flopped between her legs, she stared straight ahead

listlessly. How was she going to get through the weekend with her sanity intact? Beside her, the phone rang as if in direct response to her silent plea. She leaped on the receiver with pathetic eagerness.

"Sadie, it's Claudia. We have a problem."

A shiver of apprehension raced down her spine and she took a deep breath. Claudia knew about the sex-on-the-desk thing. A rush of heat washed up her chest and into her face. How was she going to explain what had happened to her friend when she didn't even understand it herself? Claudia was so professional, so committed to doing a good job. And Sadie had let her down.

"Sadie, are you there?" Claudia asked as the silence stretched.

"I'm so sorry. I want you to know that up front," Sadie said.

"Well, that's really sweet, Sade, but I think you're going to feel more pissed off than sorry when I tell you you've lost your weekend," Claudia said.

Sadie pulled the phone from her ear and stared at it a moment. Slowly it dawned on her that Claudia didn't know about her and Dylan, and that there was some other crisis to deal with.

"Sure, that's okay. What's up?" she asked.

"Mac Harrison has chicken pox," Claudia said, referring to the actor who played the part of Kirk on the show. "Can you believe it? He visited his niece, who was infected but not showing. Bingo, he's covered in spots. We have to pull him for two weeks."

Claudia sounded thoroughly pissed.

"I'll be at the office in half an hour," Sadie said reassuringly.

"Chicken pox. My first test in the hot seat, and it's *chicken pox*. I can't believe I have to dip into the emergency funds to work around a stupid kid's rash."

"It can be quite, um, uncomfortable," Sadie said, trying to repress a giggle at Claudia's utter disgust.

"This is going to look so great in the soapie mags and TV

guides," Claudia said morosely. "Our hottest star down with the pox."

Sadie burst out laughing. After a moment's silence, Claudia joined in.

"Okay, I'm overreacting a little," Claudia admitted after a moment.

"It's cool. You're allowed. It *is* a stupid thing to catch."

"Don't worry, I've already had words with Mac," Claudia said. "I've warned him that next time it had better be something headline-worthy like flesh-eating virus or botulism."

"I'll see you in twenty," Sadie assured her friend through her laughter.

She didn't bother changing out of her old denim cutoffs, flip-flops and tank top. She didn't even bother putting a bra on beneath her tank top—at the best of times, a bra was pretty much a token gesture anyway, given the size of her bust. Claudia had seen her in worse, and if she was going to work like a dog all weekend, she might as well be comfortable.

She regretted her decision the moment she walked into the office and saw Dylan talking with Claudia in the kitchen area. She stopped in her tracks, suddenly acutely sensitive to the fact that she had far too little clothing on. Dylan broke off what he was saying when he saw her, his dark gaze raking her from head to toe. Sadie stuck her hands into her front pockets and willed an extra couple of inches onto the bottom of her cutoffs. They were her car-washing shorts, and while they weren't exactly Daisy Duke hot pants, they ended a good distance above her knees. She could feel the heat in Dylan's gaze as it ran up her bare legs. Goose bumps broke out over her body, and she suppressed a shiver. Why wasn't she wearing a bra? And how could a simple look have so much power? Especially a look from a man she didn't like?

"Thanks, Sade. I owe you one," Claudia said, oblivious to the crackle of awareness surging back and forth between her two key story people. "I figure between the three of us we can at least pinpoint the size of the problem today. If I have to, I can reschedule next week's shoot to give you more time to rewrite the replacement scenes."

"Sure. Not a problem," Sadie said automatically.

She was deliberately not looking at Dylan. She could see him in her peripheral vision, but she could not risk looking at him directly. She was already too aware of the fact that he was wearing a pair of low-slung jeans, the denim faded and soft enough to outline every muscular bulge in his legs. And she didn't need to look more than once to have an image burned onto her retina of the way his ratty, slightly shrunken T-shirt moulded the hard planes of his chest. It sported the Lakers' logo in faded lettering, and didn't quite meet the waistband of his jeans on one side. His feet were bare, an innocuous circumstance that for some reason made her palms feel hot and sweaty. God help her, even his *feet* were sexy.

"Where do you want to work? The story room? One of the offices?" Claudia asked.

She instinctively turned toward Dylan's office, since it was the closest, and Sadie and Dylan both spoke at once.

"No!"

Claudia's eyebrows shot up. "*O-kay.* Story room it is, then," she said, shooting Sadie a what-the-hell-was-that look as they moved toward the larger meeting room.

Sadie smiled weakly and shrugged a shoulder, regretting the gesture the moment she felt her breast jiggle. A bra, a bra, her condo for a bra. Never had underwire, lace and various bits of tiny hardware seemed so appealing.

Sadie waited until Dylan chose a seat before pulling out a chair as far from him as possible. Claudia sat between the two of them and started handing out the scripts in question. There were ten one-hour scripts in all, two weeks' worth. A substantial tower of paper.

"Okay, how do we want to handle this?" Claudia asked, throwing the floor open to her experts.

To Sadie's surprise, Dylan deferred to her with a quick look in her direction.

"Right. Um, sure." Why was she surprised that he hadn't tried to take the lead? She was the boss, right? Somehow, she always expected him to try to bully her or beat her down, but she was beginning to understand that Dylan didn't ever do what was expected of him.

"Let's break these up, find out what we're up against. I'll handle the first four scripts, since I'm probably the most familiar with the material, and you two take three scripts each."

Sadie leaned forward to grab a handful of tiny Post-It notes, forgetting her sans bra condition until the front of her tank top gaped. She didn't need to look up to know Dylan was looking at her. She could feel his eyes on her like a caress.

Swallowing self-consciously, she slid a pile of Post-it notes toward both Claudia and Dylan.

"Tag anything with Kirk in it, or any mention of him. Once we ascertain what we have to pull him out of, we can come up with a reason for his absence and a replacement story to slot in," Sadie instructed.

Claudia and Dylan nodded their understanding, and for the next few hours there was nothing but the rustle of paper and the scratch of pens as the three of them ploughed through the scripts. Slowly, Sadie's monumental awareness of Dylan faded to manageable proportions. As long as Claudia was there, they had the ultimate buffer for the insane physical attraction that seemed to exist between them. Even if Sadie wanted to take advantage of it, she couldn't with Claudia on hand. Not that she wanted to, of course. Dylan was everything she disliked in a man. And they had a deal—a very sensible, rational deal not to let anything happen between them again.

By 4:00 they had a blueprint of what needed pulling out and

replacing. Across the ten episodes, Kirk was in nearly forty scenes spread over six sets and one location shoot.

By 7:00, they were all jangling with coffee nerves, but had formulated a solution to their problems. Once Mac was clear of his quarantine period, they would shoot a scene explaining that his character was heading off to help his brother with a business crisis across country, and paste it in during the tape edit. Story wise, Loni would be angry that he was leaving at a time when she was still grieving the loss of their unborn child. Since the shooting scripts were ten weeks ahead of the stories Dylan and his team were plotting at present, Kirk's abandonment of Loni at this difficult emotional time only added weight to their decision to divorce in subsequent weeks.

When they'd finished mapping out the arcs they would be slotting in to take the place of Kirk and Loni's scenes, Claudia breathed out a sigh of relief and pushed a hand through her hair.

"Wow. That's great, guys. I can't believe we got through all that so quickly."

Sadie was faintly surprised, too. But once they knew what they were up against, she and Dylan had worked together like a well-oiled machine. There was a special form of shorthand that developed between simpatico story people on television drama that allowed them to finish each other's sentences and outline moments without going into every tiny detail. Sadie had experienced it with a couple of colleagues in her time, but she had never expected to be so in tune with Dylan that they would understand what the other was going to say before it was said.

But that was the way it had been. He suggested an idea, she fleshed it out, they both spoke up with the pay-off scene at the same time. Her excitement about a moment fed his energy, and ideas flew across the table. Claudia sat between them, her brow furrowed with concentration as she tried to keep up.

"You know, it's like you guys are speaking another language when you get going like that," Claudia said as she went over her notes. "I don't even know what half of this stuff I wrote down means!"

Sadie laughed self-consciously. "It's a story-table thing. It's hard to explain."

"Well, whatever it is, it's solid gold. I was feeling incredibly guilty about this stupid dinner I have to go to, but you guys have got this whipped. Once you've fleshed out those replacement scenes in story line form, I'll farm them out to a couple of freelancers to write up the dialogue and we'll be ready to rock and roll."

Sadie barely heard anything that her friend said. She was too busy registering the fact that Claudia was standing and collecting her bag and car keys.

"You're going?" Sadie asked stupidly.

"Like I said—I've got a dinner with the organizing committee for the People's Vote Television Awards," Claudia said.

Sadie shot a panicked look toward Dylan, then immediately regretted it. What was she expecting him to do, second her plea for Claudia to remain as chaperone between them? His dark gaze was unreadable, and Sadie dropped her eyes back down to her notes.

"I'll check in again later, okay? If you need me, I can swing back around after the dinner," Claudia said on her way out the door.

And then they were alone again.

6

DYLAN SCRIBBLED a pointless note in the margin of his scratch pad. Out of the corner of his eye, he could see Sadie's blond halo of hair, the silky mass even more tousled than usual after an afternoon of plot wrangling.

If he shifted his head a little more to the side, he would also be able to see the sweet swell of her breasts in the bright aqua tank top she was wearing. He didn't need X-ray vision to know she wasn't wearing a bra—that fact had been apparent the moment she'd walked in the door. All afternoon he'd been resisting the urge to feast on the soft outline of her nipples through the stretch fabric of her top. But he was only human, after all. He was bound to slip up sometime. Like…now, for instance, with Claudia gone and the coast clear.

He shot a glance toward the end of the room. Sadie was resting her head on her hand, her elbow propped on the table. Her full lips were pursed around the end of her pen, her eyes fixed on the page in front of her. His eyes dropped to caress her breasts. Their curves pressed full and proud against her tank top, two pert, perfect handfuls. He shifted a little in his seat, remembering the weight of her in his hands, the way she'd moaned with need as he'd taken one of her nipples into his mouth. His fingers curled into his thighs, wanting to touch, as well as look. His groin tightened, and even though he knew it was an exercise in self-torture, he couldn't pull his eyes away. Her nipples were very sensitive, he remembered, but she'd liked it when he bit her there, his tongue rough against the pebbled silk of her skin. He moved his tongue against his teeth, remembering how she'd tasted. As if they were responding to his lust-laden thoughts, Sadie's nipples hardened into two erect nubbins, poking proudly through the thin layer of cotton that was all that separated her from his roving gaze.

"Stop it!"

Dylan's gaze shot from her chest to her face and he saw she was staring at him, her brown eyes frustrated.

"I wasn't doing anything," he said, aware that he sounded more than a little caught out.

"Yeah, you were. You were staring. We had an agreement," she said.

"Then you should have worn a bra," he fired back.

"You're the one with bare feet," she said belligerently.

He made an exasperated noise. "Not quite the same thing, I'm sure you'd agree?"

She blushed, and avoided his eyes. "Don't look at me like that. I don't like it."

"Parts of you do," he said before he could help himself.

She pierced him with her gaze. "You don't even *like* me. Remember?"

"You're the one with the erect nipples, baby."

"Right. So you don't have a hard-on right now?" she demanded.

"That's right, I don't," he fibbed.

"Liar."

She stood abruptly and moved around the table toward him. Dylan fought the urge to cover his incriminating crotch with his notepad. This conversation was juvenile enough as it was.

"Ha!" she said as she spotted the thick ridge his erection made in his jeans.

"Okay, you got me—I have a hard-on. Big deal. It's a well-known fact that penises are indiscriminate. I, however, am not."

"Ditto for my nipples," Sadie asserted defiantly. "I have no control over their bad taste."

"Fine. We've got that covered. How about we do some work so we can get out of here before Monday?" Dylan suggested tightly.

"Great idea. Let's do that," she agreed.

For the next two hours, they plotted the specifics of the replacement scenes. Dylan's hand began to cramp from his intensive note taking, and his growling, empty stomach became louder with each passing moment.

When a particularly loud, demanding hunger rumble shattered the silence of the room, Sadie rolled her eyes.

"I take it you're hungry?" she asked, as though that were an incredibly unreasonable thing.

"Us humans need to recharge every now and then. We can't just find a handy power socket like you robots," he said.

Sadie harrumphed, clearly irritated by his smart-ass comments.

"I'll order a pizza. Anything you don't want on it?"

"Anchovies and olives," he said.

She made another harrumphing noise.

"What? Have I offended the World Anchovy Convention now or something?" Dylan demanded, exasperated.

"No. It's just… I don't like them, either."

There was a small silence, broken when she pushed herself up out of her chair.

"I'll go phone in the order."

He watched her butt all the way out the door. For the life of him he couldn't work out why he found her so appealing. Okay, she had a hot body. Great breasts, great ass, amazing legs. And she was wild in the bedroom department. But there had been plenty of other women in his life who'd ticked all the same boxes, and none of them had ever had him on a knife's edge the way Sadie did.

It had to be the added fillip of their shared history. Something about not liking her, about wanting to dominate her and prove to himself and her that he was worth something.

As motivations went, it was pretty immature. But, as he'd said to Sadie earlier, penises weren't exactly known for their discrimination. Apparently the rest of him wasn't, either.

SADIE SLID THE TWO pizza boxes onto the freestanding counter that served as a communal table in the kitchen. Gesturing for Dylan to take a stool, she slid onto one herself and flipped the first box open.

"God, I'm starving," she said. The moment she caught sight of the super supreme pie, her mouth started watering like crazy.

Dylan shot her an unfathomable look before reaching for a big slice. She pulled her own gigantic piece from the box and started eating, determined to get through the evening as quickly as possible. Food for ten minutes, then back into it. If they kept plowing through, they would be out of here in the early hours and she could have a small break before she had to deal with Dylan again on Monday morning.

Dealing being the operative word. He was becoming an increasingly vexing issue. Or, more accurately, her reaction to him was becoming increasingly worrying. Take the staring incident for example. She'd felt his gaze on her like a physical thing. Hot and hard, and she'd been powerless to stop her body from responding. It was pathetic. She was a grown woman, not a teenager anymore. Dylan's dark good looks shouldn't have so much power over her.

The silence stretched between them as they munched on pizza. Sadie's nerves ratcheted even tighter. She was too aware of him, too self-conscious about herself, also. Something had to give.

"So, what are you thinking in story terms for next week?" she asked suddenly, falling back on work as the perfect distraction.

"More tension with Kirk and Loni over J.B. And I want to crank things up with Angel and Jack. I was thinking some kind of big class test that Jack's really wound up about and Angel gets in the line of fire."

"I did a bit of research on this during the week," Sadie said in between mouthfuls. "There are tons of programs in place to catch kids with learning difficulties and physical disabilities. We need to be realistic about whether a kid like Jack could go undiagnosed for so long."

To her surprise, Dylan swore under his breath and dropped his half-eaten slice of pizza back into the box.

"Right now, across the country, there are hundreds of thousands of kids with learning disorders, and only a small portion of them have been diagnosed. It's all very well to say the system will catch them, but there has to be a will to help. And there are too many overworked, under-resourced teachers out there shuffling problem students from one class to the next to win themselves a bit of peace and quiet. Trust me, this shit happens every day."

His eyes were blazing dark heat, and his face was tense with suppressed frustration. Sadie saw that she'd struck a chord and she held her hands up in a make-peace gesture.

"Okay, clearly you're more informed on this subject than I am," she conceded.

His gaze slid away from hers. "We did a story on it on *The Boardroom*," he said.

Sadie frowned as she mentally ran through the episodes she'd seen. She hated repeating another show's dynamics. It was impossible to avoid using the same themes and starting points—there were only so many ideas in the world—but it was important to tell the story differently each time. Finally, the episodes he was talking about came to mind.

"I remember. The head honcho's kid had dyslexia, didn't he?" she asked.

Dylan froze in the act of biting into his pizza slice.

"You watch the show?"

Sadie shrugged a shoulder casually. She'd caught all the first season, and most of seasons two and three. She'd been hooked despite knowing he worked on it. His involvement aside, it was a compelling concept, with a great cast and strong, honest scripts.

"I caught it here and there, when I was in," she disclosed.

He eyed her searchingly for a beat or two before resuming his attack on the pizza.

"Anyway, I think the important thing with this Angel/ Jack/Calvin triangle is that we remember Angel is our core cast member. We need to keep the focus on her."

Dylan nodded his agreement, too busy with food to respond verbally.

"You did a nice job with the small nuances between her and Jack this week," Sadie said. "Have you had any thoughts about how you're going to bring things to a head?"

Dylan paused to take a swig of cola before answering.

"Yeah. I was thinking about the school prom. We can dress Angel up, and make Calvin look pretty good, in a geeky kind of way. Plus, there's nothing like a little public humiliation to bring things to a head."

Sadie's pizza turned to cardboard in her mouth. She swallowed the tasteless lump and slid the largely uneaten slice back into the box.

"I don't think the prom's a good idea," she said stiffly.

Was he doing this on purpose?

She eyed him closely, but he looked completely guileless.

"Why not? We can shoot it on location somewhere, deck out an old gym in crepe paper and crappy lighting. Give all those stay-at-home moms a good dose of nostalgia."

He doesn't remember. The thought ripped through her like a peal of thunder. The thought that her humiliation meant so little to him made her push her stool back with a screech of metal legs on tiled floor.

"I don't think the prom's a good idea. You'll have to come up with something else," she said.

Shoving her hands into the pockets of her cutoffs, she hunched her shoulders and headed for the ladies' room.

Washing her hands under the warm water, she shook her head at her overreaction. The problem was, the past kept bleeding painfully into the present with Dylan dogging her every footstep. Her stupid physical reaction to him was just one manifestation of the phenomena, along with her irrational emotional reactions to the things that he said.

Running more water onto her fingertips, she brushed coolness across her brow. She had to stay calm and in charge, and she had to protect herself. Most of all, she had to separate herself from Angel's story. It may have started out as her story, but it was never going to stay that way—the collaborative nature of television meant that the end product never resembled the original idea. She needed to be professional.

Unfortunately, the woman in the mirror didn't look very professional right now. Her hair was wild, her cheeks lightly flushed, and she had trouble meeting her own reflected gaze.

She needed to get away from Dylan. And the only way to do that was to get the work done, pronto.

DYLAN CRUSHED the pizza boxes and squished them into the trash can. His gaze kept sliding to the door to the ladies' room, where Sadie had disappeared more than ten minutes ago.

She was upset about something. That much was obvious. It hadn't escaped his attention that every time they discussed Angel she came on pretty strong about the way things had to be. It also hadn't escaped his attention that he had some pretty concrete notions where that story was concerned, too. He knew why he felt that way—he identified with Jack, Sadie's two-dimensional bad boy. He'd imbued him with his own history, invested his own memories and emotions in the kid. He didn't have a clue what was driving Sadie, however.

As he washed his hands at the kitchen sink, he went over the last few minutes of their conversation before Sadie had disappeared.

They'd been talking about Angel and what the crisis moment might be. He'd raised the idea of the prom…Dylan froze, water dripping from his hands as he at last got what he'd done.

He wasn't a saint, but he'd never set out to deliberately hurt anyone in his life—except for that one time at the school prom when Sadie had stood in front of him, all prim and proper and eager to play Lady Bountiful to his ignorant peasant. He'd taken one look at her ridiculous tissue-stuffed dress and stitched-up little smile, and all the rage and disappointment and fear inside him had come welling up.

She'd deserved it. He'd told himself that ever since he'd woken the next day filled with regret. She'd had no qualms about humiliating him in front of his peers; he'd simply been returning the favor. But it still wasn't a memory he was particularly proud of. Which was why it wasn't exactly on high rotation in his mental hit parade. Which explained why he'd been stupid enough to bring it up with Sadie.

He shook his head at his own thick-headedness. For a moment he toyed with the idea of apologizing, but everything in him balked at the idea. She wasn't about to get down on bended knee and beg him to forgive her for what she'd done to him all those years ago. He'd be damned if he was the only one eating humble pie.

The slap of her flip-flops on the tiled floor signaled her emergence from the washroom, and he swung around to face her. She looked cool and determined, very businesslike. Good. That was exactly the right attitude to get them through the night.

"Let's get this done," she said.

He followed her back to the story room, resolutely resisting the need to eye her butt the whole way.

"I think we should split the workload down the middle," she said as they resettled into their chairs. Without Claudia in the room, the distance between them seemed almost comical.

"Sure, that makes sense," he said. Even if he hadn't agreed— which he did—he'd have done it her way. Anything to get this over and done with.

Sadie shuffled through the stack of flagged scripts, sorting them into two piles: the first pile for her, made up of the four scripts she'd reviewed personally and one script that Dylan had reviewed, and the second pile for Dylan, made up of the remaining two scripts he'd reviewed, plus Claudia's three.

"There you go," she said, sliding the pile across to him.

"Thanks. I'm going to go work in my office," he said, collecting his notes and the scripts.

"Sure. I'll probably be in my office, too," Sadie said.

He'd made it to the doorway when he heard her sharp intake of breath. Glancing over his shoulder, he saw that Sadie was staring at the open pages of the script he'd reviewed earlier in the afternoon. The familiar highlighted phrases and underlining of words that was second nature to him in combating his dyslexia seemed to jump off the page as she lifted stunned eyes to him.

"You're dyslexic." It wasn't a question, it was a statement.

Too late Dylan realized that he shouldn't have brought *The Boardroom* into their discussion over dinner. When he'd been working on the show, it had seemed natural to use his particular form of dyslexia as a basis for the show's character. As a result, all the therapies and strategies shown on-air had mirrored his own. Since he'd been stupid enough to put the reminder in her head, Sadie had only to look at his heavily marked up pages to put two and two together.

"Yes," he said. He told himself it didn't matter. Lots of people knew he was dyslexic. He wasn't ashamed of it. It was part of who he was. But he was old enough and cynical enough to understand that some people weren't above using his difference as a weapon.

"When did you— When were you diagnosed?" she asked faintly. She'd gone very pale, he saw.

"In my early twenties."

"My God." The eyes she lifted to him were tortured. "I'm so sorry."

Dylan frowned. This was the last thing he'd expected from her.

"It's no big deal. I work around it," he said carefully.

"No. I mean… I'm so sorry about what I did. I thought you didn't care. I mean, I knew you cared because of that time in the locker room, but then I tried to help and you said those things… I didn't understand, or I never would have…" She stood, and he saw that she was shaking and that tears had filled her eyes. "No wonder you were so angry with me at prom."

Dylan frowned, trying to piece together what she was saying.

"What do you mean, you were only trying to help?" he asked fiercely, eyes boring into her. Suddenly he knew this was very, very important.

She shook her head, tears spilling over her cheeks now. Dashing them away with her hands, she moved toward the door.

"Just—just give me a minute," she said, her voice thick with unshed tears.

Dylan stood obediently to one side as she walked briskly toward the ladies' room for the second time that evening. It wasn't until the door had swung shut on her delectable ass that he got it. A collage of images and conversations and memories fell into place in his mind.

Sadie's voice, explaining about Angel. *She thinks he's a god. She adores him… She would never try to get him to look at her… It's about small moments. She doodles his name in her book, then has to hide it when he looks across… She tries to shield him when the teacher has it in for him.*

Suddenly he could see it as plain as day in his mind—Sadie sliding her forearm across her notepad, her gaze darting nervously his way as he sat beside her. Sadie shooting her hand into the air every time Mr. McMasters prowled by Dylan's desk to check on his work. Sadie leaning across when he was scrambling to fudge his book review, offering unsolicited advice despite his obvious resistance.

All of it intended to help him. Because she'd loved him.

"Shit."

He strode toward the bathroom, a million thoughts and feelings vying for top billing in his mind. Slamming the door open, he found Sadie in an open cubicle, seated on the closed lid of the toilet. She lifted her tear-streaked face, startled.

"Angel is you, isn't she?" he demanded harshly.

He watched as she made an effort to pull herself together.

"Listen—"

"Did you have a crush on me or not?" he asked.

Her shoulders dropped in defeat and she put her head back in her hands. "Yes."

"Goddamn!" Curling his hand into a fist, Dylan slammed it unthinkingly into the wall. She gave a startled yelp as the plaster crumbled, leaving a large, fist-size hole in the wall.

Ignoring the stinging in his hand, Dylan rounded on her.

"Do you have any idea how much I hated you? How much I blamed you for me getting kicked out of school?"

"You got kicked out of school? Because of what I did in class that day? Oh, God."

Fresh tears welled up and slid down her face.

"You should have said something. You should have written me a poem or ridden past my house or something like an ordinary person," he said.

That night at the prom… He'd wanted to destroy her. And she'd only been offering up her shy, teenager's love.

For almost half his life she'd been the focal point for all the rage he felt toward the people who'd let him down and found him lacking.

And it was all a big, fat, stupid mistake.

Spinning on his heel, Dylan slammed out of the bathroom before he could put another hole in the wall.

WHEN SADIE EMERGED from the bathroom Dylan was running his hand under the cold water tap in the kitchen He flicked a glance her way before returning his attention to his reddened hand.

"There's ice in the freezer. I'll make you a pack," she said.

"Thanks."

Pulling a fresh dishcloth from the drawer, Sadie filled it with ice and tied it in a knot. She handed it to Dylan wordlessly.

"I'm sorry about what I did at prom," Dylan said after a long silence. "I was half-cut, but that's no excuse. I wanted to tear you down."

"I know. I guess I wanted to do the same to you, too."

The anger had faded from Dylan's face. For the first time, she saw him as a whole person, not simply the adult version of her teen crush, or the manifestation of all her insecurities. He was still a very attractive man. But she could see the humor in him, the cleverness. The kindness. He wasn't even close to the arrogant egotist she'd painted him as.

"I wish I'd known about your dyslexia," she said hopelessly.

"That makes two of us," he said wryly.

"I can't believe they kicked you out of school because of what I did that day. I thought you went because you wanted to."

"Probably did me a favor in the long term. I was never going to graduate, not with my marks. And if I hadn't left school, I wouldn't have wound up at the Burger Barn, and I wouldn't have met Harry."

Sadie frowned, and Dylan obviously read her confusion.

"Harry's kid had dyslexia. He was the one who worked out what was going on for me."

"Lucky."

"Yeah."

"How's your hand?" she asked.

Dylan flexed it experimentally. "I'll live to fight another wall," he said lightly.

Sadie managed a half smile. Everything had shifted. Nothing was the same, even her memories.

"After the prom—it must have been pretty bad," he said.

Sadie shrugged. "I survived."

"Still. I was an asshole."

Sadie shrugged again, but something nudged a confession from her. "It was the first time I'd done that, you know. Stuffed my top. I wanted to impress you so badly." She shook her head at her own foolishness. "I must have been the only seventeen-year-old titless wonder in the state."

Dylan's eyes dropped to her chest. "If it's any consolation, I'm pretty impressed now."

Sadie blushed and tucked a stray piece of hair behind her ear.

"Please. We both know my chest is never going to set the world on fire."

The moment she'd said it, she knew how it sounded: like a plea for reassurance.

"You said something before. About a time in the locker room…?" he asked.

Her relief that he'd chosen to ignore her moment of weakness faded. She *so* didn't want to explain about playing voyeur all those years ago.

"Forget it," she said lightly, waving a hand dismissively. "It wasn't anything important."

Dylan raised an eyebrow.

"Not knowing this stuff has caused enough problems for both of us, don't you think?" he said.

He wasn't going to let it go. She sighed, prepared to be embarrassed all over again.

"One day after gym class, I heard you singing in the boys' change room. I—I snuck in. You were in the shower."

One of Dylan's eyebrows shot up and a slow grin spread across his mouth.

"Dear me. Little Sadie Post. Who would have thought?"

Sadie finished the rest in a rush. "I saw how cut up you were about failing the Lit test we'd just taken. Before that, I always thought you didn't care about school."

He nodded slowly. "So you decided to help out," he guessed, filling in the blanks.

"Yeah. Stupid, huh?"

He eyed her steadily. "Misguided, maybe."

She shrugged, feeling an odd lightness in her chest. It was all on the table between them. No more misunderstandings, no more anger or blame. A clean slate.

"So, how much did you see?"

Her head shot up and she saw that he was eyeing her speculatively now.

"What?"

"In the shower. How much did you see?"

She smiled faintly, remembering the perfection of his teenager's body.

"Everything."

"I guess you were a lot naughtier than I ever imagined."

She felt his eyes drop to her chest and didn't need to check to know that her nipples were doing their usual "look at us" thing for him.

"So what did you think? About what you saw?" he asked.

She realized he'd taken a step toward her. The sensible thing would be to take a step backward, let him know that she wasn't interested.

She didn't.

"It was the first, uh, penis I'd seen. I didn't know what to think."

He took another step. Excitement licked along her nerve endings.

"What about later? Did you think about it later?"

His eyes were hooded, intent. Her gaze dropped to his mouth. She remembered how it had felt on her skin, so hot and wet.

"Yes. In my bedroom at night."

He stopped an arm's length away.

"Did you ever touch yourself and think about me?" he asked, his tone smoky and low.

She couldn't look away. Didn't want to.

"Yes. I used to pretend it was you, your hand…" she whispered.

She could see a pulse jumping in his neck.

"I think it's time we made some new memories," he said.

She caught her breath as he reached out and wrapped his hands around her rib cage. She could feel his thumbs nudging the underside of her breasts, and her body ached with need. He studied her chest intently.

"I think you've got some serious rethinking to do about these breasts of yours," he said. Before she could do anything to stop him, he'd grabbed the hem of her tank top and whipped it up.

"Hey!" she protested, but he tugged it over her shoulders and threw it to one side.

Instinctively she crossed her arms modestly over her chest, but he reached out and gently pulled them away. Then, his eyes locked with hers, he slowly slid his hands up her torso and onto her breasts.

She groaned, her knees almost buckling with pleasure. His hands were big and warm and just right.

"Definitely," he said, agreeing with her mindless expression of need. He began kneading her breasts gently, his thumbs rasping back and forth over her already-tightened nipples.

"You have great breasts, Sadie," he said, his gaze still intent on the body part in question. "Very responsive. And your nipples… Did I ever tell you that coral-pink is my favorite color?"

He began plucking at her breasts, and she had to squeeze her knees together to stop from slithering to the floor in a liquid mess.

"The thing is, they don't only look great, they taste great, too," he said. She let her head sag back as he ducked his head to suck a nipple into his wet, hot mouth. Every flick of his tongue sent shafts of pleasure rocketing through her body. Damp heat pooled between her thighs, and she reached for his shoulders for support.

She gave a little moan of despair when he lifted his head. His eyes were glazed and very dark as he looked into hers. Her body felt heavy with desire, and she could feel her pulse echoing thickly in the heat between her thighs. As though he knew exactly what she needed, Dylan's hands slid down her torso to the stud on her cutoffs. She held her breath as he popped the stud free and unzipped her fly. She bit her lip as he slid his hands into the loosened denim and smoothed them around her hips and down inside her panties to clasp her bare bottom.

She closed her eyes and began to pant, her knees seriously rubbery now.

There was the hint of laughter in Dylan's voice as she flopped toward him.

"Stay with me, baby," he said as he caressed her bottom briefly before pushing his hands down. Her cutoffs and panties went with them, and before she knew it she was stepping out of them, leaving her naked before him.

His gaze raked her from head to toe and she was almost frightened by the animal need she saw in his face before he reached out and wrapped his arms around her. The next moment she was being lifted, and she felt cool laminate beneath her bare butt as he placed her high on the dining counter.

"Dylan…" she said, the cold change startling her out of the sensual haze she'd fallen into.

"Shh," he said, and she shivered with anticipation as he pushed her knees apart and slid his hands up her thighs. "Last time…last time was too fast, Sadie," he said. "This time, we're going to take it slow."

She felt the rasp of his stubble on the tender skin of her inner thigh, and watched as his dark head moved closer. The first touch of his tongue on her clitoris made her tremble with need.

"Yesssss," she groaned. She felt Dylan grin against her thigh.

Then he was laving her with such skillful intensity that she could do nothing but collapse back onto the table and writhe with pleasure. His tongue was by turns firm and rough, then delicate and butterfly light as he teased her. She clutched at the edge of the counter and panted for breath, gasping when he slid one finger, then two inside her. Instinctively she tightened herself around him, and he slid his free hand beneath her bottom to hold her in place and lift her more firmly against him.

His tongue was everything. So hot. So deliciously rough, but at the same time so needfully, delicately smooth. His fingers taunted her further as he traced her inner lips, sliding inside her again and again as she became increasingly frantic with desire.

She was sobbing her need by the time all the tension inside her dissolved and she came, a pulsating wave of release. She bucked her hips, pressing herself into his embrace, his name on her lips.

For a long moment she could do nothing but breathe. The thump of her own heart sounded loud in her ears. Then she registered Dylan's kisses on her inner thighs, her belly, as he worked his way back up her body. The tug of his mouth on her breast made her moan, half in protest, half in surprise. Even after the most thorough, complete orgasm of her life, she was still ready for more from this man.

When he lifted her this time, she wrapped her legs around him and plunged her tongue deep into his mouth. He walked them toward the low-slung couch that occupied one wall of the kitchen zone, his muscles bulging beneath her hands as he lowered her down onto it.

She gave a whimper of dismay as he left her for a moment, but she swiftly saw he was only undressing, ripping his T-shirt off and tugging his jeans down impatiently. His erection sprang free from his boxers, and she watched with greedy eyes as he rolled a condom on.

Then he was lying on top of her, and she was wrapping her thighs around him as he slid inside her with one smooth, powerful thrust.

It was so good. He filled her utterly, and when he began to move inside her, every nerve ending vibrated with pleasure. Clutching his hard male butt, she urged him closer still, tilting her hips to encourage the deepest penetration possible. He grunted his satisfaction, his hips flexing as he drove into her. Sadie sought his mouth with hers and their tongues mated in time with their bodies, each kiss deeper than the last. The crisp curls on his chest rasped against her highly sensitized nipples, and she felt herself climbing toward release again.

"Yes," Dylan whispered in her ear. "For me, Sadie. One more time for me."

He slid his hand between their bodies to find her clitoris, and she arched with pleasure as he thumbed it rhythmically. He shifted his weight higher, bringing the shaft of his erection into firmer contact with her mound, and she cried out as she rushed into climax yet again. As though her pleasure fed his, his body went stiff with tension, and she felt the muscles of his back convulse as he shuddered into her.

"Sadie," he groaned into her hair. "Sadie."

For long minutes they remained locked together, their breathing slowly returning to normal, heart rates gradually calming. After a while, she began to register the prickle of the couch upholstery beneath her, and the weight of Dylan's hipbone pressing against hers. But she didn't want him to move. They'd have to acknowledge what had happened then. For now, it was enough that she'd just had the most amazing sensual experience of her life.

Her conscience didn't give her much respite, however. There were too many things to consider. Not the least of which was that they were at work—again—and that Claudia might take it upon herself to pop in to check on their progress at any time. Dylan must have registered the sudden tightness in her body, because he pushed himself up on his elbows to look down at her.

"Too heavy?" he asked.

"Claudia said she might come back," she said.

A grin split his face. She marveled for a moment at how handsome he was with his dark eyes dancing with merriment.

"I'd like to see her face if she caught us like this," he said.

"I wouldn't." She wriggled her hips, and Dylan obligingly rolled off her. Immediately, perversely, she missed his heavy weight.

Scooping up her clothes, she padded barefoot and naked toward the washroom. Dylan followed her, and she turned in surprise when he put a foot in the door to prevent her from locking the unisex shower cubicle behind her.

"Haven't you ever heard of conserving water?" he asked innocently.

She wasn't about to protest. She was too busy mapping the perfect contours of his body. This was the first time she'd had the chance to truly appreciate seeing him fully naked—her locker room excursion all those years ago not included—and she feasted on him hungrily.

His shoulders were broad and leanly muscled, his chest

firm, his pectorals nicely defined and dusted with curly, dark hair. The mat of dark hair held sway till it reached his belly, where it tapered down to a steadily diminishing arrow that directed attention to his crowning glory—a heavy, thick penis that was even now stirring under her avaricious inspection. Strong thighs and well-shaped calves completed the picture. All in all, every woman's fantasy.

There was no way she was going to say no to sharing the shower with him.

"I think I'd better tell that I only had one condom on me," Dylan warned as she reached out to smooth a hand over his shoulder.

"I know. And Claudia might be coming back," she murmured distractedly.

They settled for hands and lots of slippery soap, each pushing the other to the edge and over in the steamy warmth of the shower. Her skin pink with hot water and desire, Sadie stepped out into the dressing area first, toweling herself sparingly with the one towel on hand so that Dylan wouldn't be left with a wet rag to dry himself with. Sliding into her panties, shorts and tank top, she felt as though she was climbing back into her rational self at the same time.

What had just happened was…incredible. Mind-blowing. Amazing. But it also raised more questions than it answered. Even though the bone-deep ambivalence she'd felt about her attraction to Dylan had dissolved thanks to their mutual disclosures, she wasn't stupid enough to think that she and Dylan suddenly had a green light to get it on.

For starters, he was her subordinate, and she owed Claudia her loyalty and full support. Second, Sadie wasn't exactly in a place to start a relationship right now. If all had gone according to plan, she'd be Mrs. Greg Sinclair right now, a married woman. She hadn't even begun to deal with the fallout from what Greg had done to her, and she knew that emotionally she was a disaster area.

Last, Dylan didn't exactly strike her as Mr. Monogamy. In fact, she suspected he was probably a seasoned pro at love-'em-and-leave-'em flings. A man didn't get that good in the bedroom without lots of practice. She was already dangerously attracted to him. She'd be a fool to play with fire.

By the time Dylan had dried himself off and emerged from the shower room, Sadie had her game face back on. The quiet reserve in Dylan's face told her that he'd been thinking about the consequences of their actions, too. She didn't bother beating around the bush.

"This can't happen again," she said.

Dylan shrugged a shoulder. "We've obviously got some serious chemistry going on, Sadie. Sometimes you can't fight nature."

"Yeah, well, we're going to have to." She pushed a hand through her heavy, damp hair, lifting her arms to begin plaiting it away from her face. "Whether we like it or not, I'm your boss. The last thing I should be doing is…what we've been doing," she finished in a rush. "We need to keep things strictly professional."

"I thought we'd already tried that. Even when we hated each other's guts, it didn't work so well."

Sadie flinched at his casual reference to hating her.

"I didn't mean—you know why I felt how I felt," Dylan said, frowning.

"Which is another reason for us not to get involved. There's too much history, too much bad old stuff. And I'm not looking for a relationship right now," Sadie added boldly.

Dylan looked startled. "Nobody said anything about marriage and kids."

She managed to not blush. Barely.

"I've just come out of a serious relationship. I'm really not interested in anything, casual or otherwise," she said stiffly.

Dylan narrowed his gaze and looked as though he wanted

to argue, but finally he shrugged. "Waste of some damn fine chemistry," he said lightly.

"We'll live," Sadie said drily.

Scooping up her notes and marked-up scripts, she headed for the door.

"I'll be in my office," she said.

"Sure."

She felt his eyes on her the entire way, but it wasn't until she'd shut her office door that she admitted to herself that she was disappointed by his easy capitulation.

You're not interested, remember? she told herself. Perhaps if she repeated it a thousand times, she'd believe it.

7

IT WAS THREE in the morning by the time Sadie left work, and she was so exhausted she almost didn't register the large bouquet of flowers leaning against the door to her condo when she got home. A mixture of irises and lilies, they smelled fantastic and she blinked at them stupidly for a few beats.

Who would have sent her flowers? The awful suspicion that they were from Greg was confirmed when she let herself in and managed to find the small card taped to the wrapping on the bouquet.

Sadie, the note said. *To let you know I am thinking of you. Love, Greg.*

Only a handful of words, but enough to release a tidal wave of anger inside her. Tiredness gone, she stormed around the house, dragging cupboards open and riffling through drawers until she'd amassed a pile containing everything that Greg had ever left behind in her condo: an old sweatshirt, a couple of pairs of boxers, a set of cuff links, a thriller novel, some vitamin C tablets, his favorite brand of toothpaste and his toothbrush, a six-pack of beer and some chili pickles from the fridge. Shoveling it all into a garbage bag, she dropped the bouquet on top and made the trip to the basement to toss it all.

How dare he. Those three words kept reverberating around her mind as she prepared for sleep. Her eyes were squinty with anger in the bathroom mirror as she brushed her teeth, and she spat out her toothpaste with vengeful vigor.

Thinking of you. What a champ. How damned *generous* of him to be thinking of her after he'd humiliated her in front of her family and friends.

Climbing into bed and pulling the covers up to her chin, she suddenly remembered what she'd been doing with Dylan just hours ago. A smile curved her lips—a feline, smug, very feminine smile. While Greg had been thinking of her, she'd been thinking of Dylan. For the first time in two weeks, that didn't seem like such a bad thing.

DYLAN WOKE SLOWLY the next day. His eyes felt dry from long hours in front of the computer, and he peered at the alarm clock warily. He relaxed a little when he saw it was midday— he'd managed to get a reasonable amount of sleep, despite being so wound up when he went to bed the previous evening. Mentally reviewing his options for the day, he tossed up between hitting the gym or going for a surf before he started in on some of his own writing. Then he remembered what had happened between him and Sadie, and a big smile curved his mouth.

Folding his arms behind his head, he grinned at the ceiling, reliving some of the highlights of their liaison. There was no doubt about it, Sadie was a sexy, sexy lady. And now that they both understood what had really happened between them all those years ago, there was no guilt or discomfort attached to the acknowledgment. He could lust after her with impunity. His smile broadening, Dylan realized that he planned to do just that.

As far as he could see, there was nothing stopping them from fully exploring the chemistry between them. He certainly hadn't had his fill of her long, lean body, and he suspected she was every bit as eager to have a rematch with him—even if she wasn't quite ready to admit it to herself just yet.

Remembering her reference to having recently ended a serious relationship, he frowned. What man had been stupid enough to let a delicious goddess like Sadie slip through his fingers? Still, one man's mistake was another man's opportunity. More specifically, his opportunity.

To his mind, Sadie's desire to remain unattached didn't in any way preclude the two of them having a very adult, very X-rated fling. It wasn't as though he was interested in commitment. And Sadie was clearly keen to remain footloose and fancy free. Having a short, hot affair would suit both of them down to the ground.

He just had to convince her of that. He scratched his belly and laughed out loud as he remembered the uptight little speech she'd given him when he'd emerged from the shower last night.

We need to keep things strictly professional. Who was she kidding? Did she really believe that the animal attraction that burned between them was going to fade away because she'd drawn a line in the sand?

Of course, if they both concentrated really, really hard and were on their very best behavior, it would probably be possible for them to keep things work-only.

What a pity that he'd never been very good at behaving himself.

THERE WAS A DEFINITE lightness in Sadie's step as she swung through reception on Monday morning. Her early-hours purge of Greg's belongings had been very therapeutic—along with the sensational sex she'd enjoyed with Dylan. For the first time in a long time, she felt in control and on top of things. Now that she and Dylan understood one another, *Ocean Boulevard* would no longer be a war zone. Her life could finally start to get back on track.

Her self-confident buzz lasted about as long as it took for her to clap eyes on him. He was lounging near the photocopier, and she was almost floored by the kick of pure, unadulterated desire that rocketed through her at seeing him again. The mere sight of his strong, broad shoulders and sexy, rounded butt were enough to send her heart hammering against her ribs—then he turned and a slow grin curved his mouth and she thought she might have an orgasm on the spot.

He was just so…

And he made her feel so…

And she just wanted to…

"Morning, Sadie."

Two small words, but they were heavy with intent. She fought the urge to cross her legs and squirm.

"Dylan. Hope you had a bit of a break yesterday?" she asked, making an effort to at least sound professional, even if every other part of her mind and body was rampaging in Slut Land.

"Not really. But it was no biggy." He was still grinning, his eyes making lazy forays up and down her body.

She shivered and tried to ignore the throb of heat between her thighs. She was at work. She had to remember that she was at work.

"Um…good," she said stupidly.

She turned blindly toward her office and nearly walked into a desk. She didn't need to look back to know his grin was even wider now. Could she be any more gauche?

She gave herself a stern talking to as she unpacked her satchel and booted up her computer. They might have called a halt to hostilities, but that didn't mean it was a free-for-all now. He was her subordinate, and she was grieving her relationship with Greg, and…

She sat at her desk and shook her head to clear it. She couldn't concentrate on anything, especially the reasons why she and Dylan couldn't have sex again. All she wanted to do was stride across the office, tear his clothes off and have her way with him.

The very strength of her desire was the wake-up call she

needed. If she wasn't careful, this thing with Dylan was going to get out of control—and she didn't do out-of-control. Very deliberately, she made herself remember all those nights she'd lain awake as a teenager, dreaming of him. *That* was what was firing all this need—repressed teen lust. And she had to get a grip on it because even though she and Dylan had reconciled their differences, she was absolutely certain that he would not welcome the attentions of a grown woman with a reconstituted adolescent crush.

She bit her lip as she admitted a truth to herself: she didn't want to feel this strongly about anyone. Not after what Greg had done to her. She didn't want to be exposed or vulnerable in any way. Not for a long, long time. Maybe not ever.

She had a brief flash of how it had felt standing outside the doors of the church, knowing she had to go in and face everyone. She never wanted to feel like that again.

A few minutes of mindless letter opening and e-mail reviewing calmed her somewhat. Lust receded, and common sense once again ruled the roost. As usual where Dylan was concerned, she was overreacting. He was an attractive man, and she'd had sex with him. Big deal. Once the angst of their teen relationship was taken out of the equation, that was what it boiled down to. They were both adults, and they'd both agreed that it couldn't happen again. Ergo, it was a nonissue. Simple.

The stockade of rationality she'd erected around herself was good till midmorning when she bumped into Dylan in the kitchen. Yet again he gave her a leisurely once-over, his eyes undressing her shamelessly.

"How goes it, boss?" he asked.

How did he manage to make such an innocuous collection of words sound so decadent?

"G-good. Have you brought the team up-to-date on the changes from the weekend?" she asked, dragging her gaze from the chiseled perfection of his mouth.

"Yep. All sorted."

He moved closer, and she opened her mouth on a little gasp and took a step back, only to feel the sink at her back.

"It's okay, only after a coffee," he said. Very casually, he leaned across her, stretching to grab a mug from the shelf behind her.

He was so close she could feel the heat radiating from his body, and the scent of his aftershave surrounded her. She stared at the stubble on his jaw and the crisp curls peeking out over the neck of his shirt. Her fingers itched to touch him, to trace the curves and dips and hollows of his hard man's body. She felt dizzy with desire, and she bit her lip to contain a needy whimper. Then, as he withdrew, mug in hand, he shifted minutely and his arm brushed across the tips of her breasts. Instantly they sprang to life and she sucked in a much-needed lungful of air.

"You want one?" Dylan asked.

Yes, please, her wanton self sighed. It took a moment for her to realize that he was referring to coffee. She blinked, trying to corral her thoughts.

"Um, no. I'm fine, thanks." She had to get a grip. She was at work, for Pete's sake. Talking to an employee. A man she'd just vowed never to sleep with again.

Then her gaze slid down his belly and dipped below his waistband. What she saw there made her eyebrows shoot toward her hairline. He had an erection. She stared at the unmistakable bulge in his jeans and licked her lips instinctively. She could almost feel the weight of him in her hands. He was so thick and long, and she wanted to touch him so badly—

"Okay, fair's fair. I brushed your breasts on purpose but that's out of line," Dylan said, a growling note in his voice.

Sadie blinked and tore her eyes away from the main event. "What?"

He stepped closer, his dark gaze heated. "Don't look at me like that unless you're going to follow through."

"You brushed my breasts on purpose?" she asked, the import of his words finally sinking in.

"Hell, yeah."

"Why?"

He made an exasperated noise. "Why do you think? You want me to draw a diagram?"

"But we had an agreement," she said, both shocked and thrilled by his blatant confession.

"Uh-uh. You made a suggestion, but I never agreed to it. I said it was a shame to waste so much chemistry. Which it is."

He was grinning again, and suddenly she got it. He was trying to seduce her. Okay, not *trying*—succeeding. If she wasn't very careful.

"I can't sleep with you again," she said, lowering her voice and glancing over her shoulder nervously. "I shouldn't have slept with you in the first place."

"Relax. This is a television production company, not the White House. No one's going to impeach you if you have a bit of fun."

She stared at him, digesting his words. "A bit of fun," she repeated flatly.

"A lot of fun," he corrected himself. He moved closer, his voice dropping an octave. "A whole lot of very fun fun."

Sadie swallowed hard and tried to ignore the fact that her thighs had gone up in flames. He was so attractive. And she wanted to give in so badly.

"I can't," she said. "I'm sorry, but I can't."

Hair flying, she spun on her heel and retreated to her office.

TWO AND A HALF WEEKS later, Dylan shoved a T-shirt into his backpack with more vigor than was absolutely necessary. There had been a bit of that going on lately—fridge door slamming, swearing at motorists on the freeway, growling at his team at work. It didn't say much about him as a person, he knew, that a few weeks of sexual frustration were all it took to turn him into a stand-in for Oscar the Grouch.

It had been a long time since he hadn't gotten something he wanted. All his early failures had made him hungry for success, and it was a taste he'd become used to. Except now he'd struck out. Because he wanted Sadie, and she was staunchly maintaining her *professional* stance.

It was driving him crazy.

He'd tried everything—standing too close to her, flirting, suggestive comments, arriving early at work so they could be alone, staying late for the same reason. The sexual tension between them crackled like an electrical storm—and still she hadn't folded. Meanwhile, he was so damned horny that he was about ready to explode.

A million times he considered giving up, moving on, calling one of his old girlfriends or asking out the receptionist who kept giving him extra special smiles every morning. But it was Sadie he wanted, not anyone else. She haunted his dreams, and taunted him all day at work with her tight jeans and short skirts and clinging tops. He was at his wit's end.

Which was probably why he was less than thrilled to be going away for a "bonding" weekend with the writing team. Two nights and three days in the Big Bear Campgrounds in the San Bernardino National Forest hiking, orienteering and team-building with his fellow writers. In his present frustrated condition, sharing a three-person tent with Luke and Ben was about as welcome as a prostate exam. Only the thought that Sadie would be sleeping a few feet away had stopped him from putting his foot down and staging a mutiny. Fresh air, green things, a change of scenery—surely something had to give. Jaw set, he stuffed a box of condoms into his backpack. The act of an eternal optimist, he admitted, but he wasn't ready to give up yet.

He'd opted out of carpooling to the park, preferring to take

the Ducati and leave himself an escape route. Locking up the
house, he stowed his pack on the bike and slid on his helmet.
Pulling down the visor, he gave himself up to two and a half hours
of travel time fantasizing about having Sadie in his arms again.

"WE ARE SO LATE," Sadie said as she opened her condo door to
Grace and Claudia.

"Don't blame me. I was at Grace's place at eight on the dot,"
Claudia said pointedly.

"Hope was upset. She'd forgotten I was going away," Grace
said apologetically.

Claudia shot Sadie a frustrated look and bent to heft
Sadie's backpack.

"Is this everything?" Claudia asked, already heading out the
door.

"All set," Sadie said, ushering Grace out into the hall so she
could lock up.

"It's that bastard boyfriend of hers," Grace said, obviously
feeling as though she owed them a further explanation. "He
keeps calling and sending flowers. When is he going to get the
message that she's not interested in an abusive asshole?"

"What I want to know is how he got your number in the first
place," Claudia said as they stepped into the lift. "You're
unlisted, aren't you?"

Grace shrugged helplessly. "Hope called him. She said she
had to ask him to send her things over."

Claudia shot another look Sadie's way. Sadie knew exactly
what she was thinking: Hope was playing both ends against the
middle. It had been three weeks since she had moved in with
Grace, and there was still no sign that she planned on picking
up the threads of her life. She'd taken no modeling assignments,
and was already asking Grace to cover her expenses while she
was between jobs. Sadie had visited her friend the previous
weekend and been privately appalled at the squalor that Hope

had reduced Grace's normally tidy apartment to. Added to the discovery that Grace had given up her bedroom to her sister after she complained that the sofa bed was uncomfortable, and Sadie was inclined to agree with Claudia's assessment that Hope was shamelessly using her unfortunate situation to full advantage.

"Maybe I should stay," Grace said as they emerged outside Sadie's building. "You guys don't need to bond with me. We're already bonded."

"It's a team thing," Claudia said firmly as she beeped the trunk of her car open. "We're all going."

"You've said about a million times that you think this is a dumb idea. Will it really make a difference if I'm not there?" Grace asked.

Sadie hid a smile behind her hand. It was true that Claudia had very vocally denounced the coming weekend as a big fat waste of time and money. The weekend had been the previous producer's idea, but since it had been fully paid for in advance, Claudia had had to honor the booking. She'd been grumbling about it on and off since she'd started with the show.

"If Sadie and I have to go, you have to suffer, too," Claudia said as she tossed Sadie's bag in with the other luggage. "We're like the three musketeers—if one of us has to pee hiding behind a bush in the woods, the rest of us have to, as well. It's an unwritten rule of our friendship code."

Grace's green eyes remained troubled, and Sadie squeezed her arm.

"Hope will be fine. Serena's in town if she needs anything, right?"

Grace pulled a face. "Serena's not exactly Mother Earth in situations like this."

Sadie refrained from saying that she couldn't imagine a situation where Serena would ever be Mother Earth. The woman was so highly groomed she practically had a glossy veneer.

"Still, if Hope needs company or advice, Serena is there. It's only two nights," Sadie reassured.

Grace nodded, sliding into the backseat and putting on her seat belt.

"We're the ones you should be worried about. We could be mauled by a pack of wild bears," Claudia said as she started up her car and pulled out into traffic.

"Except bears don't hunt in packs," Sadie said wryly.

"I still can't believe we're not camping near an amenities block. How am I going to survive without my shower?" Claudia moaned.

"There's a lake, isn't there?" Grace said.

"So the whole team is going to go skinny-dipping together? That's a little too much bonding for my comfort," Claudia said.

Sadie stared at the streetscape passing by as she automatically imagined Dylan striding confidently into a pristine blue lake, his glorious body buck-naked.

As if she needed more fuel for the sensual fire that had been smoldering inside her for the past two weeks. She was practically jumping out of her own skin she was so frustrated, and Dylan wasted no opportunity to remind her what she was missing out on. He somehow arranged to be sitting next to her in every meeting, then he spent the entire session brushing her thigh with his or rubbing shoulders. She'd lost count of the number of times he'd cornered her in the kitchen, standing too close to her and reaching across her body for a mug or the coffee canister.

She should call him on his behavior, she knew, but even though she found it torturous and frustrating in the extreme, it still excited her so much that she was loathe to give it up. She'd already said no to anything actually happening between them. What harm could a little flirtation do?

The fact that Dylan had been starring in her increasingly elaborate nightly sexual fantasies had nothing to do with anything. Sometimes, when she said it to herself with a great deal of conviction, she almost believed her own lie.

The truth was, if Greg hadn't been sending her a bouquet every few days, she'd probably have given in to Dylan's sensual lures within the first week. But every time she came home to find a fresh display of lilies or roses or gerberas on her doorstep, her determination to protect herself was renewed. She'd given all the flowers to the local nursing home, but she hadn't been able to stop herself from reading Greg's notes. He wanted her to forgive him. And he wanted to talk. He even said he still loved her. She was half-surprised that he hadn't tried a phone call by now, but she figured he was using the flowers to soften her up first. It all made her so angry and sad. Perhaps that was why she hadn't shut down Dylan's flirtation. When she was with him, she felt alive and beautiful and desirable.

"How's work on the feature special coming along?" Claudia asked, drawing Sadie from her moment of introspection.

"Good. Great. Dylan and I have broad stroked some ideas. I'm hoping to have the structure in place by the end of next week, then we can assign a team to it and flesh it out," Sadie said.

"Great. Have I told you how excited I am about the fact that it's a wedding episode?" Claudia enthused.

"About fifty times," Grace said wryly.

"Weddings are so good for ratings. We are going to bury *Heartlands* with this episode," Claudia said, referring to the soap that aired at the same time on a competing network.

Sadie heard Grace giggle in the backseat, and couldn't stop herself from joining in.

"What have I done now?" Claudia asked.

"We love your competitive streak," Sadie explained. "It's so soap. If you were a soap heroine, you'd have hair that could take men's eyes out, and shoulder pads you could hang glide off."

Claudia grinned. "If *you* were a soap star, you'd have fake eyelashes, breasts up around your earlobes and skirts so small the audience would need a magnifying glass to find them."

Sadie turned to include Grace in the conversation. "And our Gracie…" she said.

"Gracie would be the queen of the soap," Claudia announced unequivocally. "The big-hearted vamp who is always misunderstood, and who can never escape her humble beginnings. And her tits would also be up around her ears."

They all dissolved into laughter. The rest of the trip east passed in gossip, laughter and singing, and Sadie found herself relaxing for the first time in weeks. She'd been so busy feeling guilty around Claudia about jumping Dylan, then feeling guilty about avoiding Claudia because she felt guilty, that she'd unconsciously distanced herself from both her friends. It was good to bask in the warmth of their companionship again.

The sudden transition from tarmac to dirt road signaled their nearness to their destination, and within twenty minutes Claudia was pulling into a clearing on the side of an apparently endless bright blue lake. The rest of the team's cars were parked to one side, and Claudia parked her SUV in the shade beneath a huge pine tree.

Sadie slid from the car and stretched her arms high over her head, sucking in a big lungful of fresh air.

"Careful. You don't want to O.D. on all that fresh air all at once. We're from L.A., remember."

She almost jumped out of her skin as Dylan stepped around the tree. Immediately all her hard-won relaxation evaporated as her eyes ate up his tall frame. He was wearing a pair of beaten-up khaki hiking shorts, thick socks, well-worn boots and a faded red muscle shirt. He looked supremely edible, and she had to shove her hands into the pockets of her jeans to stop herself from reaching out to touch his strong, tanned arms.

"You have to acclimatize. Small breaths. Give the pollution a chance to contaminate the fresh air in your lungs," he said.

Even though she'd become used to the way his eyes slid over her so suggestively over the past few weeks, she still felt a thrill as he made a leisurely inspection of her body. There was so much heat and promise in his look, she almost melted out of her jeans.

Since she figured that was pretty much what he'd intended, she forced herself to stiffen her backbone.

"Tell me, does this whole bedroom-eyes routine work with other women?" she asked conversationally.

"Mostly."

"Well, don't let me ruin your averages. Feel free to move on to pastures greener," she said. She ignored the lurch her stomach made at the thought of Dylan with another woman. But it was bound to happen. Better to face it head-on than to have it sneak up on her.

"Hmm. Have I ever told you that I thrive on challenges?" he said, leaning against the tree trunk and reaching up to pluck a pine needle from a low-hanging branch.

She watched his long, strong fingers play with the foliage for a beat. She could almost feel his hands on her, sliding beneath her clothes. She should say something, let him know that she was one challenge he could never conquer, but somehow she couldn't find the energy to talk.

"So, where are these stupid tents we're supposed to be sleeping in?" Claudia asked as she exited the car.

Sadie wrenched her eyes away from Dylan's hands and tried not to look like someone who'd been watching her own personal adult movie in her head.

"There's a professional guide over near the lake," Dylan said, gesturing toward a tall guy in a ranger's hat and khaki uniform who was standing with the rest of the story team.

Her face pulled into a grimace of distaste, Claudia started across the clearing, obviously intent on taking things in hand. Grace moved to stand beside Sadie, tucking her arm through her friend's. There was a distinct warning in the glance Grace sent Dylan's way. Despite now knowing the truth about their shared history, Grace still considered Dylan too good-looking and confident to trust. Nothing personal, she'd explained to Sadie, more of a life philosophy thing.

She tugged on Sadie's arm to get her walking.

"Let's go check out the lake," she said.

Dylan pushed off from his lounging position against the tree. "Great idea."

Before Sadie could retreat, he'd grabbed her other arm. She stiffened at the warm brush of his skin on hers, and Grace shot her a curious look.

"Water's cold, but clear as a bell," Dylan said conversationally as he led them toward the lake. Sadie finally managed to slip her arm free as they neared the shore.

"Wow. What a great color," Grace said, shading her eyes with her hand.

Sadie stared out at the stretch of blue water, trying to concentrate on nature's bounty instead of the tall man standing beside her.

"Just what we all need to relax, don't you think, boss?" Dylan said. She nearly jumped out of her skin when she felt his hands land on her shoulders. The next thing she knew, he was kneading her tight muscles, his fingers and thumbs turning her insides to mush. She was on the verge of moaning out loud when Grace pointedly cleared her throat.

"I've got a sore spot right here, since you're spreading the love around," Grace said, indicating her left shoulder.

Dylan shrugged good-naturedly. "At your service."

Sadie choked back the instinctive protest that found its way to her lips when he lifted his hands from her shoulders and moved to stand behind Grace. Grace gave her a wink, as if to let her know she was happy to take a bullet for a friend. Sadie forced a smile and turned back to the clearing.

"I'm going to go see about those tents," she said.

She'd been here five minutes, and already she was hot and bothered.

It was going to be a long weekend.

DYLAN STUFFED the last fold of the three-person tent into its carry bag and sat back on his heels. Ben and Luke were nearby, packing up their sleeping mats and other camping paraphernalia, both their faces dark with stubble, their expressions decidedly grim after a night of little-to-no sleep. None of them was a regular camper, and the uncomfortable sleeping arrangements had not inspired any supernatural bonding to date. Dylan figured they would have done better with a karaoke machine and half a dozen bottles of tequila, but who was he to judge?

The sound of laughter called his gaze across the campsite to where Claudia, Grace and Sadie were talking with Dan, their guide. Daring Dan, as Dylan had mentally dubbed him over the past twenty-four hours. It was obvious to anyone with an optic nerve that Dan thought all his Christmases had come at once, having scored a bevy of beautiful women to squire across the wilderness for two days. As he'd led them on hikes and supervised various activities, Daring Dan had been doing his utmost to impress the ladies in the team. Particularly Sadie. As Sadie threw back her head and laughed again, Dylan felt his lip curl. It looked like it was working, too, if the number and volume of Sadie's laughs were anything to go by. He narrowed his gaze on Dan, taking in the other man's tanned legs and brawny, muscular arms. It had been a long time since Dylan had had cause to be jealous of another man, but he felt a distinct stirring of the green-eyed monster as he watched Dan gazing into Sadie's eyes. If Dylan didn't pull off some fancy footwork soon, all his weeks of flirting—fore-foreplay, he'd told himself every time frustration threatened—would have simply laid the groundwork for Dorky Dan to swoop in and grab the girl.

"Great to see Sadie looking so happy again, eh?" Luke said to Ben.

"Yeah," Ben agreed.

Dylan turned to his fellow tentmates, intrigued.

"You talking about Sadie's ex?" he asked, taking a stab in the dark.

"The butthead," Luke said, shaking his head with disgust. "May his dick drop off with a bad dose of scrum pox."

"Too good for him," Ben said.

Interesting.

"So their breakup was bad?" Dylan asked, trying to sound supercasual.

Ben made a rude noise. "Just a little. I still can't believe Sadie toughed it out and told everyone in the church to come back to the reception and party hearty. My personal definition of courage," he said.

Dylan froze. "Her ex stood her up at the altar?" he asked, incredulous that anyone could be so callous.

"Yep. And Sadie went back to the reception and partied her ass off. Man, what a night," Luke said, smiling reminiscently.

"Sadie's never said a word," Dylan said more to himself than anyone else. There'd been a lot of wedding talk lately, too, since the feature-length episode centered around the nuptials of two of the show's favorite characters. Yet Sadie hadn't even dropped a hint that she'd almost been married herself.

Ben shifted uncomfortably. "Yeah. Guess she doesn't want to talk about it."

"Which means we shouldn't be gossiping," Luke added, looking guilty now.

Dylan could only admire Sadie's ability to inspire such loyalty in an industry rife with backstabbing, gossip and innuendo. It was a testament to how well she was liked that he hadn't heard this irresistible story sooner.

"When did all this happen?" he asked.

"Right before you came on board," Luke said.

Of course—the trip to St. Barts. Not a holiday, a *honeymoon*. A honeymoon Sadie had taken on her own. Suddenly the glance she'd shot at Claudia in that first meeting made sense. He was the last person she would have wanted to know about her personal pain.

His gaze slid across the camping ground to where she was kneeling beside her backpack, running a comb through her long hair. Her face was pensive as she stared off into the forest, unaware that anyone was observing her. He felt a sudden, fierce surge of protectiveness toward her. What kind of a spineless creep humiliated someone they cared about like that? Getting cold feet was one thing, but allowing Sadie to get to the church before delivering the bad news smacked of cruelty and cowardice in equal measures. Dylan's fingers flexed as he imagined the short, sharp conversation he'd have with the guy if ever he got the chance.

Obviously sensing his gaze on her, Sadie met his eye. One eyebrow quirked up inquisitively as she called him on staring at her. Then she shook her head to signal her continuing determination to keep him at bay, a small smile curving her lips.

For the first time, her saucy determination to both deflect him and inflame him didn't win an answering smile.

Why hadn't she told him?

Even as part of him acknowledged that Sadie had every reason not to make herself vulnerable to him, the other part of him was offended that she hadn't trusted him with her recent pain. They'd slept with each other. They'd confessed and forgiven old hurts. And for the past few weeks they'd worked hand-in-glove in the most simpatico creative working relationship of his career.

But she still hadn't told him.

Irrational or not, he wanted her to trust him. Almost as much as he wanted to press his body against hers again.

Clipping his smaller pack onto the tent pack, Dylan shouldered the whole monstrosity. Dashing Dan had another exciting orienteering quest for them to bond over today, he knew, and he sauntered his way across to where the rest of the team was clustered.

Making it sound as though he was handing out bars of gold bullion, Dan detailed the day's activities.

"We'll be breaking up into teams of two, and each team will take a different route to the same point, which will also be our last camping spot. The first team home wins a secret prize," Dan said, waggling his eyebrows as though he was talking to a bunch of preschoolers.

"Goody," Dylan muttered under his breath. Claudia was standing nearby, and she smirked, clearly as annoyed by their guide as he was.

"Okay. I'll give you a few minutes to sort yourselves into pairs, then I'll start sending you off into the scary wilds," Dan said brightly.

Seeing a prime opportunity, Dylan stepped sideways and slid his arm over Sadie's shoulders. She'd already turned toward Grace and Claudia, clearly about to barter who would be going with whom, but he cut her short.

"Sadie and I can be a team," he said, managing a passable imitation of Dan's perky tones. "Good bonding exercise for story ed and script producer."

Sadie opened her mouth to protest, but Dylan talked over her.

"Come on, Sadie—for the show," he said.

"That leaves you and me, Gracie," Claudia said.

"Excellent. That works out perfectly," Dylan said, already steering Sadie toward Dan.

"A nice long route," he said to the blond-haired guide. "Sadie and I have got a lot of bonding to do."

Dan gave him a wary look and rather reluctantly handed over a plastic-wrapped map and compass.

"This should take about four hours. Don't forget your lunch kit."

Sadie waited until they were collecting their meal bags from the group's provisions before speaking up.

"I'm not sleeping with you again, Dylan," she said quietly.

"Who said anything about sleeping?" he said innocently.

ALL I HAVE TO DO is say no, Sadie told herself as she followed Dylan up a rock-strewn track. *If he tries anything—a kiss, say, or maybe if he tries to touch my breasts—all I have to do is stand firm.*

Great in theory—except for the treacherous bolt of desire that darted through her belly at the thought of Dylan's hard body on hers. God, when they'd all gone swimming yesterday afternoon, she'd nearly hyperventilated. The sight of his lean body in board shorts had forced every sane thought from her mind. Only the presence of her work colleagues had stopped her from jumping him there and then. Now she was stuck alone with him all day, and she was desperately afraid that she didn't have the willpower to keep him at bay. She wanted to be with him so much. But she also knew that she was dangerously attracted to him, and on more than just a physical level. The potent cocktail of high school crush, present-day chemistry and creative compatibility was heady in the extreme—and she couldn't afford to risk falling for Dylan in a big way. She didn't ever want to feel the doubt and pain of loving someone again. It was Greg's legacy to her, and one she was determined to learn from.

"I think we go right here," Dylan said as they reached a fork in the track.

Sadie leaned over his shoulder to consult the map. "Isn't it left?" she asked, frowning at the squiggly lines and colored bits on the page in front of her.

Dylan gave an exaggerated sigh and turned the map around

for her. "We're going this way," he said, indicating their direction. "It's a right turn."

"Okay, sure." She shrugged.

They started walking again, and this time Dylan fell into step beside her rather than pulling ahead.

"Why is it women are such bad map readers?" he mused.

"I don't know. I guess it must fall into the same category as why men can't put the lid on the toothpaste or the toilet seat down," she said.

"I'll give you the toothpaste, but not the toilet seat. I happen to believe that the toilet's natural state is seat-up. Therefore, women are the domestic vandals because they consistently leave it down."

"What an interesting and, coincidentally, self-serving theory," she said.

"I'd be a traitor to my sex if I said anything else."

"And we wouldn't want that."

"Hell, no. My sex is very important to me." The look he shot her was loaded with meaning.

"Do you ever stop thinking about sex?"

"Not when you're around."

His honesty surprised a laugh out of her, and she shook her head at his blatant agenda.

"Not going to happen," she said firmly.

"Are you going on about that whole us-having-sex thing again? That is so last week," he said.

"Really. So if I stripped off all my clothes and said, 'Let's go for it,' you'd say no?"

"To be honest, I don't know. Let's give it a go, and see what happens." He stopped in the middle of the track, crossing his arms over his chest and adopting a patient waiting expression.

She couldn't help laughing again. He was too sexy and too charming for his own good. Or her own good.

"Nice try. I almost didn't see the cunning trap you'd laid for me," she said.

"No trap. Just two adults who happen to really, really want to get naked with each other."

She wished it was as easy as that, she really did. She'd never desired a man more.

"How long have we been walking?" she asked, determined to change the subject. It was too much fun bantering back and forth with him like this. Too much fun, and too dangerous.

"An hour. Hungry?"

"A little. But I can wait," she said. If they ate too early, they'd be hungry again before they reached the night's campsite.

"You're good at this self-denial thing, aren't you?"

"The best," she said wryly.

"Tough-skinned Sadie Post. Is that why you braved it out at your wedding reception?"

It was such a bolt from the blue that she stopped in her tracks and gasped.

"Who told you?"

"Did you really think that a secret that good was going to stay secret for long? This is *television* we're talking about here."

She frowned down at her feet, unwilling to look him in the eye and unable to sort through her mixed-up emotions. The one saving grace in the whole sordid disaster that was her wedding day had been that Dylan was unaware of it. She hated the thought of him knowing she had been so soundly and publicly rejected. Even though intellectually she knew the fault lay with Greg, she felt branded by what he'd done to her. Shop-soiled and substandard.

"I don't want to talk about it," she muttered, resuming walking.

"Do you still love him?" he asked from behind her.

She spun around to face him. "The man stood me up at the altar. What sort of a doormat do you think I am?"

"Just checking. Not need to disembowel me."

Again she started walking, picking up the pace now, eager to get to the campsite and away from Dylan's too-knowing gaze.

"Have you spoken to him since?"

"I don't want to talk about it."

"Not once, huh? Has he tried to talk to you?"

Her mind flashed to the flowers and the notes.

"There's nothing he can say to me that I want to hear."

"Excellent. You know what would really piss him off? Finding out you were having a hot and heavy affair with a coworker."

"I'm not going to sleep with you, Dylan."

"Again with the sleeping. Sleeping is the last thing I want to do with you."

Cresting a rise, Sadie automatically took the right-hand track in the fork that presented itself.

"Okay, I am not going to screw you. Better?"

"I'm a little offended by your crude terminology. I prefer horizontal mambo," Dylan quipped.

She snorted her amusement and kept powering down the track.

"That's not going to happen, either."

"Well, you could always talk to me. I'll accept that as a compromise."

He sounded very serious all of a sudden and she shot him a look out of the corner of her eye. Big mistake. He was watching her like a hawk.

"Why didn't you tell me?" he asked.

Immediately she knew what he was talking about.

"My wedding is none of your business."

"We work with each other. We've slept with each other. Perhaps I'm mistaken, but I was under the impression that we were becoming friends, too."

He was sincere, she could hear it in his voice. She sighed and pushed damp tendrils of hair off her forehead.

"It's humiliating. I don't exactly like to think about it."

His hand landed heavy and warm on her shoulder, forcing her to stop.

"Do you really think your friends and family think any less of *you* because of what happened?"

"Even if they don't, they certainly feel sorry for me. That's worse, trust me."

In those weeks after the senior prom, there had been a lot of pity from the nicer kids in her classes. She'd much preferred the ridicule and relish from the popular kids. Pity only made her feel more whipped and pathetic.

Dylan shook her a little, enough to make her jaw click shut and get her undivided attention.

"Forget it. Forget all that bullshit. You are an amazing woman, Sadie Post. Sexy and smart and kind and funny. Most men would cut off their left arms to even stand close to you."

His intensity vibrated in his voice, and his dark gaze bored into hers, and for a second she saw an alternate her in his eyes—a blond, confident Amazon who took no prisoners and could pick and choose her men.

"Your ex was a moron. That's the only thing that wedding of yours proves," Dylan said.

They stared at each other for a beat. As if pulled by gravity, her gaze dropped to his mouth. She could remember exactly what he tasted like....

"We need to keep walking," she said, stepping away from danger.

He didn't say a word, just fell in behind her. They trudged in silence for another twenty minutes until they could hear the sound of rushing water. They emerged into a small clearing before a slow-flowing river. Sadie was about to cross over a small footbridge when Dylan spoke up.

"Hang on a minute. We're not supposed to cross a river."

"What?"

"The river is not on our route." He frowned down at the map, one finger tracing across its surface.

"We must have taken a wrong turn," she said, shrugging. "We should go back."

He shook his head. "It was ages ago. If we keep going forward, we can get back on route."

"I don't know. Even if it adds an hour, wouldn't we be better off sticking to the route?"

Dylan shot her an assessing look, then began to very deliberately fold the map. She watched as he stuffed it into his pocket.

"What are you doing?"

"We're going to risk it," he announced. His eyes dared her to protest.

"But—"

"Live a little, Sadie. It won't kill you."

He started off over the footbridge, and she stared after him angrily. She might not be a big rebel or risk taker, but she wasn't a Sunday-school teacher, either. She could be spontaneous and survive.

Just because she wouldn't have sex with him didn't mean she was chicken.

Resettling her pack onto her shoulders, she started out after him.

"Good girl," he called over his shoulder.

"Get stuffed."

His laughter only irritated her more. They walked in silence for another hour, hunger and thirst finally forcing them to stop. Dylan spent the whole of their lunch break poring over the map.

"Well? Has your big gamble paid off, cowboy?" she asked him waspishly. Her feet were sore and her shoulders ached, and she wanted to click her fingers and be magically transported back to civilization.

He had a peculiar look on his face when he looked up. Half chagrin, half amusement.

"What is it?" she asked, a finger of foreboding sliding down her spine.

"We're lost," he said.

8

AFTER SHE'D FINISHED yelling at him for being a smart-ass and leading them astray, they spent a futile two hours trying to backtrack and only succeeded in getting more lost. By late afternoon they were both tired, sweaty and hungry. When they found themselves near the river again, Sadie sent up a howl of despair.

"This is ridiculous!" Thoroughly frustrated, she kicked viciously at a small rock, only to let out an even louder howl when she discovered it was actually the tip of a much bigger rock buried in the ground.

Dylan stared intently at the slowly meandering water for a beat, then began to shrug out of his backpack straps.

"What are you doing?" she asked when she'd finished hopping around on one foot.

"It's getting late. We're going to have to spend the night here, then find the others in the morning. It shouldn't be too bad—we're only an hour or so from where we went wrong in the first place. In the morning, we can double back and then complete the original route to the campsite."

"What a brilliant idea," she said. "It was even more brilliant when I had it four hours ago."

"Now, now, gloating is an ugly indulgence," he said as he dumped his pack on the ground.

Harrumphing to herself, she slid her arms out of her own backpack straps and gave a groan of relief as she circled her shoulders.

"Let's get this tent up before it gets dark," he said.

He sounded remarkably chipper, and she shot him a suspicious look. He looked pretty chipper, too.

"Just because we're stuck together for the night doesn't mean I'm going to sl—" She caught herself in the nick of time. "I'm not doing the horizontal mambo with you," she corrected herself.

He shrugged as if it was the last thing on his mind.

"Your choice."

She shot him another suspicious look but he was concentrating on unfolding the tent. She pitched in, and in five minutes they had the igloo-shaped tent erected and pegged down.

"Shelter taken care of. What else do we have?" he asked.

Sadie threw the compressed roll that was her sleeping bag into the tent.

"One sleeping bag. No sleeping mat—unless you have one?" she asked hopefully.

"Nope. Luke and Ben had all that stuff. We were sharing the load," Dylan explained wryly.

They both emptied out their backpacks. He had a small penlight torch and a box of matches. She had a packet of mints, a small bar of chocolate and a travel pack of tissues. The good news was, they both had toothpaste and toothbrushes, so dental hygiene emergencies were covered off—and Dylan had brought a jumbo box of condoms.

"You really are an arrogant jerk, you know?" Sadie said, hefting the condom box in her hand.

"A man can dream. Plus, I might have scored with someone else."

"Don't you think that you're sleeping with enough of the staff already?" she asked sharply.

"Dan might have been a Dan-ette. Outdoorsy girls are hot."

"Sure they are." Sadie tossed the box of condoms at him. "Hope all that rubber keeps you warm while I'm snuggled in my sleeping bag tonight."

He narrowed his eyes at her.

"I bet you that you will be begging me for one of these condoms before I'm begging you to let me into your sleeping bag," he said.

She thrust her hand out instantly.

"Done. What are the stakes?"

He got an evil glint in his eye, and she shook her head. "Something else."

He frowned, then smiled broadly.

"The loser has to do anything the winner says," he said.

"How old are you again?"

"You said something else. Those are my stakes."

"Fine—anything the winner says, within reason. Barring you-know-what," Sadie clarified.

They shook hands.

"I can think of far better things to make you do than have sex with me," Dylan said as he sat and started unlacing his boots.

"Like?" she asked, following his lead. The cool air felt delicious on her over-heated feet.

"Like ordering you to come to work naked," he said.

She gave an inarticulate squawk of alarm.

"I'm not saying that's what I'd ask for—but I could, theoretically," he quickly explained.

"Good luck with that one," she said.

She almost swallowed her tongue when he stood and stripped off his T-shirt. His hands were on the fly of his hiking shorts before she found her voice.

"W-what are you doing?"

"Going for a swim. What are you doing?"

She could only stare as he dropped his shorts and boxers in one smooth move, leaving him standing naked and magnificent in front of her.

He waved a hand in front of his groin to try to attract her mesmerized attention.

"Hello? Didn't anyone ever tell you it's rude to stare?" he asked, a sly smile on his lips.

"Didn't anyone ever tell you that it's rude to take off all your clothes in public?" she countered.

"We are so not in public," he said, shaking his head. "In fact, this is about as private as it gets. Don't you think?"

He shot her a very saucy look, then turned toward the river bank. She watched his perfect butt until it disappeared into the water.

A trickle of sweat ran down between her breasts and she scratched at a patch of dirt caked to her ankle.

"You should come in—the water's fine," Dylan called.

Sadie crinkled up her nose. Her hair felt stuck to her head with sweat, and she sniffed her armpit surreptitiously to confirm that her deodorant had failed hours ago.

The problem was, getting naked with Dylan was about as safe as smearing herself with gravy and jumping into the lion's enclosure at the zoo. She didn't trust him. He'd been trying to get her into bed again for weeks. Most of all, however, she didn't trust herself.

The sound of splashing filtered up from the river, and she stared down at her red, sore feet. Maybe she could paddle around a little…?

A whoop of pure joy sounded, and she saw that Dylan had climbed out of the river so he could stand on a rock and jump back in again.

"Damn it!" She stood and started shucking her clothes before she could think twice. The water was too inviting, and she was too hot and sticky.

Dylan stopped fooling around and stood bolt-upright in the waist-high water when she emerged from the bushes to stand naked on the edge of the river.

"Oh, thank you, Lord," he said fervently.

Sadie fought the need to cover her crotch and breasts with her hands in classic Eve posture.

"Stop staring."

"Stop being so damned sexy then. My left leg for a camera so I can capture this moment for all eternity," he said.

His avid scrutiny should have made her feel more self-conscious, but instead she felt a surge of confidence. She'd never been mad about her body—too skinny, too tall, not curvy enough in all the girly places—but all of a sudden she felt sultry and sexy and irresistible.

"That's right, work it, baby," he encouraged as she thrust her breasts out a little as she took her first step into the water.

"Oh. My. God!" She squealed as icy-cold water closed over her ankles. "Are you insane? This water is arctic."

"It's good for you, Norsca-fresh," he said. Before she could retreat, he lunged forward and grabbed her wrists. The next thing she knew, he'd pulled her into the center of the slow-moving current and icy-cold water was enveloping her body.

Gasping, she tried to push away from him but kept encountering warm, well-muscled chest.

"Y-you b-b-bastard," she said, teeth chattering.

"It's invigorating. Wait a moment, it gets better."

Grinning hugely, he pushed himself away from her and began a slow, leisurely stroke against the current. Sadie wrapped her arms around herself and shivered, turning back toward the shore. Invigorating her ass—she was getting out.

But she'd barely taken two steps on the pebbled riverbed before she started to feel a warm tingling in her arms and legs. Her body was adjusting to the coolness of the water, and she realized she was barely shivering anymore.

"See, what did I tell you?" Dylan said as he floated by. Sunlight caught on his water-slicked limbs, gilding his body briefly. She blinked, momentarily dazzled.

Giving herself up to the experience, she sank down so that

everything but her eyes was submerged. Above her, trees stretched their branches from either side of the river, creating a canopy of green overhead. Birds cried out nearby, and a warm wind sighed through the trees. Her hair fanned out behind her, and she floated, allowing the current to take her.

Dylan's hand shot out to anchor her as she drifted past.

"Careful there, water nymph. Don't want you floating downstream and giving some fisherman the treat of a lifetime," he said.

His hand felt incredibly warm against her skin—too warm. Dropping her legs to the riverbed, she pushed herself upright. Water sluiced down her breasts and belly, and her hair clung to her head, neck and back.

Dylan pressed a hand over his heart.

"If you had any idea how good you look right now," he said, taking a step toward her.

She saw the intent in his eye, and panicked. Because she wanted it so much, too, she turned tail and splashed toward the shore.

"Time to get out," she said over her shoulder.

He didn't try to stop her, and she had five minutes to herself to sluice the water from her skin and pull on fresh clothes from her pack before he padded up from the water. Even though she wanted to stare at his beautiful body, she turned her back to allow him the same privacy. She was the one who didn't want to have sex, she reminded herself. Somehow, that small but rather important fact kept slipping her mind.

"You can look now, Sister Sadie," he said after a few minutes.

She blushed and glanced across to see that he'd pulled on a clean T-shirt with his hiking shorts.

"Should we try to make a fire?" she asked, glancing toward the sky. The light was fading already—soon it would be too late to rummage for firewood.

"Sure," he shrugged. "Don't suppose you were ever a Girl Guide?"

"Nope. And you definitely weren't in the Scouts."

"Good call. How hard can it be, anyway?"

After ten minutes of scavenging they'd amassed a decent pile of wood. Dylan selected smaller pieces for kindling, and tested the rest for moisture.

"Some of it's a little damp, but I guess the heat'll fix that, right?"

With dusk well on its way, they huddled around the ring of rocks they'd constructed and waited for the kindling to take. After five matches had burned down to nothing, they exchanged worried looks.

"We need something dryer," Sadie said. She scanned their campsite. Eventually her eye landed on their map.

Dylan shook his head when she went to collect it.

"Not the brightest idea you've ever had, Sparky," he said.

"We won't burn all of it. Just the bits we don't need. Like this stupid key bit. And this bit on the front with the picture of the smiling ranger," she explained, tearing off the pieces in question as she spoke.

Soon she'd nibbled away at the map until only the very necessary sections were left, leaving them with a small, precious pile of paper scraps.

"Here goes nothing," Dylan said. A tiny flame danced on the end of the match, then licked tentatively at a paper scrap as though tasting it. With a flare of light, the paper burst into flames, and they sent up a cheer as the kindling began to burn.

"We rock," Dylan crowed.

"Oh, yeah, we're real survivors," Sadie agreed drily.

They had a good fire going by the time darkness had fallen. They sat side by side watching it, their back to the tent.

Sadie's stomach grumbled, and she winced.

"How long do we wait until we eat the chocolate?" she asked.

"You can have it all." Dylan shrugged.

She shot him an assessing look. "Are you trying to be a gentleman?" she asked.

"How am I doing?"

"Not too bad. The whole lying-about-how-cold-the-water-was thing lost you some points, but offering me all the chocolate is definitely a powerful strategy."

"Thanks."

She smiled, crossing her legs. She really enjoyed his company. In fact, she couldn't imagine anyone else that she'd rather be lost in the wilds with.

The flames were mesmerizing, and it seemed perfectly natural to start talking as the night grew older. Dylan told her about his parents, how they'd always thought he was a waste of time. His dad was dead now, but he'd set his mother up in a little house down the coast. He didn't visit often—he felt guilty about that, but her glass-half-empty negativity made him angry, and his visits always ended in acrimony.

In turn, she told him about her parents' deaths, how she'd been angry for so long afterward but had finally come to terms with their absence from her life. Splitting the bar of chocolate, they talked about work, swapping war stories and gossip and laughing till their sides ached over in-jokes.

Finally their stockpile of wood dwindled and the fire began to fade.

"Bedtime, methinks," Sadie said. In the last dying light, she brushed her teeth and washed her mouth out with river water, being careful not to swallow. She could see Dylan doing the same on the other side of the campfire as she stowed her gear away and crawled inside the tent.

Untying her shoelaces and sliding her shoes off, she admitted to herself that she was nervous. And excited. She was very, very attracted to this man. He was the most exciting lover she'd ever had, and he made her laugh almost as much as he challenged her creatively and intellectually.

She frowned into the darkness as she unzipped her sleeping bag. Dylan's very attractiveness scared her so much. If Greg hadn't turned out to be a wimpy jerk, she'd be married right now. Would she have still found Dylan as attractive if her marriage had gone ahead? And if the answer was yes, what did that say about her feelings for Greg—and for Dylan?

She pulled her knees up tight to her chest and rested her chin on them, fretting. She didn't trust herself anymore. She'd put all her eggs in Greg's basket, and he'd dropped them spectacularly. She simply didn't trust herself not to make the same mistake twice.

What did she know about Dylan, after all? Yes, he had a hard, sexy body, and he seemed to instinctively know how to please her. He was a successful writer, a sensitive observer of other human beings. But he was also thirty years old, and still single. Not once had he mentioned a serious relationship in his past, a failed marriage or a live-in girlfriend. What did that say about his ability—or willingness—to commit?

The tent flap rustled, and she stiffened as Dylan entered.

"I put the fire out, in case Smokey the Bear was on patrol," he said.

"Okay."

Uncurling her body, she lay on her back and shuffled as far to one side as she could.

"What are you doing?" he asked after a moment.

"Making room so you can share the sleeping bag," she explained.

There was a small silence. "Let me get this straight—you're *asking* me to share the bag?" he asked.

She smiled. "Forget the bet. Unless you want to freeze to death?"

The sound of him sliding into the unzipped bag answered

her question. She rolled onto her side facing away from him. For a moment they were both quiet, then Dylan cursed under his breath.

"I swear there are about a million rocks underneath me," he said grouchily.

"Think of it as therapeutic. Like a shiatsu massage."

"You obviously have a much better imagination than me," he said.

She tensed as she felt his arm slide around her waist as he snuggled up to her back.

"Ah, Dylan?"

"Yes?"

"What the hell do you think you're doing?"

"Conserving body heat. I'm sure Ranger Dan would approve. I believe the Native Americans call it spooning."

She couldn't help herself—she laughed. And she didn't push him away. It was much warmer with him curled against her back, even if it was doing crazy things to her heart rate.

He felt so good. Hard, hot. Masculine. Her breath caught as she remembered how he'd looked naked. She curled her hands into fists and pressed them against her chest, just in case they took it upon themselves to reach out and touch him without permission.

His breath tickled the back of her neck, and she shifted her position minutely, hoping he couldn't feel how quickly she was breathing. Her new position brought her into firmer contact with his hips, and she stilled when she felt something very firm and hard nudging her bottom.

"Dylan," she said warningly.

"It's not my fault. You're a beautiful, desirable woman, and I'm only human." He shrugged. "Ignore it. It'll go away."

As if to prove his point, he tightened his arm more securely over her body and snuggled in closer.

Sadie stared into the darkness. *Ignore it*. He wanted her to ignore his erection, even as he pressed it against her backside.

She tried counting sheep, but all she could think about was how easy it would be to turn around and slide her hand down between his legs to take him in hand. She licked her lips, imagining taking him in her mouth.

"I can't do this," she said after five minutes of pure torture. "I can't sleep with…*that* pressed up against me."

"Okay. I'll take care of it," he said.

She felt an abrupt chill as he rolled away, then heard the metallic whisper of his zipper. There was a rustle of clothing, then his arm brushed hers as he began to move rhythmically.

She froze. "What are you doing?" she demanded.

"What do you think I'm doing? I'm taking care of it."

Instantly her mind filled with an image of how he must look—his own large hand wrapped around his swollen shaft, his eyes half-closed as he slicked his palm up and down, up and down. Desire flooded her like a tidal wave. There was no way she could lie here while he touched himself like that—not when she was the one who wanted to do the touching so badly.

"Damn," she muttered under her breath. Then she reached for the waistband of her jeans.

She felt him still as she wriggled out of her jeans and panties. "What's going on?"

"What do you think is going on?" she asked, deliberately echoing his earlier words as she pulled her bra and T-shirt over her head.

"I think—I hope—that you're taking your clothes off," he said.

"Bingo. Now get your hands off my property," she said, pushing his hands away from his erection.

"Yes, ma'am," he said. She heard the smug amusement in his voice and knew she'd played right into his hands.

"Laugh it up, buddy," she said, getting a firm grip on him. "Wait till you can't walk tomorrow."

"A risk I am more than prepared to take."

She felt him lean toward her, and she automatically angled her head to meet his kiss. His tongue was hot and wet as he invaded her mouth, and she moaned encouragingly as his hands slid over her breasts.

He alternately plucked at her nipples and smoothed his palms over her breasts as they kissed, long, slow, deep kisses that made her ache to have him inside her. She could feel how wet she was, ready for him to fill her, and she shifted her hips impatiently.

"We've got all the time in the world," he whispered in her ear as he began to nibble his way down her neck.

"You've got too much clothing on," she said, tugging impatiently at his T-shirt. He obliged by pulling away from her for a moment to struggle out of his T-shirt and shorts. The hot press of his naked skin against hers was so welcome that she laughed with relief.

"Amen," he said, ducking his head to pull a nipple into his mouth. She smoothed her hands over the planes and angles of his shoulders and back, slowly working her way around to his belly. Trailing her fingers through his hair, she found his erection again. Gently pushing him away from her breasts, she encouraged him onto his back. Stopping first to tongue his flat nipples to full arousal, she began to blaze a trail down his chest.

"Sadie," he said warningly as she slithered lower.

"Shut up."

Holding him firmly in one hand, she ran her tongue across the velvety head of his erection. She could feel his belly tense beneath her other hand, and she smiled to herself and took him fully into her mouth.

He made an inarticulate, needy sound, and she began to swirl her tongue over the head of his erection, sliding her hand simultaneously up and down his shaft. He tasted amazing, and she gloried in her power as he shifted restlessly beneath her hands.

"Enough," he said suddenly, his hands clamping onto her shoulders to pull her away. Before she knew what was happening, she was on her back and he was on top of her, his hardness nudging at her wet, swollen entrance.

She lifted her hips, silently encouraging him to take her. But every time she tried to force his penetration, he retreated a little, and she knew he was grinning, despite the fact that she couldn't see his face.

"You enjoying yourself there?" she panted.

"Oh, yeah. But not nearly enough yet," he said. She felt the faint friction of his body sliding down hers, and then his hands were curling around her inner thighs, pushing her legs apart. The first, hot dart of his tongue on her sensitive center almost set her off, and she fisted her hands into the sleeping bag and groaned.

"Let it go, baby. No one's here to hear you."

As though he'd given her permission to do something she'd always wanted to, Sadie began to vocalize her pleasure. She moaned. She cried out. She talked dirty, encouraging him as she came closer and closer to orgasm.

"*Yes.* I want you inside me, Dylan," she finally demanded, sliding her hands into his hair and trying to pull him away.

"Go away, I'm busy," he said, his voice muffled by his close contact with her body.

"Get up here now!" she ordered, giving his hair a far from gentle tug.

"Ow. That hurt."

She had his attention now, and she sat up so she could reach his erection.

"Where's that jumbo box of condoms?" she asked impatiently as she slid her hand up and down his shaft.

"Would it be really crass for me to mention a certain bet at this stage in proceedings?" He laughed as he reached for his backpack.

"What do *you* think?" she said, her breath catching in her

throat as she heard the telltale crinkle of a foil packet. Any second now, and she would have what she craved.

He settled his weight between her legs, his erection pressing against her slick inner lips.

"I think that you are almost too hot to handle," he said, then he flexed his hips and plunged inside her.

She bit her lip and tried to contain the cry of ecstasy that came to her lips, but it was too much, and she was already falling apart, her muscles pulsating around him. His voice whispered in her ear as she quivered and clutched at his back, encouraging her, pushing her further over the edge. And all the while he thrust inside her, his butt tensing and relaxing, his breath coming in panting gasps.

As the last ripples of her orgasm left her, she rocked her hips back and wrapped her legs around his hips. Locking her ankles together, she answered each of his thrusts with one of her own, hands clawing at his shoulders, teeth bared as she began to climb toward release yet again.

His hands slid up and down her body, tracing the curve of her hip, dipping into the crease of her backside, smoothing over the sensitive skin beneath her arms. His head dipped, and she felt the wet firmness of his tongue on her nipples, and suddenly she was coming again, her head thrashing from side to side, her back arching as she cried out his name.

She felt him tense, too, then his big body shuddered, and he pressed his face into her neck and whispered her name as he came.

He slumped on top of her, spent, and she soothed circles on the smooth skin of his back, relishing the weight of him between her thighs. She felt completely, utterly satisfied.

After a while, he rolled off her and Sadie sighed. A long moment passed and slowly she registered that his breathing had deepened. She nudged him with her elbow.

"Don't go falling asleep," she said.

"Don't worry. Sleep is the last thing on my mind," he said.

"Just as well. Because like I said, I will not sleep with you," she said, mocking her earlier promise.

"I got that. And I respect it, believe me."

She knew he was smiling. She was, too—the broad, smug smile of a satisfied woman who knows she's about to get more of the same.

Getting lost, it turned out, definitely had its advantages.

THE NEXT MORNING, Dylan woke with a crick in his back from the rocky ground and a numb arm from where Sadie had fallen asleep resting on his shoulder. Lifting his head, he stared down at her face. Even in sleep her mouth was curved into a smile, and he wondered how he'd ever convinced himself she was uptight or shrewish. As he watched, her eyelids fluttered and her mouth opened on a soft sigh. He knew the exact moment that she came to full consciousness—she tensed, then immediately rolled away from him.

Smiling wryly to himself, he clenched and unclenched his fist a few times to get his circulation going, and waited for her to say something.

"What time is it?" she finally asked in a very subdued voice. Not quite the same saucy vixen who'd kept him awake all night with her passionate demands—but he'd expected as much.

"A little after six, I think. If we start out soon, we might be able to catch the others at the camp before they pack up and come looking for us."

"Okay."

He watched as she fumbled around for her clothes, trying to gather them while holding a corner of the sleeping bag to her chest for modesty.

"But first, I figured we should have another swim," he said, rolling to his knees.

She froze and stared at him, her eyes widening as he backed

out of the tent and stood in the clearing, stark naked. He could read the longing and regret in her face, and knew exactly what she was going to say. He didn't want to hear it.

"Dylan—" she began, but he reached in to grab her ankle.

"After our swim," he said.

In the end, he had to carry her down the bank and toss her into the deepest part of the river, and they splashed around and swam and floated for twenty minutes before clambering out of the icy water. She was shivering as she tried to pat herself dry with yesterday's T-shirt, and he pulled her close, warming her with his body. Being close to her had its usual inevitable effect and soon they were kissing and he was backing her into the tent and sliding into her with a sigh of relief. This was what he craved, only this, he thought as he buried himself inside her. He was utterly captivated by her—the little hitch she got in her breathing when he entered her, the greedy way she eyed his body, her amazing responsiveness. Moving languidly, he prolonged each thrust, glorying in the slide of his body inside hers. Her head began to move restlessly from side to side, and he captured her mouth with a kiss. She sucked his bottom lip into her mouth and dug her fingers into his butt, urging him to go faster, harder, deeper. He resisted, keeping it slow, building them slowly, savoring the pleasure.

Only when she was sobbing and he was shaking did he step up the pace, and within seconds she came apart beneath him, her cries of ecstasy echoing in the clearing. He held her close as he found his own peak, her name on his lips as he lost himself inside her.

They lay staring up at the peak of the tent for a while before she finally stirred.

"When we go back to L.A...." she said, her voice heavy with regret.

"I agree. We should probably keep things under wraps. No need for everyone to know our business," he said easily.

She blinked, then stared at him.

"We can't do this again," she said as if it were the most obvious thing on earth.

"Haven't I heard that before? Wait, it's coming to me…. I've got it—that's what we said the first time, yeah? And the second time. And again last night. Seeing a pattern here?" he asked.

She sat up and pulled her knees to her chest, looping her arms over them. He resisted the urge to touch the delicate vertebrae of her spine. Sometimes she seemed infinitely fragile, even though he knew she was as tough as nails.

"What are you suggesting? An affair?"

"Do we have to label it?" He shrugged. "We like each other. We have great sex. I want to see you again. Isn't it that simple?"

She shook her head.

"It sounds simple. I want to believe it's that simple. But I've never done anything like this before, Dylan. I'm a boring old monogamist from way back," she said self-deprecatingly.

"Is that a roundabout way of asking if I think we have a future?" he asked. He always made a point of laying his cards on the table up front—that way no one could complain that they didn't know the score.

"No. God, I'm supposed to be married. I just… I don't know," she said.

He sat up beside her, mirroring her position.

"I'm not looking for commitment," he said baldly. "You should know that going in. I won't ever lie to you."

She nodded. "So…it's just sex?" she asked.

"Mostly, yeah. It's pretty amazing sex though, wouldn't you agree?" he said lightly. He smoothed a hand down her bare, vulnerable back, and she shivered in reaction.

"Oh, yeah," she said ruefully.

He slid his hand up to her nape and captured the back of her head. Pulling her close, he kissed her, a thorough, deep, intense kiss that sent both their pulses racing.

"You can't walk away from chemistry this good," he murmured against her mouth.

"No," she whispered back.

He felt a surge of triumph. He had her.

As if making a decision had lifted a burden from her shoulders, she brightened visibly as they packed the tent and made their way back to the fork where they'd taken their first wrong turn. Two hours later they crested a rise and ran smack-bang into the rest of the team, obviously on a rescue mission.

"You're alive!" Claudia said, rushing forward to capture Sadie in a fierce embrace. "I've been so worried about you."

Grace grimaced at Sadie's mystified expression. "Hey, what did you expect? We make up drama for a living. By midnight, we had you in a coma, dying from snake bite, trapped by some hill-dwelling cult, or dead from a grizzly bear attack."

"Wow," Sadie said.

"Yep. You guys being plain old lost wasn't good enough for us," Grace said.

"Well, it was plenty good for us," Dylan said.

Sadie shot him a loaded look, and he could see the memories flicking across her mind's eye. All of a sudden, he wished the rest of them to hell. He wanted to be lost with her again, just the two of them.

"Thank God, it's all over," Claudia said as they made their way back to the team's camp. "I am never camping again. There's something so wrong about not having access to running water."

"And hair dryers," Grace said, fingering her hair. "I feel like one of those troll things from *Lord of the Rings*."

Dylan watched as Sadie fell into step with her friends, a frown pleating his forehead as she began to laugh and talk easily with them. After a few minutes of waiting in vain for some acknowledgment from her—a glance, the casual brush of her arm against his—he realized what was wrong. He was jealous. Immediately, he gave himself a mental kick in the pants. Was he so sexually obsessed with Sadie that he begrudged her spending time with her friends? Ridiculous. Ahead of him, Sadie laughed at something Grace had said and slipped her arm around her friend. His frown deepened. Yep, definitely jealousy. He was officially pathetic.

With Dan supervising, they made short work of packing up the campsite, and another hour's walk led them back to the clearing by the lake where their cars were parked. As they approached the clearing, Dylan managed to edge Sadie away for a private word. It was the first time he'd got a word in edgewise since they'd rejoined the others, and he couldn't resist the temptation to touch her. Sliding a hand along her hip, he hooked a finger inside the waistband of her jeans and rubbed the bare skin he found there.

"Ride back to the city with me on my bike," he said quietly.

She looked surprised. "That'll look pretty obvious, won't it?" she suggested.

All of a sudden he wanted to tell her to forget about what everyone else thought. What did it matter if their work colleagues knew they were involved? But he knew that it mattered a lot to Sadie, particularly in light of her friendship with Claudia. He shrugged.

"I'll say you lost a bet. Technically, you kind of did," he said.

Her eyes flashed with laughter, and she hid a smile behind her hand. "Okay. Let me tell Claudia. She can take my pack for me."

Another win. He patiently stood to one side as Sadie said farewell to her friends and the rest of the team, managing to bite back on the urge to remind her that she would be seeing them all again at nine the following morning. Finally she was strapping on his spare helmet, sliding onto the bike behind him and wrapping her arms around his waist.

"Hold on," he said, starting the engine. The Ducati surged forward as he let out the throttle, and then they were bouncing their way long the dirt road. Twenty minutes later, they turned onto tarmac, and he opened up the throttle. Sadie gave a yelp of excitement and tightened her grip on his torso, and he grinned behind his visor. She might not recognize it yet, but Sadie Post had a thrill seeker inside her just waiting to get out.

They made short work of the trip home, despite stopping for snacks twice and sex once in a secluded strip of forest outside of the L.A. basin. He'd never been one for the great outdoors, but he was beginning to appreciate certain aspects, that was for sure.

Sadie began giving directions as they neared her condo in Santa Monica, and nearly three hours after leaving the campsite he parked the Ducati outside her building.

Tugging her helmet off, she slid from the bike and smoothed her hands down the front of her jeans nervously. Even with helmet hair she looked infinitely desirable.

"Do you want to come up?" she asked tentatively.

He cocked his head to one side, trying to read her. "Do you want me to come up?" he asked.

Her eyes slid off him for a second, then she nodded. "Yes. Is there such a thing as having too much sex?" she asked worriedly.

"I don't know. But I think it's a bold experiment we're conducting," he said as he pulled off his helmet. Stowing them both in the storage compartment beneath the seat, he followed her into the elevator. Her hair was deliciously mussed from a combination of the helmet and the wind, and he pushed her against the wall and nuzzled her neck.

"You smell like smoke from the campfire," he said.

She smiled and murmured approvingly as he cupped her butt and pulled her closer for another kiss.

The elevator chimed as it reached her floor, and they pulled apart reluctantly.

"Hold that thought," she advised him as she extracted her house key from her pocket.

He followed her hungrily as she lead the way to her door, casting a saucy look over her shoulder as she let him inside.

"The bathroom is to the left, if you want to freshen up," she said, then she stopped dead in her tracks as a tall, good-looking blond guy stood up from the couch where he'd obviously been waiting.

The color drained out of Sadie's face and she rested a hand on the hall table as though she needed support.

"Greg," she said.

Dylan's eyes narrowed as every muscle in his body tensed. The ex.

Perfect timing. Not.

9

SADIE DIDN'T KNOW where to put herself. Horribly aware of Dylan standing behind her, she stared at her ex-fiancé.

"What are you doing here?" she asked for lack of anything else to say.

"I had to see you," Greg said, his blue eyes wide and sincere.

She shook her head. "What if I didn't want to see you?"

"I know I don't deserve a second of your time after what I did, but please, hear me out," Greg said. She'd never heard the note of entreaty in his voice before. He was a successful man, an investment banker, and she'd never once seen him second-guess himself or sound anything less than supremely confident. Until now.

"I can't believe you let yourself in," she said, falling back on the mundane because she didn't know what else to do.

Should she talk to him, allow him the chance to state his case? Seeing him in the flesh again, she felt oddly detached. She assessed him objectively. He was a handsome man, by anyone's standards—a young Robert Redford, only a little taller and a little broader in the chest. He had a deep voice, he dressed well, he was well educated, usually kind, often funny. A little over a month ago, she'd been confident she loved him and wanted to build a life with him.

Now he looked about as familiar to her as a generically attractive model from a men's clothing catalog.

"I'm sorry, Sadie. Just give me a chance to explain, and if you don't want me hanging around, I'll be gone," Greg said.

The heavy, warm weight of Dylan's hand landed on her shoulder as he stepped forward.

"Or I can make him be gone a hell of lot sooner," he said. She didn't have to look at him to know what expression he was wearing—his tough-guy look, the one that had served him so well for all those years at Grovedale High.

"Who the hell are you?" Greg asked, the tendons in his neck standing out as he scanned Dylan from head to toe.

"It's all right," she said, holding up a hand.

The attitude radiating off Dylan was palpable. She had the horrible feeling that this scene was going to become even more fraught if she didn't keep these two bristling alpha males away from one another. One of them had to go, and Dylan was the natural choice. Apart from the fact that she'd never been engaged to him, he was also closest to the door.

"I think you should go," she said, turning to face him.

"Me?" His voice rose with incredulity. "You're kidding."

"The sooner I hear him out, the sooner he's gone from my life," she said, not bothering to modulate her tone for Greg's benefit. He didn't deserve consideration for his feelings.

Placing her hand on the small of Dylan's back, she encouraged him toward the door.

"I'll see you at work tomorrow," she said.

For a moment he resisted the pressure of her hand, then he strode toward the door. The look he gave her was fierce as she opened the door for him.

"Call me tonight," he said.

She nodded absently, too blown away by Greg's sudden appearance to think straight. She was also too slow on the uptake to avoid the kiss Dylan dropped on her mouth. Even in the most awkward situation imaginable, her knees still went weak. For a dazed moment she watched his tall, rangy frame walk down the hall.

"You're seeing that guy?" Greg asked.

When she turned to face him, his expression was stricken.

"Do you really think you have the right to ask that?" she asked.

Greg's jaw jutted mulishly. "Yes, I do."

Her hands found her hips.

"Pretty rich coming from the guy who ditched me at the altar. How do I know you haven't been off screwing some bimbo for the past few weeks?"

"I'm not seeing anyone else. I love you, Sadie."

"Forgive me if I'm a little unconvinced on that one, being of the actions-speak-louder-than-words school of thought," she said.

She was surprised at how calm she sounded. In the days following their wedding, she'd been angry with him, hurt and confused. But now when she reached inside herself to the dark place where she'd stuffed all her feelings, all the heat was gone.

Very deliberately, she moved into the living room and took the seat opposite him as he, too, sat. Folding her hands into her lap, she checked the clock on her mantelpiece.

"You've got five minutes—ten if it's really interesting," she said coolly.

Greg leaned forward, the picture of earnestness.

"Sadie, I'm a jerk. I regretted what happened the second it was too late to turn up at the church. You are the best thing in my life, and I was a fool for not realizing that," he said urgently.

"The reception went for four hours, Greg. You could have turned up at any time and put me out of my misery. The *least* you could have done was turn up at the church to tell our friends and family—let alone me—in person that you'd changed your mind. I haven't been dumped via a note since I was in the fourth grade."

Greg ran a hand through his hair, ruffling it out of its usual smooth perfection. She registered for the first time that he was wearing his best suit and favorite tie—dressed to impress. She hardened her heart. Too little, too late.

"I found out something recently, something that freaked me out," he said. His blue eyes were tortured as he gazed across at her. "My dad's having an affair."

Sadie shook her head. Greg's parents were pinups for conjugal bliss—still happily married after more than forty years together, devoted, interested in each other and the world. They traveled regularly, worked for the community despite being retired, and by the sparkle in their eyes still enjoyed a regular sex life.

"That can't be right," she said.

"I saw them out together. She used to live up the street from us when we were kids. I confronted Dad and he admitted they've been seeing each off and on for years." Greg looked devastated, and despite all that had gone wrong between them, she felt for him. He idolized his parents, his father in particular. She'd lost count of the times he'd held his father up as the image of the man he wanted to be—faithful husband, successful businessman, devoted family man. She'd thought it was the image of what she wanted in a man, too.

"I'm sorry. I take it your mom doesn't know?" she asked.

"No. This has been going on for years, Sadie. You know what he said when I told him I'd seen him? That he loved Mom, but she wasn't enough. That no woman was enough to satisfy a man for a lifetime."

The disgust in his tone gave a fair indication of how he'd responded to his father's comments. Greg ran his hand through his hair again, leaving it sticking up in an endearing spike.

"I was furious with him. I wanted to beat him to a pulp. But then I started thinking. All my life, he's been the best man I know—and he couldn't stick his marriage out and play by the rules. What hope did that leave for us?"

She stared at him, everything slotting into place.

"You didn't turn up because you didn't think we could make it work?" she asked.

"I didn't think *I* could make it work. Everyone says I'm a

chip off the old block—it's a goddamned family joke. I love you too much to do that to you, Sadie. I freaked. I thought I could do it, but on the day of the wedding I took one look at my father and knew I couldn't risk it."

It made sense. She could see how upset he was now, could imagine how wounded and confused he must have been to discover his much-idolized father had feet of clay.

"What's changed? Why are you here?" she asked.

"I have to know you're okay. That's the most important thing. And…and I want to know if you can forgive me. I'm not my father. It's taken a few weeks for me to work that one out." Greg gave a self-deprecating grunt of disgust. "I love you. I want nothing more than to spend the rest of my life with you. But I understand that I may have forfeited my chance at that when I screwed up at the wedding."

Sadie stared at him. She had never imagined, even in her wildest dreams, that Greg would someday present her with an excuse that she would be prepared to accept. But staring at him now, seeing the pain and suffering and anger in his face, she understood that he'd been through the wringer recently. His perception of the world had been shattered. He'd lost his rock, his true north. And he'd panicked. Intellectually, she could understand what had happened.

"You should have told me, talked to me," she said.

"As ridiculous as it seems, I didn't want you to think badly of Dad." Greg shook his head at his own poor judgment. "If you look me in the eye and tell me it's over, that you feel nothing for me at all, I'll walk away and never bother you again. But if you're willing to give me a second chance—" Greg broke off, his eyes pleading with her.

She stared at him, moved despite herself by the wounded hurt she could see in his face. For the first time since her wedding day, she allowed herself to remember what it had felt like to wake in his arms, reliving for just a second the warm

sense of protection and peace he'd offered her. As if she'd
opened the floodgates, a thousand other memories swamped
her: the smell of his freshly starched shirts, the neat way he had
of folding the paper to make it easier to read, his secret love of
reality television shows, the deep bass of his laughter when she
surprised him with a joke, the tender light in his eyes as he
kissed her good night….

She'd been ready to hitch her star to his and set off on the
adventure of a lifetime. She'd imagined bearing his children,
growing old with him…. She'd built a whole future around her
relationship with him. And he was sitting here telling her that
she didn't have to abandon her dream—if only she could
forgive him and learn to trust him again.

As if sensing her ambivalence, Greg eased forward on the
couch until he could drop his weight down onto one knee. It
should have looked ridiculous, pathetic—a grown man literally
begging her to take him back. But his back was straight, his
eyes clear and honest, his expression intent. All the old feelings
hammered at the door to her heart. She'd felt safe with this
man—adored, loved, admired.

Without her consciously willing it, her mind flipped to the
man who'd just walked out of her apartment with long-limbed
grace. Dylan was the antithesis of Greg, an almost perfect
polar opposite. Dark where Greg was blond, impulsive and rebellious and messy where Greg was safe, measured and neat.
He was a walking disaster area compared to Greg, even when
Greg's altar-abandonment was included in the deal. Dylan had
openly admitted he was not looking for a relationship. He'd
made it clear that while he liked and respected her, what they
had going was based on sex and nothing more. In short, he
offered her nothing—and Greg was offering her everything.

Again.

But there was one thing that Dylan had brought into her
world that Greg never had—she'd never felt as sexy in her life

as she'd felt in Dylan's arms. And she'd never been as bold or as driven or as daring, either. He'd branded her body with his touch, and she craved the feel of him inside her from the moment he pulled away until the second she had him again.

It had never been like that with Greg. With anyone, for that matter.

But great sex did not a great relationship make. In fact, great sex did not an *anything* make, according to Dylan I'm-not-looking-for-commitment Anderson.

"Don't give me an answer now," Greg said, reaching for her hand.

She didn't pull away. Why was she thinking about Dylan when Greg was laying himself out in front of her?

"Think about it, please? Then come out for dinner with me Friday night," he said.

"I'm sleeping with someone else," she blurted suddenly, almost as though she was hoping the decision would be taken out of her hands if she revealed what had happened with Dylan.

Greg's face hardened momentarily, but then he swallowed hard and nodded tightly.

"I kind of figured that," he said. "And you're right, I don't have the right to be jealous or hurt or angry, even though I am."

His hand was warm and firm on hers, his touch familiar. She swallowed a sudden rush of tears.

"Okay. Dinner Friday night," she slowly agreed.

He smiled for the first time since she'd opened the door, a tentative expression of hope.

"Thank you." Lifting her hand, he pressed a brief kiss to the back of it before pushing himself to his feet.

"I'll pick you up at eight, okay?" he said.

She didn't watch him leave, and it wasn't until he'd been gone for five minutes that she realized that she hadn't asked him for his key back. Her thoughts in turmoil, she stripped off her clothes. Under the steamy warmth of the shower, she at last let go of the ironlike grip she'd kept on her emotions since she'd seen her uncle Gus waving her limo on in the front of the church all those weeks ago. Like a fist unclenching inside her chest, the emotions came tumbling out. Tears slid down her face, sobs racked her body, her hands clutched at her torso as she let it all go—the hurt, the anger, the confusion, the fear. She cried until the water ran cold, then toweled herself dry and dressed in her comfiest pair of flannelette pajamas.

At last, she felt as though she had said goodbye to the life she might have had with Greg. She'd let it go. Apart from the sting of humiliation from that awful day at the church, she regretted nothing. She'd loved him. Now she didn't. It was over. His visit had brought her the closure she needed.

But the acknowledgment that things were well and truly over with Greg forced her to face a more dangerous truth that had been making itself at home in her heart for the past month. There were no more excuses to hide behind.

She was falling for Dylan.

It wasn't just about sex. It had never really been just about sex. His charismatic attraction went way beyond the physical for her. He was the smartest person she knew, and incredibly talented. She admired the steely drive and determination that had helped him to turn around the bad hand life had dealt him. And, yes, he was the best lover she'd ever had, or could ever imagine having. When she was with him she felt like the most desirable woman in the world. He challenged her, excited her, amused and touched her. He made her feel alive in a way she'd never felt before.

And he wanted nothing from her but sex.

Tucking her feet beneath her on the couch, she acknowledged that she'd been a fool to sleep with him again. Deep inside, she'd known she was in danger, and she'd tried to resist. But the chemistry between them was so hot, and her feelings for him so deeply entwined with her childish crush on him that she'd been a sitting duck.

He was irresistible. And only a very foolish, self-destructive woman would continue to indulge her taste for something so addictive. Because Dylan wanted only one thing from her—her body. He'd told her so over and over—and she was a fool if she didn't believe him.

For the first time in what felt like a long time, everything was very clear in her mind. She knew what she had to do.

Now she had to find the strength to do it.

DYLAN KEPT ONE EYE ON the clock from the moment he arrived home. One hour. Two. Full night descended, and still Sadie didn't call. What was keeping her? He'd told her to call him. He was worried about her, wanted to know that her asshole of an ex hadn't twisted her in knots or put a big guilt trip on her. So what was taking so long? Surely she wasn't still talking to the jerk?

By ten he was grinding his teeth to powder as darker thoughts plagued him. Images of Sadie and her blond ex fighting tooth and nail, then sinking to the carpet to enjoy a passionate bout of make-up sex. The thought of another man touching her slender body was enough to boil his blood.

By eleven, he was officially going crazy, and he reached for the phone—only to put it down again as he imagined what he'd say if Greg picked up on the other end. Only when the clock hands were twitching ever closer to the witching hour did he give in to impulse and dial her number.

She sounded sleepy—exhausted—when she answered the phone after several rings.

"Hello?"

"It's me." He practically growled at her. "You said you'd call."

"Oh. Sorry, I forgot."

"Are you all right?" he forced himself to ask when instead he wanted to demand an accounting of every second since they'd parted.

"I'm fine," she said. There was constraint in her voice, and jealousy twisted through his gut like a snake.

"Look, if he's still there I don't want to cramp your style," he said stiffly, ready to end the call.

"You're not," she said. "And he's not. We talked for a few minutes, then he left. I've been…working through some things."

The tension in his shoulders faded and he unclenched his jaw. So, Blond Adonis hadn't smooth talked his way back into Sadie's bed. Yet.

"What did he want?" He rolled his eyes at his own unsubtlety. He was coming across like a nosy neighbor or a cranky parent. Or a territorial lover. "Sorry, you don't have to answer that," he quickly added. "It's none of my business."

She was silent for a beat, then she said very quietly, "Thanks for calling, anyway."

Her voice sounded husky, as though she'd been crying. Now he really wanted to know what had gone down, but he'd already blown his chance. He also wanted to smooth away the small frown that he knew beyond a doubt was between her eyebrows right now, and hold her in his arms until she relaxed into sleep.

"Try to get some rest. I'll see you tomorrow," he said gently.

"Okay. 'Bye."

He lay awake staring at the ceiling for a long time after ending the call, unable to stop thinking about her. If the ex hadn't turned up, she'd be curled in his arms again. He felt as sulky as a kid deprived of a favorite toy. But it was more than that. He felt…edgy. On guard. Not unlike the territorial lover he'd impersonated during their phone call.

Which was ridiculous—because Sadie wasn't his. He'd made it more than clear to her that he wasn't interested in a relationship.

Punching his pillow into shape, he told himself to let it go. He had a week of plotting ahead of him and he needed a clear mind

He hadn't let anything distract him from work and his career for a long time. And now was definitely not the time to start.

Despite himself, however, he wasn't thinking about work when he finally drifted off to sleep—his dreams were full of a certain tousle-haired woman with toffee-brown eyes and a body that he couldn't seem to get enough of.

He was first into the building the next morning, and he tapped away distractedly on his notebook computer until he heard her brisk step in the foyer. Like an overwound Jack-in-the-box, he sprang up from his chair and strode out to meet her. Immediately, he felt ridiculous, as though he was racing to see her or something, and he forced himself to alter course and dawdle by the photocopier so that when she finally saw him he looked as though he was doing anything other than wait for her.

"Hi," she said, and he could hear the uncertainty in her voice. Uncertain because of something to do with what had happened between them? Or uncertain because of what had happened between her and Blondie?

"Hi." Because he hated not knowing where he stood with her, and because he still felt cheated out of having her in his arms the previous evening, he locked gazes with her and made a slow approach. "You sleep well?"

She shook her head slightly, then shrugged. "Not really."

"Yeah? I have the perfect cure for insomnia," he said.

Her eyes widened as she realized what he intended, but by then his fingers were already sliding through her hair as he angled his mouth over hers and pressed his body against the perfection of her curves.

She tasted of minty toothpaste and freshness, and he tightened his grip on her hair and deepened the kiss as desire licked along his nerve endings. One touch, one kiss, and he wanted her. Rational self out the window, he began backing her toward his office. She went willingly, groaning and moaning softly as his hands discovered her body once more, but when she brushed against the door frame of his office she stiffened in his arms.

"Dylan," she murmured against his mouth, turning her face away from his kisses.

Even though everything in him burned to show her that she wanted him as much as he wanted her, he backed off.

"Let me guess—Claudia will be here soon?" he said lightly, determined not to mention her damned ex again.

"Greg asked me out for dinner on Friday night," she said, hands dropping to her sides.

"And you're going?" he asked. A tight feeling stole into his chest. He told himself he was angry with her for giving her jerk ex a second chance when he so patently didn't deserve one.

"Yes."

"Wow, he must be a real silver tongue," he said. Even to his own ears he sounded like a petulant teen.

She flinched, then frowned. "It's dinner, that's all."

"And we all know what happens after dinner."

What was wrong with him? It was as though some other man had control of his tongue all of a sudden—some bitter, jealous guy with an ax to grind.

"That's not true, Dylan. You and I never made it to dinner," she said in deceptively dulcet tones. "We were too busy having sex on your desk, as I recall."

Shooting him a furious look, she brushed past him and strode toward her office. Dylan lifted his eyes to the ceiling and cursed his own stupidity. Shoving the hair back from his forehead, he took off after her.

"Sadie, wait," he said.

Her pace slowed and she finally turned to face him. The jut of her hip and her single raised eyebrow warned him he'd better talk fast.

"I'm sorry. I was worried about you last night. I know this guy did you over pretty good. I suppose I was feeling protective."

The cool expression in her eyes thawed.

"He wants to get back together," she admitted.

"What do *you* want?" he asked. He told himself it was none of his business what she decided—he had no claim on her. Had spent his entire adult life avoiding having claims on women, in fact.

"I don't know. I now understand why he didn't show. I don't like it, but I understand it. But I don't know if I feel the same way about him anymore."

She lifted her eyes to his then, and he caught a flash something soft and gentle and hopeful inside her. Something tentative and infinitely fragile. And even as part of him gave a primal roar of triumph that Greg had been vanquished, the other part of him froze in its tracks and became very, very cautious.

He wanted Sadie in his bed. He desired her enormously, couldn't stop thinking about her. But he wasn't the man to offer her love and marriage—and that was what that vulnerable, hopeful, soft look was all about. He wasn't stupid. Emotions were his stock-in-trade, the tools and materials he used to craft the television dramas that had made his career. Sadie was beginning to think beyond sex. And he didn't have anything else to offer.

His thoughts slid to the film script he'd completed recently, and to the other partially fleshed-out ideas crowding his computer. Next year, he had a tentative arrangement to work with an up-and-coming director on a movie, shadowing the guy's moves so he could start to learn some behind-the-camera craft. Once he was confident he wouldn't look a fool, he'd start working on a deal to direct the low-budget script he'd had in his bottom drawer for the past few years. Then there was the production company he wanted to set up... There was too much undone in his life yet for him to even consider settling down. He wasn't ready yet. Not by a long shot. He'd spent so much time being the dumb kid, he still had a lot of ground to cover. He had plans, dreams, goals. He couldn't even think about tying himself down before he'd conquered every challenge he'd set for himself.

"I guess the only thing you can do is wait and see," he said slowly. Noncommittally. Cautiously.

She stared at him for a long moment. Then her gaze dropped and her expression became shuttered.

"Yes. I guess you're right," she said.

She smiled, a polite gesture that didn't reach her eyes. Then she retreated to her office.

Making his way to his own turf, Dylan tried to name the strange sensation that had darted through his belly as she'd smiled her tight little smile and turned away.

He'd felt as though he'd fumbled something very important. He shook his head sharply before sitting behind his desk. It wasn't his place to judge what Sadie decided to do. It was her life, after all. There was nothing between him and Sadie except sex. Great, sweaty, noisy, earth-shaking sex, but still only sex. It was her decision, end of story. It was none of his business.

But when he saw her talking to her ex-fiancé at the local café at lunchtime, it felt very much like his business. He stopped on the other side of the street and stared as Greg reached for her hand and talked earnestly. She didn't drag her hand away or slap him or even shake her head. She listened. She didn't take her eyes from his face once.

Jesus, she was actually considering taking the jerk back!

Dylan couldn't believe it. Until that moment, he'd had himself convinced that she was in no danger of making such a huge, monumental mistake. But he'd seen it with his very own eyes. She was giving the jerk a second chance.

He forced himself to go on his way, but for the rest of the afternoon his attention was shot to hell. He was good for about three minutes' work before his thoughts once again cycled back to Sadie. It really burned him up that Biff-the-amazing-disappearing-fiancé thought he could wander back into her life and pick things up where he'd left them. And that Sadie would even consider letting a bastard like that back into her life…

In Dylan's book, any man who was self-centered enough to leave Sadie to face a church full of friends and family on her own was a sniveling, crawling, yellow-bellied lowlife. There was no excuse big enough, sincere enough, tragic enough to make Greg's no-show acceptable. In short, the putz didn't deserve Sadie, and would never make her happy.

Half a dozen times he fought the urge to march into her office and demand that she tell Greg to take a long walk off a short pier. But Dylan was the last person who could offer her romantic advice. The parameters of their relationship did not include cozy heart-to-heart chats about her future. And any attempt to change those parameters would send the wrong message Sadie's way—and he didn't want to hurt her. More than anything, he didn't want to hurt her. That was what this was all about, after all.

It wasn't until the end of the day that he found the solution to his dilemma. A slow smile spread across his face as he considered the idea from all angles and decided he liked what he saw.

Sex was the cornerstone of his relationship with Sadie. He knew without asking that the fire between them burned hotter, faster, higher than anything she'd ever experienced with Greg. Clearly the guy was wrong for her, for a whole bunch of reasons—and Dylan had until Friday night to prove as much to Sadie. Pushing himself out of his chair, he strode toward her office.

ONE MINUTE she was writing up her notes on last week's block, and the next Dylan was sitting on the corner of her desk and leaning too close.

"You busy tonight?" he asked casually.

She pulled back in her chair a little, trying to put some

distance between them. As though that was going to diminish her feelings in some way.

"Um…not really," she said.

She gave herself a mental slap. Why hadn't she told him that she was busy? She couldn't keep seeing him. She should have told him as much when she'd arrived for work this morning. But for a ridiculous moment there, when he'd asked about Greg, she'd hoped. She should have known better. Dylan had never lied to her about how he saw their relationship.

"Good. I was thinking I could cook for you. Have I ever told you about my hot tub?"

"No," she said.

She hadn't had any problem meeting Greg and telling him her decision at lunchtime today, and she'd almost married him. So why was she having so much trouble drawing a line under her fling with Dylan? It should be easier, not harder.

Steeling herself, she straightened her shoulders. It was time to be smart.

"Dylan, I don't think we should—" She broke off as he smoothed a hand up her arm. A wave of heat ricocheted its way around her body, warming every extremity before settling between her thighs.

"It's on the deck—completely private, no one can see in," he said, gliding his hand up onto her shoulder and rubbing at the hard ridge of her trapezius muscle with his thumb.

His hand on her skin felt incredible. Her eyelids dropped to half-mast and she tried to marshal her thoughts. But somehow the image of Dylan, naked and hard in a hot tub, kept popping into her mind.

"Nice?" he asked, deepening the massage.

"Mmm."

Sliding off the desk, he moved to stand behind her so that he was massaging both of her shoulders. She gave a small whimper of helplessness as her muscles melted and her nipples sprang to attention.

"That's better," he said. She shot a look upward and saw that he was enjoying an unfettered view down the neck of her top.

Very aware that they were at work, she shot a glance out into the main office, but it was after five and most of the staff had gone for the day.

"Relax. Enjoy," Dylan murmured.

She knew she should tell him to go, let him know her decision. But an energy-sapping, resolve-dissolving lassitude was settling over her. Suddenly, the only thing she could think of was that she wanted him, needed him.

Leaning forward, he pressed a kiss to the slope of her shoulder.

"Come to dinner," he said.

He slid his hands over her shoulders and down into the neckline of her T-shirt. She let out a mew of pleasure as his palms covered her breasts. She knew she should be worried about a million things—her professional reputation and emotional health being at the top of the list—but all she could do was close her eyes and shiver as his thumbs found her nipples.

"Come to dinner," he whispered in her ear.

Despite all the reasons not to, her lips formed a single word.

"Yes," she breathed.

His hands stilled abruptly as he withdrew from her top.

"Great, I'll see you at seven," he said as he headed for her door.

Sadie stared after him, suspicion narrowing her eyes. Why did she suddenly feel as though she'd just been managed?

HIS HOME WAS NOTHING like she'd expected. She'd anticipated hard edges and dark colours, but he'd filled his contemporary cliff-top home with fifties-era furniture with clean lines in warm, bold oranges and reds. The walls were neutral, decorated with beautifully mounted retro movie posters. Other movie memorabilia was also on display—an old clapperboard from

MGM, the lens from a camera, and in the corner an ancient theater light bounced light off the ceiling.

"This is nice," she said.

Being a nosy writer, her eye was drawn to the collection of papers scattered across the coffee table. Dylan's notebook computer was resting on one of the couch cushions nearby, the screen filled with text. He was working on a screenplay, she saw.

"You never stop working, do you?" she asked.

He shrugged. "Writers only have a small window to establish themselves in this town. Once we hit forty, no one wants to know us unless we've got some weight behind us."

"I never think about this stuff. I just write what I like," she said a little shamefacedly. She'd never been as career minded as she should be.

"I like the stuff I do," he said. Was it her imagination, or did he sound a little defensive?

"So, what's it about? Your screenplay? Or are you going to make me sign a confidentiality agreement first?"

He shrugged. "It's a teen movie. Vampires, high school stuff. You know."

She blinked, surprised. Teen schlock was the last thing she'd imagined Dylan writing. His TV work was so emotional and sophisticated.

"It's commercial, but so what? It's what the studios are looking for," he said. Definitely defensive.

He began shuffling his paperwork together. She lay a hand on his arm.

"I'm not judging you, Dylan. I love vampire movies. If I looked surprised it was only because it's so different from your TV work, that's all."

His shoulders relaxed a notch. "Sorry. Olly gives me a lot of shit for selling out. He doesn't get that no one is ever going to make his movie about two old men on a fishing trip. Or, even if they do, no one is ever going to go see it."

It was important for him to be successful. She understood that he was still trying to shake off those bad years of being the class idiot.

"Everyone dreams in their own way, I guess," she said diplomatically.

He looked as though he wanted to argue the toss a little more, but then he shook his head, smiled and gestured toward a doorway to his left.

"You're probably hungry, yeah?"

The kitchen boasted plain white cabinets and polished oak countertops, the simple lines giving an impression of serene calm. Partially sliced vegetables added a splash of color on a chopping block—green and red peppers, tomatoes, lettuce, onions.

"Fajitas," he explained, picking up the knife.

She studied him as he concentrated on the food, trying to define what it was that made him so fatally attractive to her, why she'd pushed aside all logic and traipsed across town to put her heart in more danger this evening.

He was the most dazzlingly attractive man she'd ever met, various movie stars included. Perhaps because he'd always appealed to her. Or maybe it was something else, something more intrinsic to who she was and who he was. Whatever—he made her breathless just by existing. The mere thought of this dinner had kept her on edge since she'd left work—already she could feel the damp heat of her own desire between her thighs, and he hadn't even touched her yet.

She thought of the screenplay spread over his coffee table, and the long hours he put in on the show. He was such a dynamic man. When she was with him, she felt so alive, so energized. He always kept her on her toes, challenging her world views, teasing her, goading her.

Suddenly she realized what she was doing—standing in his kitchen, staring at him adoringly.

This has to stop, she told herself. A heavy feeling stole over her. This had to be the last time. The heat she was feeling, the fascination, the pull—she was a goner if she didn't step back from the edge before she tumbled over. No more dinners, no more banter, definitely no more sex. Tonight had to be her swan song, her goodbye. Her last taste of paradise. A sudden desperation gripped her and when she looked down, her hands were shaking.

"Do we have to eat now?" she asked, aware that there was a needy quaver in her voice. If this was going to be her last night with him, she had to make enough memories to tide her over for a long time.

"Not hungry yet?" he asked.

Unable to respond, she reached for the buttons on her shirt, sliding first one, then another and then another free. He followed her movements slavishly, his meal preparations completely forgotten. Exhaling lightly, she flicked her shirt open and slid her arms from the sleeves. She heard his sharp intake of breath as he saw her new bra—naughty see-through black mesh with a single bloodred poppy embroidered high on one cup. Sliding a finger into her mouth, she sucked on it briefly before sliding it inside the thin fabric of her bra. Her nipple pebbled greedily, eager for his touch.

"That's an excellent idea, it being a warm night and all," he said.

His eyes locked on hers, he slid his own shirt off, revealing his impressive chest. Her heart skittered in anticipation and she squeezed her thighs together, already imagining him there.

Then, to her astonishment, he turned back to the vegetables. "Maybe we should eat first, on second thought," he said.

She stared at him for a moment, lust fizzing through her veins as the rhythmic sound of his chopping filled the room.

She was about to object when his mouth quirked and the corners of his eyes crinkled with amusement. Laughter and desire bubbled up inside her in equal measures as she understood what he was doing—teasing her. Without hesitation, she reached for the zipper on her skirt. Two could play at that game. Her black mini slid down her legs to reveal the garter belt and stockings she wore beneath. And nothing else.

She'd fretted over making such a bold statement before she'd come over, but now she felt a fierce wash of satisfaction as the smug look froze on his face as his gaze traveled up and down her body. There was a long moment of tense silence as desire crackled between them like electricity. Then, wiping his hands on a towel, he reached for the snap on his jeans. Her gaze gravitated to the hard length of his erection as he pulled his cargo pants and boxers down over his hips and kicked them off.

Sure she'd won, she took a step forward—but he turned toward the stovetop to collect a frying pan.

"Dinner will probably be about five minutes, if you want to pour yourself a glass of wine," he said.

She stared at the perfection of his tight male butt and broad, strong shoulders, shocked to the very core. Surely he wasn't going to deny her? Not now?

He spoke without turning around.

"When I was a kid, I wanted this toy truck at the local shop. Mom wanted to buy it for me, but Dad insisted I earn it. So they bought the truck, and they kept it in the cupboard until I'd mowed the lawn and washed the car enough to pay it off. It took four weeks, but that truck was the best toy I ever had. Mostly because I had to wait for it. The magic of anticipation, I guess."

The tension in her shoulders eased as she got it. He wanted to see how long they could wait. Stretch it out until they couldn't take it anymore.

If anything, the idea only increased her desire. For the next five minutes he concentrated on cooking the chicken and beef and serving up the fillings in a series of neat white bowls, and she tried to get her breathing under control. Soon they were sitting opposite each other at his kitchen table, highly aroused and unbearably aware of each other.

Noting the tremor in his hand when he passed the platter of tortillas, she felt marginally relieved. She wasn't the only one struggling with the concept of delayed gratification here.

As the meal progressed, she sipped at her wine sparingly, but she felt drunk with need. Every time his eyes slid over her body, she imagined his hands following in their wake, and she grew more and more aroused. The cool of the timber chair beneath her bottom, the brush of her own arms against the sides of her breasts, the strong flavors of their meal—every sensation seemed heightened, magnified.

Aware that she couldn't last much longer, she decided to up the ante. Shifting her legs apart, she shamelessly ensured that he could see the dark, wet heart of her. His gaze arrowed in on her with single-minded intent, and she thought she had him… Then he reached for a tortilla and began methodically assembling another fajita. Frustration choked her as he polished off his creation in two big mouthfuls, licking the juices from his fingers with sensuous gusto. She shivered—she wanted his tongue on her, his hands on her, his hardness inside her, and anticipation was driving her crazy.

By the time he was serving her fresh berries with vanilla whipped cream and crunchy meringue, she was ready to admit defeat. He managed to brush her shoulder half a dozen times with his erection as he spooned berries into her bowl before adding a dollop of cream. As he sank into his chair opposite her, she finally cracked. She was practically sliding off her chair with lust, and she could take no more.

Her chair slid back abruptly as she stood. Her stiletto heels clicked on the floorboards as she walked around the table. Very deliberate, she shrugged out of her bra, dipped her fingers into the cream on top of his berries and smeared a generous amount over each nipple. Then she straddled him, almost groaning as she felt his hard shaft press against her slick heat.

"I want the truck," she said boldly.

He went very still, then he grinned hugely before ducking his head to her breasts. The first touch of his mouth on her nipples nearly made her scream, she was so turned on.

He sucked the cream from each tip with greedy abandon, then he was lifting her onto the table, shoving plates out of the way as he spread her before him. His dark gray eyes glinting with desire, he reached for his dessert bowl. She shivered as he dropped a handful of berries onto her belly, squirmed as he smoothed cream onto her thighs. Then she could do nothing but gasp as he set himself to the task of devouring her.

By the time she'd emerged from the haze of lust he'd woven around them, it was the early hours of the morning. She left him sleeping in his bed. All the way home, she trembled with remembered desire and the determination to put an end to their affair first thing the next day. She had to pull out before it was too late. First thing tomorrow, she would end it. Definitely.

10

SHE TOLD HERSELF the same thing every day for the next three days, but each night she wound up in his arms again. She was never quite sure how it happened. One minute she would be on the verge of telling him they were over, the next she would be agreeing to dinner again. Tuesday night it was a picnic after-hours in the Getty Museum, courtesy of one of Dylan's friends who worked on security. The next it was dinner at a little restaurant in the hills he knew. Afterward, he pulled over on the way home to make love to her against the side of the car, whispering praise for her passion in her ear all the while.

She should have said no to it all. But she couldn't. She was out of control, running full pelt down the steepest slope of her life with no way of stopping.

And slowly, insidiously, she began to wonder if she even needed to stop. All her life she'd despised women who ignored the warnings men gave them at the start of relationships. Dylan had been absolutely frank about his desires—sex, no commitment—and she'd believed him. But every time he looked deeply into her eyes as he slid inside her, every time he pressed a kiss to the nape of her neck, or smoothed the back of his hand across her cheekbone, she was sure she saw something more in his eyes than simple lust.

As she waited for him to answer the door to her knock on Thursday evening, she admitted to herself that she'd begun to hope that there was a future for the two of them. He cared for her. She was sure he did. She knew he respected her, that he valued her expertise, that he shared her sense of humor. Was it so crazy to think that his feelings for her ran beyond the strictly sexual?

People changed. Expectations changed, all the time. Who was to say that, no matter what intention he'd set out with when they began their fling, he hadn't discovered deeper, more longer-lasting emotions within himself? She had, and she certainly hadn't been looking for them.

"Hey."

As usual, the mere sight of him was enough to set her pulse racing. He was barefoot and wearing a pair of faded jeans and a plain black T-shirt. He looked delicious, good enough to eat.

"Hey, yourself," she said, standing on tiptoe to press a kiss to his lips in greeting.

The kiss quickly got carried away, and before she knew it he was backing her onto the couch and tugging her shirt from the waistband of her skirt.

Smoothing a hand up her legs, he lifted his head from her breast when he encountered nothing but bare skin above her thighs.

"No underwear again," he murmured, smiling his approval.

"It seems kind of superfluous when I'm with you," she said, pressing butterfly kisses to his neck and shoulder.

"Another thing to add to my list of things I worship about you," he whispered in her ear as he slid clever fingers into the damp curls between her legs.

She stilled for a heartbeat, the significance of his words resonating within her.

He didn't say love, she warned herself. But it was too late, the damage was done—his almost-declaration forced her to acknowledge the burgeoning, fledgling truth in her heart. She loved him. Probably had for weeks, even if she'd put off admitting it to herself with her stalling tactics and prevarications. She'd fallen, hard. So hard she might never get up again.

She thought about him every spare moment. She knew the exact second he walked into a room, even if she had her back to him. And she could recognize his voice in a crowd of thousands. She craved his touch like a drug—but she craved his smile and his eyes on her and his laughter almost as much. She felt a warm glow of pride every time she heard someone praise his work, and she was awed by his talent and discipline as he crafted some of the best episodes *Ocean Boulevard* had ever produced.

As he slid a finger inside her while sending his thumb on a slow, lazy pass over her clitoris, she clutched at his shoulders and rode a wave of realization and passion.

She wasn't blind to his faults. He was arrogant, impulsive, cocky. The same discipline and focus that had helped him come to terms with his dyslexia made him appear distant and cold at times. He worked too hard, pushed himself beyond what was healthy. But it was all part of what made him who he was, and she wouldn't change him for the world because she had fallen in love with him, hook, line and sinker, irretrievably, irreversibly, forever.

"You are so hot," he groaned in her ear as he fumbled with his belt buckle.

Her new self-knowledge made her tremble with an urgent need to be as close to him as she could get. She helped him release his zipper, pulling his straining erection from his boxers with eager hands.

"Now," she begged breathlessly, guiding him to the heart of her. "Now." All the thoughts and feelings and fears and desires of the past few weeks welled up inside her as he entered her, his thickness filling her, his body crushing hers into the sofa.

She closed her eyes as sensation and emotion overwhelmed her. So gentle but so strong. So fierce but so tender. So demanding but so generous. The contradictions of his lovemaking thrilled her. He felt so right, so perfect.

She loved him so much.

Her orgasm crashed over her, undeniable, intense. She cried out incoherently, hands clutching at his shoulders as she convulsed around him. She felt him tense, knew that her climax had triggered his, and reveled in the moment of closeness as he ground his hips against hers.

Afterward, he lay beside her on the sofa, his chest rising and falling sharply as he struggled to catch his breath.

She felt radiant and faintly dizzy with her newly admitted love for him. Her hands never still, she mapped the smooth planes of his body, each stroke of her hands an unspoken endearment. Turning her face toward his, she loved him with her eyes, memorizing the angles of his face, the dark spike of his too-long eyelashes, the full curve of his lower lip.

She was thinking how she craved these quiet moments after the storm had passed almost as much as she craved the storm itself when he lifted his head and smiled at her. A frown quickly replaced the smile, however, and he brushed a hand across her cheek.

"You're crying," he said, holding up his wet hand to prove it.

She'd been so lost in the intensity of the moment her tears hadn't registered. Not quite sure what to say, she simply held his eye. His frown deepened as he stared at her, then he abruptly pulled away and began setting his clothes to rights.

Aware that something had shifted, she followed suit, tugging her T-shirt back into place and smoothing her skirt down.

"Where are you going tomorrow night?" Dylan asked suddenly.

She shook her head briefly, confused. "Tomorrow night?" she repeated.

"Dinner. With Greg."

She blinked. She'd been so lost in Dylan this week that she'd almost forgotten.

"I canceled on Monday," she said without thinking.

She could feel him stiffen beside her. "Monday?"

"Yes. I had lunch with him on Monday and I told him it was over."

Abruptly he headed for the kitchen.

"I ordered take-away Chinese. It's getting cold," he said over his shoulder.

She stared after him, not quite sure what had just happened. She followed him into the kitchen. He didn't look up from spooning portions onto plates, and the silence stretched awkwardly between them.

"What's going on?" she finally asked.

He shrugged a shoulder. "Nothing."

She frowned. "Dylan," she said simply.

"You should have told me you'd canceled dinner with him," he said.

"Why?"

"Look, forget about it," he said. He sounded distant, withdrawn.

"I don't understand why it makes a difference whether I'm having dinner with Greg or not. Didn't we agree he was none of your business?" she said carefully.

"It changes things, that's all."

"Between us?"

He shrugged a shoulder. She narrowed her eyes.

"How does it change things between us? We're just about the sex, right?" she said.

He sighed heavily and ran a hand through his hair.

"You should have told me," he repeated again, looking world-weary.

"Why?"

"Because you just cried while we were having sex," he said baldly.

She flinched from the accusation in his tone.

"So?"

"So it's not just about sex any more, is it?" he said.

The look he shot her was challenging. She looked away, opening her mouth to deny his observation. But then she remembered the intensity of her feelings as he'd held her, the feeling of rightness and belonging. Was there any point in lying about her feelings when he'd looked into her eyes and seen her tears? She lifted her head. She wasn't ashamed of loving him.

"You're right, it's not. I've fallen in love with you," she said.

To her everlasting surprise, he swore and slammed his fist down onto the counter. Running his hands through his hair, he raised his eyes to the ceiling in a gesture of helplessness, then turned away from her, clearly not knowing where to put himself. Finally he shook his head, then brushed past her. She heard the slide of the screen door onto his deck, then nothing as he disappeared outside.

She stood frozen in his kitchen for a handful of heartbeats. She was shell-shocked, completely taken aback by his reaction. Then a slow anger began to burn in her belly.

He was leaning on the railing when she found him, glaring broodingly out into the night.

"I told you the deal up front," he said when he saw her. All the heat had gone out of him and his voice sounded flat and sad. "I don't want a relationship."

"I get that. What I don't get is that I just told you that I love you, and your one reaction was to swear and walk away. It's not a crime, Dylan. Or an insult."

"I don't want you to love me," he said. "I didn't ask for it."

Pain sliced through her, but she fought on.

"It's an offering, not an obligation," she said.

"It comes with about a million strings attached, and you know it," he said. The eyes he turned on her were tortured. "I didn't want to hurt you, Sadie. I told you how I felt up front. We were about fun, nothing more."

"I can't help how I feel," she said. "You think I was

looking for love? I almost got married a month ago. The last thing I expected was that I would develop these feelings for you. But I did."

He sighed heavily. "I'm sorry. I thought I was doing you a favor, helping you…"

She frowned. "What are you talking about?"

He stared out into the darkness. "When Greg turned up this week. I thought you were thinking about taking him back. The guy's a jerk—he doesn't deserve you. I wanted to make sure you didn't settle for second best."

Her eyes widened as she got it. Dinner at his place. The Getty Museum. The hill restaurant. Tonight. What she'd read as mutual attraction, two people unable to get enough of each other, was actually Dylan doing her a *favor.*

She'd thought he was as fascinated and attracted by her and she was by him. She'd thought…

"You…you… I don't even have a word for what you are. Arrogant jerk doesn't begin to cover it."

"You're too good for him, Sadie," he said gently. "I didn't want you to throw yourself away like that."

"How noble of you. How self-sacrificing. Every time you got a hard-on you must have been patting yourself on the back for pitching in for poor old Sadie," she said.

The enormity of what had just happened rose up to swamp her. Dylan Anderson had broken her heart again. All the time that she'd thought he was reciprocating her feelings, growing closer to her, losing his head the way she was losing hers, he'd been doing a good deed.

Suddenly she couldn't stand the sight of him. She felt cheated. The worst thing was, she knew the reality was that she'd cheated herself—she'd made him into something he wasn't, painted him in hero's colors and thrown herself at his feet. And now she was getting her just deserts.

Jaw set, she swept through the house, scooping up her coat

and purse on the way. She could hear him following her, but she didn't look back.

"Sadie," he said as she wrenched his front door open.

She spun to face him, holding back her tears through sheer force of will.

"Don't you dare say you're sorry," she said, her voice fierce. "I don't want your pity."

Then she stumbled out to her car and screeched off into the night.

CLAUDIA ANSWERED on the third knock, her silk robe half-tied, her hair smooshed flat on one side of her head.

"I'm sorry it's so late. I'm sorry I'm such a bad friend. But I need you," Sadie sobbed as soon as she saw her friend's sleep-creased face.

"Sadie!" Claudia said, stepping forward instantly to draw her into an embrace. "My God, what happened?"

"I'm such an idiot! How could I let this happen? Why couldn't I see?" Sadie said, wiping the tears off her cheeks with both hands.

"Calm down," Claudia said, pushing Sadie into a chair and shoving a box of tissues into her hands. "Is this about Greg? Does he want you back? Is that it?"

Sadie shook her head, a wave of shame overtaking her as she remembered how much she'd been keeping from her friend.

"It's Dylan," she said. "I've been sleeping with him. I thought I hated him, then—Oh, God, I can't believe I fell in love with him again."

Claudia's expression shifted from concerned to surprised to bewildered.

"Okay, now I'm really confused."

Further conversation was stymied by a knock at the door. Claudia shook her head and went to answer it.

"Is she okay?" Grace asked as she stepped over the threshold.

Sadie stared at her, baffled.

"Dylan called me," Grace explained as she shrugged out of her coat. "He didn't want you to be alone. When you didn't turn up at home I figured you'd be here."

A surge of rage burned through Sadie at this further evidence of Dylan's magnanimous interference in her life. For a full ten minutes she paced Claudia's carpet, railing and gesticulating and venting. Somehow, Claudia finally pieced it all together. Her dark eyes were sad as she regarded Sadie.

"I wish you'd told me. I can't believe all this has been going on and I had no idea," Claudia said.

"I'm sorry. It's the most unprofessional thing I've ever done in my life. I should have said something that first day when you told me you'd hired him, but I knew we didn't have anyone else for the story ed role. I didn't want to let you down. And now I've let you down even more," Sadie said. Suddenly she felt very small and stupid, and she sank onto the couch.

Claudia's hand cut through the air in a frustrated chop.

"Don't be ridiculous, Sadie! You slept with a colleague, that's all. I don't give a hoot. But I do care that you've been so unhappy and you haven't felt able to talk to me. You and Grace are my closest friends, and you're about a million times more important to me than some stupid job."

"I'm sorry," Sadie said quietly. "I should have trusted you. I know better."

Claudia shook her head. "Maybe if I hadn't been running around all the time playing superproducer you might have been able to talk to me."

"This is not your fault, Claud!" Sadie said.

"We all know whose fault it is," Grace said harshly. "The question is, how do we dispose of his body?"

It was such a blood-thirsty thought, delivered with such venom, that they all three burst into laughter. Near hysteria reigned for a few minutes, and the tissue box did the rounds before Sadie could talk again.

"He warned me," she said quietly. "I should have listened."

"Yeah, you're a real bitch for falling in love with him," Grace said.

"Not a bitch. Just stupid," Sadie corrected.

"It sounds to me as though he's given you plenty of encouragement to be stupid, Sade," Claudia said. "In fact, it sounds to me as though Mr. Anderson has been having himself a whale of a time, sitting on high, ordering things to suit himself."

"I knew it the moment I saw him—too good-looking to live," Grace said.

For the second time that night Sadie noted the acerbic tone to her friend's comments. Grace had always had a tongue in her head, that was for sure, but it wasn't usually this astringent.

"You okay, Gracie?" she asked tentatively. Belatedly, she registered her friend's appearance, her concern increasing as she took in the oversize polka-dot clip-on earrings, a hot-pink brooch shaped like a flamingo and the faux-fur coat Grace had teamed with a silk flower in her hair and an alarming number of mismatched bracelets on her arm. Her fingernails glittered with deep crimson nail polish, and a pair of false eyelashes clung like spiders to her eyelids. Bright red lipstick, heavy rouge and a stick-on beauty spot completed the damage.

Grace always dressed to suit her own unique style, but her look was unfailingly elegant. Tonight, however, she looked like a child who had been playing dress-up with her mother's jewelry and makeup case.

"I'm fine. You're the one who's just been screwed over by Mr. Big Dick," Grace said dismissively.

Claudia met Sadie's speculative glance with a frown. Something was definitely up. The only other time they'd seen Grace this badly put together had been when her beloved grandfather had passed on.

"Come on, Gracie, no more secrets," Claudia ordered.

"Seriously, I'm fine," Grace said. "Just a little stressed over having Hope staying with me." She almost got away with it, but her voice got caught on her sister's name somehow, and suddenly there were tears in her eyes. Grace grabbed a tissue and mopped at her face hastily.

"I'm tired, that's all," she said again.

Claudia and Sadie slid their arms around their friend's waist and waited. Finally Grace could contain the misery inside herself no longer.

"W-when I got home from the bonding weekend, Hope's boyfriend was there. She phoned him the moment I left and he flew out from New York right away."

"Has he been giving you trouble?" Sadie asked, outrage at the ready.

"Nothing like that. Turns out that the black eye was an accident. They were fighting about some girl Hope caught him flirting with, and she started throwing stuff at him. He threw things back, and something clocked her in the eye."

Claudia made a disgusted noise. "Are you sure Hope isn't the actress in the family?" she asked. "All that baloney about him hitting her."

"Your sister lied to you so she could mooch off you. No wonder you're upset," Sadie said.

Grace twisted a tissue between her fingers and shook her head. "I knew she was lying weeks ago. She told me three different versions of how she got the black eye."

Grace lapsed into silence, and Claudia squeezed her arm.

"Come on. Better out than in."

Grace shifted uncomfortably, then made a negligent gesture with her hand.

"It's nothing, honestly. I just overheard them talking about me when I got home on Sunday afternoon. It doesn't mean anything."

She was pretty convincing—except for the way her generous lips were pressed together as though she were working overtime to hold her emotions in check.

"What did they say?" Sadie asked gently. She didn't want to hurt her friend, but Grace was obviously dwelling on something, and Claudia was right—better out in the light of day than in the dark where it could turn into something bigger and scarier.

"Zane—that's Hope's boyfriend—was talking about our family. About how much alike Serena and Hope and Felicity are, you know. How beautiful they are. He said—it was a joke, really—he said that he was surprised Mom and Dad didn't throw me back when I was born. He said I let the team down and he wanted to know if I was adopted."

She said it matter-of-factly, as though she was simply reporting what she'd heard. Sadie's hands curled into fists.

"What did Hope say?" she asked, knowing only a loved one could strike a blow as deep as the one that had obviously wounded Grace.

"She laughed. She said—" Grace broke off, tears squeezing from her eyes as she remembered her sister's cruelty. She struggled to continue for a long moment. "She said I was the family mascot," she finally whispered.

Claudia swore pithily, and Sadie closed her eyes for a brief moment. She knew Grace's history with men, her lifelong struggle with low-self esteem, her complex and sometimes not-very-healthy relationships with her sisters, particularly Serena. And so did Hope. But it hadn't stopped her from betraying her sister to a fickle rat who was about as important in her life as a disposable plate.

Claudia was shaking with anger, Sadie saw. Sliding off the couch, Claudia knelt in front of Grace. Reaching out to take her hands, Claudia waited until her friend had stopped sobbing and could meet her eyes before speaking.

"Have I ever lied to you?" she asked very seriously.

Grace shook her head. "No."

"That's right. I told you that hat looked stupid the time we went to the races, and I told you never to wear dark brown lipstick again. And I'll tell you right now that that beauty spot is ridiculous."

Grace smiled faintly at Claudia's characteristic bluntness, and Sadie rubbed her hand in comforting circles on Grace's back.

"But I'll also tell you this. You are *beautiful,* Grace Wellington. You have flawless skin, the sexiest mouth I have ever seen, tits to die for and an ass that makes men's mouths water. You are stunning. What you are *not* is a stick-insect anemic blonde with a lollipop head and ribs you can play the xylophone on. No, they don't put women like you on the cover of *Vogue* magazine. Not this decade, anyway, but fortunately you're also one of the most talented script writers I have ever worked with, so you're not exactly hanging out for that all-important phone call. You're also generous, kind, funny, smart as a whip, and wicked-good behind the wheel of a car. Your sister, on the other hand, is a screw-up. She spends every cent she has ever earned, she has appalling taste in men and she told me last time she saw me that she considered reading 'over-rated.' She's also vain, selfish and cruel. So—who's opinion counts more with you? Mine or hers?"

Grace was silent for a long time, then slowly the hurt look faded from her eyes.

Claudia nodded as though she was very satisfied. "Good. That was what I thought."

Grace sniffed and took a swipe at her still-damp cheeks.

"I shouldn't have let it get to me. But I just wasn't expecting it. They were in my bedroom, the door was open. I guess they didn't hear me come in…"

"More likely they didn't care," Sadie said. "Gracie, you need to give your sister her marching orders. She's been sponging off you for weeks, spinning bullshit stories to keep you feeling sorry for her. Tell her no more—tell her her stay at Château Mooch is over."

Grace opened her mouth to protest, but nothing came out. Her jaw shut with a click, then she nodded.

"You're right."

"Kick 'em out tonight," Claudia said, the battle light well and truly in her eyes now. "They've got money. They can find a hotel."

Sadie laughed at Claudia's ruthlessness. "Man, you are one feisty little lady," she said.

Claudia planted her hands on her hips. "Are we going over there to kick 'em out or what?" she asked. "I'm in the mood to really yell at someone."

Grace took a deep breath. "Yes. Let's do it."

"Give me five minutes to get dressed," Claudia said. She swept from the room, then quickly popped back in again. Her dark gaze speared Sadie.

"Then we're finding an all-night diner and pancakes, okay, Sade? Pancakes with lots of ice cream."

Sadie nodded her agreement, and they heard the swish of Claudia's gown as she took off again.

The room was silent for a moment as she and Grace sat with their own emotions for a beat.

"I'm sorry things didn't work out with Dylan," Grace said after a while. "Despite what I said earlier, he actually seemed pretty human for a male."

Sadie smiled sadly. "You know what the worse things is? I actually think he does care for me. There's definitely more going on between us than just sex. But he's so dead-set against getting into a relationship—it's like he's drawn a line in the sand and he can't even think about crossing over it."

"He's pretty ambitious," Grace observed. "I heard him talking to his agent on his cell phone once during a break. He's got screenplays out there, concepts for new shows—he must never sleep."

Sadie nodded, remembering all the times she'd seen him starting early and finishing late, and the vampire movie that he worked on at home. No doubt that was only the tip of the iceberg, too—he probably had dozens of projects in the works.

She shook her head, forcing herself to let it go. "It doesn't really matter why. The important bit is that it's over. I can't make him want the same things that I want, or feel the same way that I feel."

Grace squeezed her hand sympathetically, and Sadie dropped her head onto her friend's shoulder.

It was good to have the comfort of her friends around her again, but nothing could stop the sadness rising inside her.

When was she going to learn where Dylan Anderson was concerned?

DYLAN ENTERED WORK the next morning with a heavy step. He'd hurt Sadie last night. He'd handled the whole situation badly, and she had every right to be pissed with him. It was probably for the best—in his experience, an angry woman got over a broken heart faster than a sad one. And he wanted Sadie to get over him, he really did. She deserved to be happy. She deserved love, with all the usual accoutrements—marriage, children, hearth and home. She'd simply made the mistake of looking for them in the wrong place.

For a moment he had a flash of how it could have been had he been a different kind of guy. He could be the one who got to grow old with Sadie, the one who got to father her children and hold her in his arms each night.

For a second, a terrible longing welled up inside him. Like a Norman Rockwell painting, the images in his mind were too pure, too shiny and perfect. He knew they were idealized, unrealistic. But he wanted them. He wanted *her,* so badly. It was the first time he'd admitted as much to himself, and the realization rocked him to the core. He'd avoided emotional involvement his whole life for this exact reason—nothing was ever going to come of him caring for Sadie Post except unhappiness.

He wasn't ready to share his life with anyone. There were still things to put in place, heights to scale, challenges to conquer. He didn't have room for anyone else. Not until he'd achieved his goals. Five years from now, once his movie career was well established. Maybe ten years—then he'd have enough money and enough points on the scoreboard to think about a wife and family.

He'd learned the hard way about having goals and achieving them—he'd still be flipping burgers in a diner if he hadn't had the discipline to beat his dyslexia. He wasn't about to set all that aside because Sadie Post set his world on fire. Too much was at stake to indulge himself that way.

She was already at her desk when he walked in, but she didn't look up when he passed her doorway. To his surprise, he saw that the lights were on in Claudia's and Grace's offices, too. Both of them gave him a cool, unflinching look when he nodded a greeting. He smiled grimly to himself as he shrugged out of his leather jacket. The wagons had well and truly been circled.

He tried to talk to Sadie a number of times throughout the day, but each time either Claudia or Grace quickly stepped up to interrupt the conversation. Those wagons again—and he was definitely on the wrong side of the circle. As the three of them exited the offices in a tight little gaggle at the end of the day, he felt a stirring of what felt distinctly like jealousy. He'd grown used to sharing his days with Sadie over the past month. He looked forward to her laughter, her sly digs, her ready wit. He knew he had no right to her friendship now—he was the last person she wanted to hang with after the ham-fisted way he'd handled himself the previous evening. But as he watched the way she tempered her long-legged stride to match Claudia's shorter one, and the way she laughingly smoothed Grace's rumpled coat collar into place, he felt more alone than he'd ever felt in his life before. He missed her already, and she'd barely been gone from his life for a day

By the middle of the following week he was desperate to speak to her. Claudia and Grace ensured they were never alone with each other, and he'd grown increasingly frustrated. He needed to know she was okay. And to apologize for being such a jerk when she'd told him how she felt. Then he could let it rest. It wasn't the whole truth, but it was good enough to get past his internal editor.

Which was why he was lying in wait for her in the parking lot on Wednesday morning, standing in the shadows of the building like a cut-rate stalker. Eventually she arrived, and he saw dark circles under her eyes as she got out of her car. Since he'd been having trouble sleeping himself, he wondered if she'd been lying awake thinking about him the way he'd been thinking about her. Not only about the sex—although he thought about that a lot. But he also thought about the way her nose wrinkled when she laughed, and the way she smelled. And the way she had of looking him dead in the eye and nailing him with a killer line.

"Sadie," he said, pushing off from the wall and striding toward her.

Her head swung sharply around and he saw the unmasked pain in her eyes before she brought the shutters down. Tucking her satchel under her arm, she pursed her lips.

"If this is about work, we can talk inside," she said.

"I wanted to see how you're doing," he said, instantly feeling like a complete idiot. It was obvious how she was doing—she was sad and lonely. About as sad and lonely as he was.

"It's okay, Dylan—I'm not about to dissolve into a screaming heap because you don't return my feelings," she said. "No need to feel obligated or uncomfortable."

She started to walk away, and he reached out to grab her arm. She flinched from him and he felt a pathetic flare of triumph. She was afraid to be close to him, afraid that the old heat would take over if her skin touched his.

"I'm sorry. About last week. I was an ass," he said, holding up both hands to assure her that he wasn't going to touch her.

"Yeah, you were. Don't worry—next time I feel the urge to tell you that I love you, I'll shoot myself in the foot or something slightly less painful."

She started to head off again, and the sight of her walking away from him burst something inside him. Before he knew it, he was talking.

"It wasn't just about the sex. I mean, for me, as well. I—I have feelings for you," he said.

She stopped, then slowly turned to face him. Her face was very still.

"And?"

He shrugged. "And I'm sorry. I shouldn't have let it get out of control, but I didn't admit to myself how I felt until it was too late."

She shook her head, bemused. "Let me get this straight. You're sorry you have feelings for me?" she asked.

"Yes. No." He sighed and ran a hand through his hair, trying to order his thoughts. "I don't mean it like that. I'm sorry if I hurt you, if I led you on. I didn't mean for that to happen. It was supposed to be fun."

"How can you lead me on if you have feelings for me, too?" she asked.

"Because it can't go anywhere, Sadie. It would only end in disaster. There's no time for us. Not for a long time. I've got commitments next year, one of the networks is interested in a show I pitched. And I've had some interest in my screenplay. I can't walk away from those opportunities. There's no room in my life for anything serious."

She stared at him for a long moment, then her eyebrows rose and a dawning light came into her eyes.

"My God. I've been kicking myself for the past few days for being stupid enough to fall in love with someone who doesn't love me back, but now I get it. *You're* the dumb ass, not me. You're going to let us slip through your fingers because you think that rewriting the past is more important than the future."

"What? This has nothing to do with the past," he said impatiently.

"Yeah? You're one of the most successful, talented, driven people I know. And you're going to miss out on life because you're so busy trying to gain the approval of all those people who let you down when you were a kid."

His head reared back as he snorted. "What a load of bullshit."

"Is it? You're independently wealthy, you have a great home, a Ducati—you've got it all. But none of that's enough for you, is it? Because you still hear their voices in your head telling you you're no good. When is enough going to be enough, Dylan? When are you going to stop trying to prove them wrong?"

He flinched, then took a step away from her. "Someone's been watching a little too much *Oprah,*" he said derisively.

"You're a fool." She reached out a hand and ran a finger along the tender skin of his inner arm. About a million neurons fired inside him all at once and a surge of desire rocketed to his groin.

"Do you really think that something so perfect comes along more than once in a lifetime? And you're going to throw it away," Sadie said sadly.

He stared at her. She closed her eyes for a long beat, almost as though she was making a wish or saying a prayer, then she opened them again and leaned close to kiss him on the cheek.

"Goodbye, Dylan," she said.

Then she walked away from him.

He let her go. It was for the best. As for the psychobabble bullshit she'd dumped on him—he knew what was going on in his own head, thank you very much. His obligation to her was over. No more loitering around feeling guilty—they were square.

The kicker came when he saw the neatly addressed envelope on his desk when he entered his office. He stared at the small card it enclosed for a few beats before letting out a short, sharp bark of laughter. An invitation to the Grovedale High School reunion. How ridiculously appropriate.

Screwing it into a tight ball, he flipped it into the trash without a second thought.

FOUR WEEKS LATER Sadie stood at the photocopier, a stack of papers in her hands. She'd finished her copying long ago, but she still hovered, shamelessly eavesdropping on the conversation she could hear drifting out from the story room. A small smile curved her lips as she listened to Dylan's humorous account of a recent restaurant outing with his friend Olly. She missed his way with words so much, the gravel he got in his voice when he was trying not to crack up and spoil a punch line, the way his dark eyes sparkled with suppressed laughter. She missed so many things about him.

Once again the familiar impulse gripped her, and she clenched her hands around her paperwork to stop herself from racing next door and throwing herself at his feet and begging him to give them a chance. It was too sad for words. She'd fallen in love with a man who was so obsessed with proving himself to the world that he'd shut himself off to all other aspects of life.

In the room next door, someone made a low comment she couldn't quite catch, and suddenly Dylan's rich, low laugh rang out. Something twisted deep inside her at the sound as she remembered the laughter they'd shared as they made love in the wilds of the Big Bear camping grounds. Hot tears filled her eyes and she blinked them away furiously. Scuttling back to the sanctuary of her office, she shut the door and faced an awful truth.

She was right back where she'd started all those years ago—she was in love with Dylan Anderson, with not a chance in hell of getting what she wanted. She might as well be Beanpole Sadie again, slinking self-consciously down the halls of Grovedale High, hanging out for any scrap of attention that the untouchable Dylan might throw her way.

The thought was so crushing that for a moment she was filled with despair. All the old self-doubt washed over her. For a second she slumped into her chair, letting her hair hang over her face the way it had all those years ago.

The sounds of the office receded into the distance as she wallowed in her unrequited longing. Why couldn't he love her the way she loved him? What was wrong with her?

Then the phone rang on her desk and she was jolted back to the here and now. Her gaze traveled across the paperwork on her desk to the posters on her wall and down to her much-loved, battle-scarred satchel on the floor as the phone shrilled out its call like a metaphysical alarm clock. Finally her gaze settled on the invitation to her high-school reunion she'd received a month ago. At the time, she'd been fresh from Dylan's rejection and she'd tossed it in the bin. Grace had rescued it and pinned it to her board.

"You never know. It might be good to exorcise a few demons," she'd said.

Now Sadie's spine straightened as her focus sharpened on the small square of card.

Shy Sadie Post was dead, never to return. She might still love Dylan Anderson, but she was no wallflower anymore, standing by waiting for him to gift her with his attention. Not this time around.

Finally the phone stopped ringing as the caller gave up, and Sadie picked up the receiver to make her own call.

"Grace, I need your help," she said when her friend picked up across the office. "I need to find a dress. A really spectacular dress…"

THE YEARS ROLLED BACK as Dylan cruised into the darkened parking lot at Grovedale High the following evening. He hadn't planned on coming. He hadn't even consciously remembered the date or time of the reunion. But somehow he'd found himself gravitating to his old stomping ground as night fell. Lines of cars filled the bulk of the lot, signaling a strong turnout—it seemed nostalgia was a big draw card. He parked his bike off to one side and sat for a moment, listening to the throb of music leaking out from the opened doors to the gym. He could just imagine all the old hits they'd dust off for the night—the big-hair bands, the bouncy-girl pop and bad electronica. Easing his helmet off, he slid off his bike and struck out into the school, veering away from the gym. He told himself he would just take a quick walk down memory lane before heading home. He didn't want to chew the fat with old school friends and play the so-what-do-you-do-now game.

The corridors were dark. He inhaled deeply, smelling dust and old school lunches and cheap perfume. He passed the door to the principal's office, pausing for a moment to eye the scarred oak surface. The times he'd sat out here, waiting to be disciplined for one thing or another…

He shook his head and moved on, passing the shadowed alcove under the stairs where he'd felt up Karla Bond, and winding up in front of the door to his most dreaded class— American Lit. On impulse he tried the door handle, but it was locked. He smiled at the symbology—it was true, you could never really go back.

Inevitably, he found himself drifting toward the gym. The

music grew louder, and finally he stepped into the cavernous space. Only it didn't seem half as big as he'd remembered, and the bleachers looked tired, the floor grimy and marked. The walls could have done with a good coat of paint, and the school logo needed a serious redesign.

The lighting had been dimmed to what someone probably thought was nightclub level, and an effort had been made to recreate the crepe-paper-fueled atmosphere of past school dances. Groups of people milled everywhere, the bulk of them congregating around a large buffet, although a few brave souls were trying out old moves on a make-shift dance floor.

Dylan hovered in the doorway, hands stuffed into the pockets of his leather jacket.

Why was he here? Two women who looked vaguely like older, tireder versions of Cindi Young and Carol Martin glanced his way, and someone who might have been a much fatter, balder version of his old friend Buddy Markham waved a greeting. Resigning himself to the inevitable, he started to make his way toward Buddy. Then the back of Dylan's neck prickled and an odd hush fell over the room. He didn't need to look to know who had just come in, but he turned around all the same.

She stood in the doorway, a glittering goddess in a shiny silver minidress, her long legs even longer than usual thanks to a pair of strappy silver sandals, her hair piled on top of her head in a do that managed to be both sexy and elegant at the same time. All around him, men were sucking in beer bellies, tucking in shirttails and smoothing hands over receding hairlines. He smiled a little grimly to himself. For a woman who'd accused him of trying to rewrite history, she was taking a pretty good stab at it herself.

Quite simply, she took his breath away. But then, she'd been doing that ever since she'd reentered his life a few short months ago.

"Sadie Post! I can't believe it!" the dumpy woman handing out sticky labels at the door screeched loudly. A stir rippled through the gym, closely followed by the buzz of excited conversation. And still every eye was glued to her.

He took an instinctive step forward, knowing how hard this must be for her. These people had witnessed her humiliation at his hands. She wouldn't be human if she didn't want to turn tail and run.

But she didn't run. Far from it. Instead, she squared her shoulders and stuck her chest out and started the long walk to the buffet table. Every male eye followed her—most of the female eyes, too. She moved with a slow, slinky, feline grace, her hips swaying seductively, a small, confident smile playing about her lips.

He wanted to cheer her on, to stand on a chair and raise a round of applause.

She was magnificent. Courageous. Stunning. And she'd once been his.

The thought stopped him in his tracks before he'd even started to move toward her. He corrected his path, aiming for the bleachers so he could keep an eye on her from a distance. He was about to sit when he saw him, the thin, gaunt face triggering a host of unhappy memories. Dylan's eyes narrowed. Same hawklike honker, same grim lips. The hair was grayer, the beard whiter, but the heavy-rimmed spectacles hadn't changed, along with the tweed jacket with its worn leather elbow patches.

McMasters. The asshole. Dylan's hands slid out of his pockets as he started walking, honing in on his old American Lit teacher like a heat-seeking missile.

SADIE'S HEART WAS BEATING at about a million miles an hour. Back home with Claudia and Grace doing her hair and makeup, this had seemed like a much better idea. But now she realized she was in way over her head. She didn't recognize a single soul, and the eye-catching dress Grace had helped her choose was drawing far too much attention.

But she couldn't go yet. She'd made a deal with herself—one lap of the gym, just to show herself that she'd moved on and put the old ghosts to rest. Taking a deep breath, she tried to calm her nerves. These people didn't matter—tonight was for her, not for them.

The buffet table seemed miles away, but finally she was standing in front of the punch bowl, an array of finger food spread out on either side of her. Lifting the ladle, she poured herself a cup, then sniffed the bright orange liquid to check for alcohol. Not surprisingly, she caught a whiff of spirits and wrinkled her nose. Still, there was something to be said for Dutch courage.

Taking a tentative sip, she gasped as the punch burned all the way down her throat. Her eyes watered, but she suppressed a cough manfully before dumping her cup on the table. Too much courage could be a dangerous thing, and she had work to do—namely, a single lap of the gym to complete.

Summoning the casually confident almost-smile she'd practiced all afternoon with Grace and Claudia, she began to saunter her way past her former classmates. A redheaded man with a prominent Adam's apple and a long-distance runner's physique gave her a nervous smile and a wave before flushing rosily. Beyond him, a brunette she vaguely remembered but couldn't quite place stared at her belligerently, her narrowed gaze assessing Sadie's dress critically.

Her cheek muscles were starting to ache, but she kept her smile firmly in place. Not for love or money was she going to show a moment of weakness.

Looming up on her left was a tubby blonde in a too-tight red dress. With a shock she recognized Cindi Young, former cheerleader and object of Sadie's adolescent envy. Unconsciously she injected some extra sass into her walk. Cindi had made her life hell after prom, never letting anyone forget what Dylan had done to her.

The end wall of the gym appeared ahead. One side down, three to go… Head high, she kept walking.

THE LAST TIME he'd seen McMasters, the guy had been leaning over him with a sneer on his face as he told Dylan in no uncertain terms that he was finished at Grovedale. He'd painted a picture of Dylan's abysmal grades, poor attendance record and patchy disciplinary record, explaining that Dylan was never going to be wearing a graduation gown on the school lawn so why was he hanging around when he was missing out on all the overtime he could be racking up on the deep fryer at the nearest Golden Arches? Between them, McMasters and the school's guidance counselor had effectively kicked Dylan out of school.

For years Dylan had wanted to meet McMasters again, stare him down and let him know in no uncertain terms that he'd written off the wrong kid. Like Sadie, McMasters had long been an integral member of the anticheering squad inside him that kept him focused and driven. He'd been proving them all wrong for years, and he intended to keep doing so.

The thought of Sadie made him hesitate for a moment. He'd been wrong about her—they'd been wrong about each other— but McMasters was a bona fide prick. He'd lorded it over Dylan in every class, belittling him at every opportunity. Even when he'd busted his balls trying to make the grade, McMasters marked him down, and Dylan intended to rub the guy's face in his misjudgment.

The older man turned toward Dylan when he was only a few paces away, and for a second his grizzled face froze with shock.

Dylan felt a surge of satisfaction—McMasters *should* be worried, because Dylan made his living working with words, and he was about to take him apart piece by piece.

Then McMasters did the unthinkable—he lunged forward,

both arms extended, and pulled Dylan into an enthusiastic bear hug.

"Jesus H. Christ—Dylan Anderson!" McMasters said, thumping him on the back with gusto. "I can't believe it. You're the last person I expected to see here. Surely you've got better things to do than slum it with us plebs?"

Dylan blinked and resisted the urge to shake his head to check nothing was loose. What the hell…?

McMasters was beaming fit to burst, his thin cheeks rosy with color.

"You know, I have not missed a single episode of *The Boardroom*. Taped 'em all, then my daughter bought me the boxed set for my birthday. Best show on TV. Just fantastic," McMasters said. "You know that episode where the guy tries to kill himself by jumping out of his office window, but the safety glass won't break? Watched it three times in a row the night it aired. Brilliant!"

Dylan stared at his former nemesis for a long beat. The righteous words on the tip of his tongue hovered, angry and accusing. Then the absurdity of the situation struck him and he began to laugh. All these years he'd whipped himself on with the thought of McMaster's disapproval. His most vengeful dreams had involved showing this man that he was wrong, that Dylan was worth something—and here McMasters was, his biggest fan.

And the big joke was that it didn't matter. His belly ached and his breath ran short as he laughed and laughed. He didn't care that McMasters thought he did good work. The earth hadn't shifted, he hadn't suddenly become a different person because he had this man's approval. He didn't feel more confident, or more of a success. He felt…nothing.

"What's so funny?" McMasters asked, a bewildered expression on his face.

Dylan sucked in air and swiped at the tears that had formed in the corners of his eyes.

"Life. Life is what's so goddamned funny," he finally managed to say.

An echo of an earlier conversation came to him as he sobered.

You've got it all. But none of that's enough for you, is it? Because you still hear their voices in your head telling you you're no good.

He flinched as the words belatedly hit home like a hand grenade.

Because Sadie was right. He'd just proved she was right by marching across the gym to McMasters, desperate to offer up his life's achievements and get an elephant stamp and a gold star from his former teacher.

He thought about the way he'd taken the job at *Ocean Boulevard* to get in Sadie's face and slap her down. More of the same. Next he'd be digging his father up and making him watch reruns of *The Boardroom*. Whatever it took to show the world that Dylan Anderson was worth something.

God, he was a fool. Sadie had been right about that, too. He thought about the endless hours of work he put in, the weekends slaving over screenplays, the early starts and late nights, the lunches and schmoozy parties and phone calls. What an empty, stupid life he'd built for himself. Sure, he'd inadvertently scored some goodies along the way—a nice house, a great bike, the respect of his peers. But he'd pushed love away—he'd pushed Sadie away—because he'd wanted this aging man in front of him to respect him.

If it didn't make him feel sick through to his backbone, it would almost be funny.

He'd lost Sadie. The best thing to ever happen to him, the most loving, amazing woman in the world, and he'd told her he didn't have *time* for her. As if taking calls from his agent and kissing some network executive's ass was more important than making love to her and laughing with her and building a life with her.

His head shot up. Sadie was here, right now. Within reach.

And even though he didn't deserve a second chance, he sure as hell was going to ask for one.

McMasters was flapping his gums about something, but Dylan tuned him out as he climbed up onto the bleachers and scanned the gym. In that dress she should stand out like a beacon, but he couldn't see her anywhere. Swearing under his breath, he turned and scanned the other half of the gym—in time to catch sight of Sadie as she exited through the double doors.

"Damn it," he cursed, lunging forward urgently.

The gym had filled since he'd arrived, and he found himself dodging impatiently past people, busting up groups, blowing off greetings from former classmates. There was only one goal in his mind—to get to Sadie.

Finally he was at the doors and his footsteps sounded loudly on the hallway of the corridor as he broke into a run.

SADIE WRAPPED her arms around herself as she made her way to her car. She'd done it. She'd been shaking like a leaf, but she'd done it. One whole lap of the gym, disdainful smile in place, just as she'd planned with Claudia and Grace. And now she could go home.

She hadn't found a miracle cure for her broken heart in her defiant circuit of the gym. She'd said it to Dylan herself—it was impossible to rewrite the past. Her former classmates would always remember her as the girl who'd stuffed her dress with tissue at the senior prom. Sure, she'd given them a new image of herself to impose over the old one, but it wouldn't ever erase the other.

Arriving at her car, she beeped it unlocked. She was reaching for the door handle when Dylan called out.

"Sadie. Wait!"

She glanced over her shoulder to see him running toward her, but she reached for the door anyway. She hadn't expected to see him here, but they had nothing to say to each other.

She got it halfway open before Dylan lunged forward to push it shut again.

"Don't go," he said, his voice low and intense.

She sighed heavily. "Didn't you get enough nostalgia inside?" she said.

"I'm an idiot. I stuffed up. You were right about everything," he said.

She stared at him. Despite everything, just being near him sent her body into a hyperaware frenzy. Her pulse kicked up, and her breath got stuck somewhere in her throat. It made her feel vulnerable and exposed and stupid, and she tried to pull herself together.

"Good for you, but I have to go now," she said.

"I was going to have a go at McMasters, but it turns out he's *The Boardroom*'s biggest fan," Dylan said, talking a mile a minute. "The guy loves me almost as much as he hated me all those years ago. Pretty much the definition of irony, don't you think?"

"That must be very fulfilling for you," she said dully. "I bet it really made your day."

Again she reached for her door handle.

"Damn it, Sadie," he said, and the next thing she knew she was in his arms and he was kissing her with a fierce intensity that brought tears to her eyes. His fingers plowed into her hair and he pressed his body against hers, backing her into her car. His tongue invaded her mouth, caressing hers, tracing her lips, and she thought she would die because it was exactly what she craved but she knew she couldn't have it.

She was powerless to stop her misery from welling up, and Dylan pulled abruptly away from her when he felt her tears on his hands.

"Don't cry, Sadie, please. I'll make it up to you," he said, cupping her face gently and wiping at her tears with his thumbs. "Let me make it up to you."

"Leave me alone," she said brokenly. "Do you know how

hard it is loving you, seeing you every day but not being able to touch you or laugh with you? Do you have any idea how hard that is for me?"

"I have a fair idea," he said drily. Brushing away more of her tears, he looked deeply into her eyes. "Sadie, even though I'm making a complete hash of it, for the past five minutes I've been trying to tell you that I love you. I can't believe that I thought getting some stupid show up with the network or finishing a screenplay or any of it was more important than having you in my life, and it pretty much ranks as the stupidest thing I have ever done, but I finally get that none of it counts for anything if I don't have you to come home to," he said.

She stared at him for a long moment. "Why?"

"Why do I love you? Are you kidding? You're the most incredible woman I've ever met. You're smart, sassy, funny. Sexy as hell. Kind, loving. Brave. Walking in there like that tonight—man, I wanted to stomp and yell for you. You want more?" he asked.

A slow hum started in her belly as his words warmed her. Despite everything, she felt a smile tug at the corners of her mouth.

"I meant, why now? Why is it okay to love me now?"

He smoothed a hand around to the nape of her neck, and she let him keep it there.

"I've spent so long running away from being the dumb kid, I guess I didn't know when to stop," he said. "The question is, can I undo the dumbest mistake of my life?"

Looking into his eyes, she trembled to see the vulnerability and uncertainty and humbleness and gentleness in him. And the love. Love for her, shining unashamedly.

"I should mark you down for handing this assignment in so late," she said slowly, thoughtfully.

A warmth was expanding in her chest, a lightness after all the darkness.

"That only seems fair. You know that other students like Sadie Post got their work in nearly a month ago?" she said, running her finger along his jaw and down his neck to his chest.

A smile teased at the corner of his mouth, and she felt the tension ease from his shoulders.

"We can't all be like Sadie Post, ma'am. She's the best there is," he said, stepping closer to her and nudging her against the side of her car.

Still not quite believing that he was hers, that they were standing here, back where it all began, holding each other and looking into each other's hearts, Sadie smiled.

"I bet if you really applied yourself, you could catch up," she said, pulling him close. "I bet you could catch up really quickly."

She kissed him, her arms snaking around his shoulders to hold him as close as she could get him. She'd forgotten the feel of him under her hands, the firmness of his muscles, the heat of his skin on hers.

"You feel so good," she murmured into his mouth.

"Not half as good as you," he said, hands sliding down to grasp her butt and haul her more tightly against his hips.

They kissed and murmured and hugged and caressed until they were both panting and weak-kneed and desperate. Breaking a kiss, Dylan pressed his forehead against hers and held her tight.

"I thought I'd lost you," he whispered.

"No," she whispered back. "I fell in love with you when I was seventeen, and I don't think I ever stopped."

"That means I've got about fourteen years of catching up to do," he said. "I like a challenge."

She gave a whoop of delighted shock as he bent and picked her up in his arms.

"Where are we going?" she asked as he started off across the parking lot.

"There has to be a private spot around here somewhere," he muttered. "It's a high school, for Pete's sake. Kids have to fool around someplace."

She laughed, happiness bubbling up inside her. He looked down at her, a smile curving his beautiful mouth.

"I love you, Sadie," he said softly.

"I love you, too."

He ducked his head to kiss her, then started walking with renewed purpose.

"You think Claudia and Grace will forgive me in time for our wedding?" he asked as he pushed open the door to the main school building with his foot.

"Wedding? What wedding?" she asked, alarmed.

"Our wedding. How does a European honeymoon sound?"

"Dylan, I love you, but I don't think I can do the whole wedding thing again," she said uncertainly.

He was breathing heavily now, and she started to giggle as he paused to check the door to a classroom. It opened, and he wiggled his eyebrows at her saucily as he walked inside.

"Tell you what," he said as he placed her smack-bang in the middle of the teacher's desk. "Why don't you think on the whole wedding thing while I take your panties off?"

She let out a shocked yelp as he slid a hand under her dress and under her panty elastic.

"What if someone comes?"

"Oh, someone will definitely come," he said with a grin.

"Dylan!" she cried as he pulled her panties off and spread her legs wide.

"Yes, Mrs. Anderson?" he said as he knelt between her thighs. Before she could object, he'd closed his mouth over her quivering flesh.

"Oh," she groaned. Reaching for the edge of the desk, she held on for dear life as his skillful tongue teased her. It had been so long, and she was so turned on, and he loved her. Quickly she began to climb. But just as she was about to lose herself, Dylan lifted his head.

"So, this wedding thing," he said.

She groaned. He laughed. "Say the magic word."

"Please?"

"The other magic word."

As if to remind her what she was missing out on, he flicked his tongue across her again and she shivered.

"Does it have to be a church wedding?" she panted.

"No. We can go to Vegas, as long as you're mine," he said, his breath hot against her thighs.

Again he laved her with his tongue, and she shuddered.

"Yes," she sighed. "Yes. Vegas, church, wherever."

"Excellent choice," he said.

And then he took her in his mouth again.

Afterward, she pressed her head against his chest and took comfort from the slow, steady beat of his heart. Finally, after all these years, he was hers, and she was his. She smiled into the darkness.

"This is the best reunion ever," she said.

"Amen to that."

* * * * *

Look for Grace Wellington's story,
the next book in the
SECRET LIVES OF DAYTIME DIVAS *miniseries!*
Look for ALL OVER YOU
by Sarah Mayberry
Available April 2007
from Harlequin Blaze

Turn the page for a sneak preview of
IF I'D NEVER KNOWN YOUR LOVE
by
Georgia Bockoven

From the brand-new series
Harlequin Everlasting Love
Every great love has a story to tell. ™

There's no way for you to know this, Evan, but I haven't written to you for a few months. Actually, it's been almost a year. I had a hard time picking up a pen once more after we paid the second ransom and then received a letter saying it wasn't enough. I was so sure you were coming home that I took the kids along to Bogotá so they could fly home with you and me, something I swore I'd never do. I've fallen in love with Colombia and the people who've opened their hearts to me. But fear is a constant companion when I'm there. I won't ever expose our children to that kind of danger again.

I'm at a loss over what to do anymore, Evan. I've begged and pleaded and thrown temper tantrums with every official I can corner both here and at home. They've been incredibly tolerant and understanding, but in the end as ineffectual as the rest of us.

I try to imagine what your life is like now, what you do every day, what you're wearing, what you eat. I want to believe that the people who have you are misguided yet kind, that they treat you well. It's how I survive day to day. To think of you being mistreated hurts too much. If I picture you locked away somewhere and suffering, a weight descends on me that makes it almost impossible to get out of bed in the morning.

Your captors surely know you by now. They have to recognize what a good man you are. I imagine you working with their children, telling them that you have children, too, showing them the pictures you carry in your wallet. Can't the men who have you understand how much your children miss you? How can it not matter to them?

How can they keep you away from us all this time? Over and over, we've done what they asked. Are they oblivious to the depth of their cruelty? What kind of people are they that they don't care?

I used to keep a calendar beside our bed next to the peach rose you picked for me before you left. Every night I marked another day, counting how many you'd been gone. I don't do that any longer. I don't want to be reminded of all the days we'll never get back.

When I can't sleep at night, I tell you about my day. I imagine you hearing me and smiling over the details that make up my life now. I never tell you how defeated I feel at moments or how hard I work to hide it from everyone for fear they will see it as a reason to stop believing you are coming home to us.

And I couldn't tell you about the lump I found in my breast and how difficult it was going through all the tests without you here to lean on. The lump was benign—the process reaching that diagnosis utterly terrifying. I couldn't stop thinking about what would happen to Shelly and Jason if something happened to me.

We need you to come home.

I'm worn down with missing you.

I'm going to read this tomorrow and will probably tear it up or burn it in the fireplace. I don't want you to get the idea I ever doubted what I was doing to free you or thought the work a burden. I would gladly spend the rest of my life at it, even if, in the end, we only had one day together.

You are my life, Evan.

I will love you forever.

* * * * *

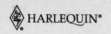

HARLEQUIN® Romance®

presents a brand-new trilogy by

PATRICIA THAYER

Rocky Mountain
B R I D E S

Three sisters come home to wed.

In April don't miss
Raising the Rancher's Family,

followed by
The Sheriff's Pregnant Wife,
on sale May 2007,

and

A Mother for the Tycoon's Child,
on sale June 2007.

Romantic
SUSPENSE

**Excitement, danger
and passion guaranteed!**

USA TODAY bestselling author
Marie Ferrarella
is back with the second installment
in her popular miniseries,
*The Doctors Pulaski: Medicine
just got more interesting...*
DIAGNOSIS: DANGER is on sale
April 2007 from Silhouette®
Romantic Suspense (formerly
Silhouette Intimate Moments).

*Look for it wherever
you buy books!*

REQUEST YOUR FREE BOOKS!

2 FREE NOVELS PLUS 2 FREE GIFTS!

HARLEQUIN®

Blaze®

Red-hot reads!

YES! Please send me 2 FREE Harlequin® Blaze® novels and my 2 FREE gifts. After receiving them, if I don't wish to receive any more books, I can return the shipping statement marked "cancel." If I don't cancel, I will receive 6 brand-new novels every month and be billed just $3.99 per book in the U.S., or $4.47 per book in Canada, plus 25¢ shipping and handling per book and applicable taxes, if any*. That's a savings of at least 15% off the cover price! I understand that accepting the 2 free books and gifts places me under no obligation to buy anything. I can always return a shipment and cancel at any time. Even if I never buy another book from Harlequin, the two free books and gifts are mine to keep forever.

151 HDN EF3W   351 HDN EF3X

Name	(PLEASE PRINT)

Address	Apt.

City	State/Prov.	Zip/Postal Code

Signature (if under 18, a parent or guardian must sign)

Mail to the Harlequin Reader Service®:

IN U.S.A.: P.O. Box 1867, Buffalo, NY 14240-1867

IN CANADA: P.O. Box 609, Fort Erie, Ontario L2A 5X3

Not valid to current Harlequin Blaze subscribers.

Want to try two free books from another line?
Call 1-800-873-8635 or visit www.morefreebooks.com.

* Terms and prices subject to change without notice. NY residents add applicable sales tax. Canadian residents will be charged applicable provincial taxes and GST. This offer is limited to one order per household. All orders subject to approval. Credit or debit balances in a customer's account(s) may be offset by any other outstanding balance owed by or to the customer. Please allow 4 to 6 weeks for delivery.

Your Privacy: Harlequin is committed to protecting your privacy. Our Privacy Policy is available online at www.eHarlequin.com or upon request from the Reader Service. From time to time we make our lists of customers available to reputable firms who may have a product or service of interest to you. If you would prefer we not share your name and address, please check here. ☐

HB07

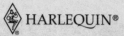